BACKS

AGAINST

THE WALL

A LAST RESORT NOVEL

NATHAN BIRR

Published by Beacon Books

Stock media provided by artisticco/Pond5, grebeshkovmaxim/Pond5, vostal/Pond5 and ValerieSerg/Shutterstock. Additional media courtesy of openclipart.org, publicdomainvectors.org, and rawpixel.com

ISBN: 978-1-7374270-7-0 (hc)
ISBN: 978-1-7374270-8-7 (sc)

www.nathanbirr.com

To my fellow travelers
who love the adventure of the open road
and always have their nickels ready . . .

CHAPTER ONE

Nicole Turner could hear her brother's voice in her head, telling her to hurry up. Her inclination was to ignore it, since it wasn't his actual voice and because the whole point of vacation was to not hurry. But Jimmy could be a little moody at times, and she didn't want to spoil what had been a pleasant seven hours since they'd left Rochester that morning. And she had been mulling for a good five minutes. So she plucked both a pack of Rolos and a Snickers bar from the shelf, justifying the decision with the knowledge that Jimmy liked Rolos and with a pledge to continue her morning run even on vacation.

Shooing away another thought of Jimmy's complaints, Nicole turned for the coffee bar, amazed at the food and drink selections of the small convenience store attached to a four-pump gas station in the middle of nowhere. She spent just a minute pondering the right size coffee cup—factoring in how many miles they had left to travel and the odds of finding a bathroom in this wilderness—before filling a medium cup. She took it and her candy to the register, paid, and then backed through the door to the parking lot.

Immediately, she was assaulted by heat. August temperatures were expected to near triple digits, but after the air-conditioned interior of the convenience store, the sun felt good on Nicole's face and arms. So too did a hot breeze in the wake of what had been a cool Minneapolis summer. So she basked for a minute, inhaling deeply in air tinged with the scent of freshly cut hay, before taking a long slurp of her mocha iced-coffee as she stared out at the barren landscape. Tan grass covered low, rolling hills as far as the eye could see, without a tree or bush in sight. The sky above was a rich, vibrant blue, dotted with cottony tufts of fair-weather clouds. But toward the horizon, it turned almost white, and Nicole was convinced it was only the haze that kept her from seeing the outline of the famed Black Hills. Or maybe it was the fact that they were still more than 150 miles away . . .

Reluctantly, thinking of the uncomfortable vinyl seats of Jimmy's fifteen-year-old Jeep Liberty, Nicole turned back to where it was parked beside the far pair of gas pumps. She stopped almost immediately. Her brother stood at the rear bumper of the Jeep, but he wasn't looking at her with exasperation. He was talking to a woman. That wasn't unusual for Jimmy, but the look on his face—something between a smirk and amused surprise—told Nicole it was trouble.

So did the woman.

Her hair was light brown with blond highlights, wavy and long. Jimmy's kryptonite. She wore a loose-fitting white shirt with faded, jagged diagonal red stripes and a dark denim mini skirt. Despite the heat, she also wore a black leather jacket short enough to reveal the shirt's stripes. She clutched the straps of a camouflage backpack in her left hand, while gesturing with her right as she talked to Jimmy. Charmed him, was more like it, as Nicole dialed in on Jimmy's expression. She bit her tongue, squinting slightly, then strode—as much as flip-flops would allow—across the parking lot.

Jimmy looked her way as she approached. She could see dimples forming through a couple days' growth of facial hair, and his blue eyes practically twinkled as he said, "Hey, Nic, this is Kira. My sister, Nicole," he added with a slight outstretched hand.

Nicole flashed him a quick onceover, then turned to Kira. Up close, she was beautiful. Her skin was flawless, her pale blue eyes covered by long lashes and dark mascara. The stripes on her shirt gave way to a rough blue field peppered with sketched stars, such that the shirt resembled an abstract American flag. A pair of aviator sunglasses were clipped over the shirt's collar. They were rimmed with silver, which matched bangles on Kira's wrist, exposed by the short sleeves of her jacket as she extended a hand.

Nicole shook it. "Nice to meet you."

"She's looking for a ride to Rapid City," Jimmy said. "We're going to Rapid City."

Nicole didn't like it, and not only because sudden changes to plans never sat well with her. Kira was a complete stranger, and while she didn't look like an ex-con or serial killer—or, for that matter, a runaway teen, even though she couldn't be *much* older than a teenager—picking up hitchhikers was generally a bad idea. A pretty face and pouty lips might be enough to persuade Jimmy, but Nicole needed more info to make an informed decision.

"What's in Rapid City?" she asked Kira.

"A Greyhound bus out of this forsaken state."

"She caught a ride from Pierre," Jimmy said. "Pierre? Pi-erre?" He looked at Kira. "Pierre," they said at the same time, Kira with a small giggle afterward, Jimmy with a grin. Nicole nearly rolled her eyes.

"I'll give you two a minute to talk," Kira said. "I have to use the ladies' room." She hefted her backpack onto one shoulder and turned, blond hair trailing behind her, and headed toward the convenience store doors. Nicole watched her over her shoulder, wondering about the combo of a leather jacket, American-flag shirt, and camo backpack. And what was so awful in Pierre that had Kira wanting out of South Dakota?

She looked back at Jimmy, who was still smiling and looking at her. The smile slowly faded. "Something wrong, Nic?"

"I'm not sure about this."

"Why not?"

"Because we know nothing about her. Why she's desperate to leave Pierre, how she got here, why she didn't get on a bus there. They must have buses in the state capital."

"Pierre's the capital? I thought it was Bismarck."

"That's North Dakota."

"Are you sure?"

"Yes, Jimmy," she said with a sigh.

3

"I thought for sure it was Bismarck."

Nicole exhaled.

Jimmy ran a hand through his dark brown hair, hair that was due for a trim. It was always due for a trim, just like his face was always due for a shave, and Nicole had no idea how he maintained either in such a stage. "Look, Nic, she said she had to leave in a hurry, just what she could stuff in a backpack, something about an ex-boyfriend, which is probably why she didn't have time to get a bus. She caught a ride with the guy who delivers pop to this and a few other places, and he was headed back to Pierre." He shrugged. "She seems like a sweet girl."

"Tell me that assessment isn't based on long hair and a short skirt."

"Nic . . ."

"Nicole."

"Right, I forgot."

Nicole drew on the straw of her iced coffee.

"Are you afraid she's some sort of cartel mule with a bunch of fentanyl in her backpack or something? Or a kleptomaniac who stole everything from her parents' safe and made a dash for it?"

"Jimmy."

"I'm serious."

"There are a lot of other things she could be besides a felon."

"Like what?"

Nicole sighed again.

"I tell you what, I'll take responsibility for her. If she causes trouble, I'll . . ."

"You'll what?"

"Buy all our snacks for the rest of the trip."

Nicole squinted at him again.

"And the gas. And have you seen the price of gas?"

She weighed her options. The unknown of Kira—somewhere between a fentanyl carting klepto and a new obsession for Jimmy—and the almost certainty of him pouting and being crabby for the rest of the day, if not the trip, if she said no. And, the very real possibility that Kira *was* just a sweet girl in need of help.

"And no more of my mix today."

Nicole huffed out something of a concession. Jimmy, a twenty-four-year-old man from northern Wisconsin, had developed a craze for outlaw country music, and had burned a CD—the newest technology available in his old Jeep—of Johnny Cash, Waylon Jennings, and Willie Nelson. He'd said it was appropriate for a trip across the badlands, but it was more than Nicole could handle.

"Fine," she said, instinctively looking back over her shoulder as Kira exited the convenience store. "But, Jimmy—Jimmy," she said, getting his attention, "keep your head about you."

"Of course," he said with a wink that made her regret her decision. Then, with instinct of his own, he lowered his eyes to her hand. "Those Rolos for me?"

CHAPTER TWO

Interstate 90 stretched across central South Dakota like a pair of long, straight, gray ribbons. Jimmy had expected endless prairie on the drive through southern Minnesota, but had hoped for more dramatic geography in the Mount Rushmore State. But save for a few features around the Missouri River, the terrain had been nothing but low, rolling farmland. With only round hay bales for scenery, Jimmy was glad to have Kira along. She had insisted on sitting in the backseat of the Jeep, and had opted for the middle seat, right in the rearview mirror. Her backpack was on one seat beside her, and she'd shrugged out of her leather jacket to reveal her patriotic shirt was a tank top, itself revealing muscular arms that suggested Kira worked out. Maybe she and Nicole could bond over exercise regimens.

"So where are you two headed?" Kira asked. "I mean, beyond Rapid City." She seemed relaxed, now that they were on the road, whereas Jimmy had sensed urgency and a touch of anxiety at the gas station.

"We're not," he answered.

"You mean that's as far as you're going? I thought you just meant tonight."

"We're going to spend a few days," Nicole said. "See Mount Rushmore, hike the badlands."

"Just the two of you?"

"We're reconnecting," he answered, while Nicole shot him a sideways glance with her almond brown eyes and slurped her iced coffee.

Kira nodded, but didn't probe.

"What about you?" Nicole asked. "Where's this Greyhound bus going to take you?"

"Hmm. Anywhere."

"Why are you leaving Pierre?"

Now Jimmy shot his sister a look, but said nothing, instead fiddling with the wrapper of another Rolo. He caught Nicole's glance back, not at him, but at the steering wheel. They were doing eighty miles per hour, but the last vehicle he'd seen westbound was an oversized load carrying a combine with tires stacked behind it, and that had been a few miles ago. He concluded he could open a piece of candy without putting them in the ditch.

"Besides the obvious?" Kira answered, gesturing out the window at nothingness.

"What brought you here?"

"Work. Sort of. Four years of high school taught me that more school wasn't for me. I tried various jobs around Columbia, then tried moving to St. Louis to see what the big city had to offer, but nothing there grabbed me either. So I thought maybe the wide-open spaces and a fresh start were the answer. I heard there were a lot of jobs in the Dakotas, picked a city so I wouldn't be completely out in the sticks, and spent the last several months doing this and that and . . ."

Jimmy looked in the mirror as he finally popped the candy into his mouth. Kira was looking down at the hem of her tank top. "I met a guy, Braden, and we hit it off. I didn't have a lot of friends since I was new to town, so his friends and family became my friends. Then I started to realize something was off."

"What was that?" Nicole asked.

"His family was crazy."

"How do you mean?"

"At first I thought they were some religious group or something, and I didn't ask many questions because I didn't really care and I liked Braden. But then . . . it started to get weird. They were kind of secretive, but at the same time seemed like they wanted to initiate me into their gang or group or whatever."

"A gang?" Jimmy asked.

"Yeah. They loved motorcycles, and motorcycle gear. That's where my jacket came from, a gift from Braden. And they were crazy about guns. Loved to shoot them, loved to own them, loved to talk about them. My dad hunted deer all the time in Missouri, so it's not like I'm afraid of guns. But they seemed obsessed. They were also big on survivalism and 'scenarios' and prepping for this and that. And they kept talking about some plan, but always in vague terms. I started to fear these guys were going to blow up a federal building or something. Then suddenly they shut me out, and I started thinking they were suspicious that I was suspicious. Braden got cold, and I was honestly relieved and ready to be done with all of them."

The highway curved south of west, causing the midday sun to shine directly on Jimmy and his black T-shirt. Even so, he felt a chill, and reached to adjust the knob of the Jeep's A/C.

"Then, Braden suddenly became clingy, like he didn't want to let me out of his sight. It was creepy, and a little scary. I found he had an app on my phone to track my location, and he kept asking me weird questions. Then he threatened me, said he loved me so much that he couldn't bear to lose me, and that if I left him, he'd find me and hurt me."

Jimmy turned to Nicole, saw wide eyes as she fiddled with the wrapper of her melting Snickers.

"That's when I knew I had to leave," Kira said. "I traded my beat-up car for an apartment when I arrived, and I've walked or bussed or ridden with Braden everywhere I go, so I had no way to leave, other than hitchhiking. I've been working at a diner, lately, and I showed up this morning for the breakfast shift, slipped out to use the restroom, and gave the Pepsi delivery guy fifty bucks to give me a lift to wherever was next. Turns out the gas station was as far away from Pierre as he goes. You were the third person I asked for a ride," she said, making eye contact with Jimmy in the rearview mirror.

He couldn't help but moving his eyes from hers to the lonely stretch of highway behind them, making sure it was still lonely.

"Do you still have your phone?" Nicole asked.

"Left it in the diner bathroom. I was afraid they were going to pull over the Pepsi truck, or come roaring into the gas station before I found a ride." She exhaled and smiled. "So thank you for getting me out of there."

"You're safe now," Jimmy said almost compulsively.

"Thanks. I'll feel even safer when I'm a thousand miles and a few states away. Somewhere warm. Arizona, or maybe Vegas."

"*Heads Carolina, Tails California*," Jimmy sang in a falsetto voice with a little twang. Not a bad Jo Dee Messina, he thought, but the look Nicole sent him suggested otherwise. With eyebrows still raised, she turned around in her seat. She swiped a strand of shoulder-length, dark brown hair from her face, and tucked it behind her ear. "Do you really think they'd come after you?"

Jimmy saw Kira shake her head in the rearview mirror. "I don't know," she said. "The way Braden was acting recently, and the way some of them looked when I asked certain questions . . . And I didn't tell you about Carter."

"Who's Carter?" Jimmy beat Nicole in asking.

"He was one of the neighbors. Relative term, because Braden's family lives on a compound outside of town, with a ton of property. They caught him snooping one night, I heard. Just a dumb teenage kid, probably on a dare with his friends. Anyhow, he suddenly disappeared. There was even talk around town that nobody knew where he was. My guess, buried under the Gardiner back forty."

Nicole flitted another glance Jimmy's way. He ignored it. "They have no way of knowing where you are now," he said, searching the mirror for Kira's pale blues. She lifted them to him and smiled a fraction. "And if we get desperate, we'll let Nicole drive. She has a lead foot."

"I do not."

"Picked it up on all those backroads through the Carolina low country."

"Carolina?" Kira asked.

"I went to USC for four years," Nicole answered.

"I thought USC was in California."

Jimmy clapped a few times.

"Hands on the wheel," Nicole said. "A lot of people make that mistake."

"You did it again," Jimmy said.

"What?"

"Dipped into your faux southern drawl."

"I do not have a faux southern drawl."

"I do *not* have a faux southern drawl," he mimicked with an exaggerated twang.

Nicole crossed her arms.

"Are you trying to tell me you picked it up honest?"

"I don't even have a drawl."

"Kira?"

From the backseat, she tipped her hand back and forth. Then she giggled again, and Jimmy couldn't help but smile at the sound.

*   *   *

The green sign announcing they were entering Mountain Time Zone stood like a lone sentinel on the border to the American West. The terrain, as it had been for miles, was nothing more than tan pastureland devoid of almost any vegetation other than grass. But the vastness, the emptiness, was appealing, especially under a brilliant blue sky. And the rolling hills were getting a little bigger, the valleys a little longer and wider. To the southwest, Jimmy could see a few buttes, and surmised they were getting close. But the next mile marker and some basic math told him they were still 113 miles from Rapid City. At eighty miles per hour, that was only an hour and a half, factoring in more road construction. Even so, Jimmy squirmed in his seat. He'd driven two hours from his apartment in Eau Claire, Wisconsin, to Nicole's high school friend's house in Rochester, Minnesota, the evening before. Nicole had spent a day there after finishing a summer job in the Twin Cities, and they had departed Rochester that morning, eight hours ago. Call it restlessness or fidgetiness—Nicole called it ants in his pants—but Jimmy couldn't sit still for long periods of time without squirming. And Nicole, who's mood still seemed a little sour, looked over again, clearly aware.

He changed the subject. "How do you feel about a stop at Wall Drug?"

"Wall Drug?"

"Yeah." They had seen billboards for the famed drug store-turned-souvenir shop since before the Minnesota-South Dakota border. The billboards advertised everything from boots and cowboy hats and leather goods to fudge and taffy, and from gold and jewelry to the free ice water and five-cent coffee that had originally made the store in the small town of Wall appeal to motorists on the highway.

Nicole had been fiddling with the radio, trying to tune in something acceptable to all three sets of ears, and now punched off the static and lowered her hand. "Why?" she asked.

Jimmy shrugged. "It's iconic, for one thing. How can you not stop at Wall Drug?"

"By driving past."

"Besides, I want to get some Western gear," he said quietly.

"Western gear? Like tack for your horse?"

"A hat."

"A hat. A cowboy hat?"

"Yeah."

"Jimmy, you work at Red Robin."

"A man is not defined by his job."

"I mean, you're not a cowboy. Just because you started listening to Alan Jackson doesn't—"

"Says the girl who twangs her vowels, blesses people's hearts, and tries to order catfish and fried green tomatoes at a restaurant in southern Minn-y-SOH-Tah."

"Are you two doing this for my benefit?" Kira asked. "Some kind of comedy routine to keep me from worrying about Braden's family?"

"No, that's just a side benefit," Jimmy said with a wink in the mirror. He turned to his sister. "Come on, Nic, just a quick stop, a cup of coffee and a quick browse through the leather goods store."

She sighed. "Fine, if it's okay with Kira."

"I guess so. I don't have a bus ticket yet, so I don't have to be there at any set time."

"If you're worried about Braden," Jimmy said, "I've been thinking about that. *If* he's after you, his family I mean, blasting down the interstate on their Harleys—"

"How'd you know?"

"You said they were a motorcycle gang, and I doubt they're all riding Japanese crotch rockets. Not in South Dakota."

"I think you're stereotyping," Nicole said.

"So be it." He looked back at Kira. "Anyhow, *if* they really are after you, they won't know if you kept going south, headed east, or headed west—if they even know you left town to the south. They might be headed for Canada, figuring you'd run for the border."

"For the border?"

He shrugged. "And *if* they happen to guess that you went west and are charging after us, the *last* thing they'd expect is for you to stop and have some cheap coffee and help me find the right belt buckle."

"If you get one of those bolo ties," Nicole said, "I'm not speaking to you anymore."

"That'd be fair. What do you think?" he asked Kira.

"Sure. That makes sense."

"Nic?"

"We can stop. The fudge does sound pretty good."

"That's the spirit," Jimmy said. "Besides, you'll need something to wash down that Snickers."

Nicole mock scowled at him, then reached for a Rolo in a dashboard cubby and pinged it off his head.

CHAPTER THREE

The billboards had become almost constant—Jimmy's audible count was at seventy-three total—in the last few miles, and the grassland broken by bluffs and buttes of sand, shale, and silt. The bluffs and buttes were in turn marred by gullies and gouges—features known as badlands. They were not technically driving through Badlands National Park, which lay south of Interstate 90, but already the features they were seeing had Nicole excited for their planned day of hiking through the park. "But first, coffee," as the T-shirt Jimmy had gotten her for her birthday a few years ago said. This of the five-cent variety, at the famed Wall Drug. Nicole had long ago learned, a good attitude made almost anything better, and she resolved to tolerate Jimmy's little Western fantasy.

It was impossible to miss the exit to Wall, which aside from the billboards and the eighty-foot-tall dinosaur marking the ramp, looked just like any other small town on the prairie. The tall pylon signs of several hotels and gas stations towered over the interchange, and as soon as they turned on the main drag, another billboard announced Wall Drug was four blocks ahead. Even so, Jimmy signaled for and made a hard left turn onto a boulevard with a grassy park in the middle and fast food restaurants, gas stations, and motels lining it.

"Uh, Jimmy."

"Trust me, Nic, it's over here."

She sighed and muttered, "Nicole."

"What?"

"My name is Nicole."

"See, that's another thing," he said as they passed a Dairy Queen, followed by a Wall Drug sign that suggested he did actually know where he was going, "you were always fine being Nicki or Nic or Nickelodeon or whatever until you went off to Carolina. Now you're 'Nicole.'"

"It is what's on my birth certificate."

"Yeah, but you're stuffy about it."

"I'm not stuffy, Jimmy. Nicole is just . . . more mature. It's hard to have a potential employer take you seriously if you introduce yourself as Nickelodeon, which I was never really fine with, by the way."

"Hmm. Fair point, I guess," he said as he turned onto what was identified as Main Street but was bounded by empty lots. Up ahead, a row of steel grain bins were an obligatory part of any Midwest town. Just before them, a few blocks from where they'd turned, a run-of-the-mill small town morphed into a commercial hub. The street widened to incorporate three rows of diagonal parking, and the sidewalks on both sides were lined with storefronts in the style of an Old West town. Signs hawked cheap T-shirts, discount souvenirs, and Black Hills gold. Towering over the scene on the right was a dark façade with a large green sign emblazoned with gold lettering:

WALL DRUG STORE ~ SINCE 1931 ~

Beneath it, an awning that covered the sidewalk was lined with yellow fabric. More signs—highlighting a café with seating for 530 people, free ice water, a travelers chapel, and a soda fountain with homemade ice cream—made the store impossible to miss. Jimmy found a parking spot in the row of spaces between the two lanes of traffic and killed the engine. "Everybody got your nickels?"

Nicole paused with her hand on her seatbelt buckle. "Tell me this whole trip wasn't a ploy for you to come out here and drink your body weight in cheap coffee?"

"Just trying to outpace you," he said with a wink back.

"Why *are* you on this trip?" Kira said as she turned sideways to dig into her backpack. "You're going to lock this, right?"

"Of course," Jimmy nodded.

She resumed rummaging through an outer pocket. "You said reconnecting. Reconnecting from what?"

Nicole shrugged. "We kind of grew apart in high school, hanging in different crowds. Then Jimmy went to college, made new friends."

"Where'd you go?" she asked looking at him.

"UW-Eau Claire."

She looked up. "Where?"

"Local college."

"Then I went to South Carolina," Nicole said, "spent most of four years down south, and got a temporary job in Minneapolis over the summer. We'd talked about this sort of a thing for a while, and decided now was the time."

"Plus we'd never been to Mount Rushmore, and what sort of red-blooded American can say that?" Jimmy asked.

Kira finally zipped up her backpack, briefly holding up some rumpled bills to show the object of her search. She stuffed them in her pocket. "Ready."

They got out and found the pavement and surrounding reflective car exteriors and windshields—not to mention the lack of breeze in the corridor of buildings—made the heat even more intense.

"Not exactly coffee weather," Kira remarked as she closed the Jeep's rear door.

"It's always coffee weather," Jimmy said. "But I bet they're making a killing on the free ice water today."

Nicole shook her head at the comment, and the fact that Jimmy wouldn't care that it didn't make sense—if he noticed. They waited for a couple motorcycles—not carrying grudge-holding, secret-hiding extremists, judging by Kira's calm reaction—to pass, then headed under the awning. Jimmy held the door, and Nicole led the way. She stopped inside a main hall, two stories tall, lined with Old West façades to various shops—a jewelry store, a bookstore, a western wear and leather goods store. Along with an American flag, various animal heads were mounted above and on a crosswalk over the hallway—deer, longhorn cattle, a buffalo. Benches offered a place to take a rest, if one was willing to share the seat with mannequin prospectors and saloon gals and an old lady smoking a cigar and holding a deck of cards. Arcade-style shooting games and coin-press machines and a carving of Buffalo Bill were just a few of the items pressing in on the hallway, which was also crowded with tourists. And this was just the main "mall."

"Let's just wander," Jimmy said as he caught up to the two women, "get the lay of the land first." He pushed forward to lead the way, and Nicole sighed, realizing this was not going to be a quick stop.

She let Kira go second, and they passed the travelers chapel, an actual pharmacy, and a western art gallery before Jimmy turned left into a short hallway leading to a large room full of souvenirs. Nicole had turned her attention to the fudge shop on the right, and was just turning her head back when she heard Kira gasp. Then she turned around and sighed.

"Something wrong?" Nicole asked.

"That big guy in the leather vest, bald head," Kira said, nodding over her shoulder.

Nicole flitted her eyes to a large, barrel-chested man in faded blue jeans and a long-sleeved black shirt covered by a black leather vest full of patches. His bald scalp was red from sun, which maybe also accounted for the almost white tone of his beard.

"Yeah?"

"For a second I thought it was Lance."

"Who's Lance?" Jimmy asked, having noticed the women stopped. He hovered behind Kira.

"Braden's uncle. The 'head' of the Gardiner family. I'm sorry, I'm going to be jumpy around anyone in leather."

"Fortunately there aren't many of them here," Nicole muttered, having seen a few dozen motorcycles parked out front.

Jimmy tapped Kira's arm. "Coffee will set your mind at ease," he said and turned. Nicole offered Kira a sheepish smile, and they followed him through the maze of souvenirs—mugs and shot glasses, keychains and magnets and nameplates, blankets and stuffed animals, necklaces and polished rocks, a host of huckleberry flavored products, puzzles and Christmas ornaments, and plenty of jackalopes. The next shop over contained T-shirts and sweatshirts with Wall Drug and South Dakota slogans. Then another store with cards and postcards, toiletries, and other miscellaneous items led them to an open room with tables and, off to their right, a serving counter.

"You eat lunch today?" Jimmy asked Kira.

"I had an energy bar at the gas station before I found you."

"Wanna grab a donut with our coffee?" he asked, gesturing at the serving counter.

"Sure."

"Nic-Cole?"

"Nice cover," she said, emitting a smile. "If you're buying."

While Jimmy led the way toward food, and Kira kept her head on a swivel looking for leather and tattoos, Nicole took in what was touted as the largest private western art collection in the country, an assortment of paintings and portraits covering the wood-paneled walls. They continued in the small dining room with booths around the perimeter. In the center, under a stained-glass mosaic, several trays of white coffee mugs were stacked next to a stainless steel urn. Between them was a small wood box with a slit in the top. "COFFEE 5¢" was burned into the box.

"Three coffees?" Jimmy asked, handing Nicole the bag of donuts he'd purchased.

"You're like a kid on Christmas," she said as he dug for nickels and she and Kira found an empty table. The entire place was busy, but at quarter to four local time, the dining room had plenty of room. Nicole pulled out a chair, while Kira slid into the booth on the opposite side of the table. Jimmy joined them a moment later, carrying three mugs of coffee. No surprise, he slid in beside Kira.

Nicole watched him for a moment, trying to decide if he was falling for Kira—he had something of a reputation for falling hard and fast—or just enamored in the presence of a cute girl. And to be fair, Kira was cute, although something about her appearance bugged Nicole. She couldn't put her finger on it, unless it was an American flag tank top, denim skirt, and white sneakers not being typical apparel for working in a diner. Then again, she could have changed and stowed her Rayon dress in her backpack.

Nicole took a bite of her donut, licking chocolate frosting off her lip. She washed it down with a gulp of coffee, which was much better than she expected.

Without staring, she focused on Kira. Something in her story bothered Nicole too, although she couldn't place it. And she didn't know if there was something that *should* bother her, something that didn't wash, or if her subconscious was finding fault because she had been opposed to taking Kira along.

"You not hungry?" Jimmy asked, looking at Kira.

"Hmm?"

"Your donut."

"Oh, yeah, sorry. Just drifted for a minute." She lifted the donut and took a bite. "So where exactly is Eau Claire? I've heard of it, but couldn't place it on a map."

"Eau Claire is easy," Jimmy said in a husky, hoarse voice. "Go to where the people speak Scandinavian, then go until they speak something else."

Both women stared at him.

"Liam Neeson, *Kingdom of Heaven*?"

Kira shook her head.

"No? Too bad, that impersonation was money."

"Worth another cup of coffee, at least," Nicole said with a fake sneer.

"Ha-ha. Eau Claire's about ninety miles east of the Twin Cities."

"You grow up there?"

He nodded. "Nicole was born there."

"Not you?"

"I was born in Minneapolis," he said. "We moved when I was a year old."

"How much difference between you?"

"Two years," Nicole said.

"Physically. Mentally she's a decade older."

Remembering the chocolate frosting on her lip, Nicole pinched off another bite of donut.

"You have any siblings?" Jimmy asked.

"No. My cousin and I were like sisters, but she was a few years older, and when she went off to college . . ." Kira waved her hand slowly in a "so long" gesture. She lowered it and lifted her coffee mug.

Maybe what was "off" with Kira, Nicole thought to herself, was sadness. She'd spoken of her dad in what sounded like past tense, had no siblings, a cousin like a sister who'd left her behind, a life story of not finding her place, now Braden and his family. Nicole had viewed Kira as a random interaction—they just happened to be at the right place at the right time to pick her up—and, if she was honest with herself, as something of an intrusive one. But maybe there was no randomness about it, and maybe it wasn't what Kira would mean to her and Jimmy, but what they could mean to her. Maybe having someone care at just this point in time was what Kira needed.

Nicole knew firsthand, having needed the very same thing herself not that long ago.

CHAPTER FOUR

"Are you sure you're okay?" Nicole asked. After stopping off in the restrooms, she and Kira had opted to browse souvenirs, neither with much a mind to buy, while Jimmy headed toward the Buckboards Clothing Store to outfit himself in the latest George Strait attire. He allegedly made good tips, so let him spend it how he wanted, Nicole figured. She'd expected Kira to go with him, but she'd opted to stay with Nicole, and now absentmindedly wandered up and down aisles.

"Yeah," Kira answered.

"You seem . . . distracted. Are you worried about them finding you?"

"A little," Kira said, fingering a keychain and letting it go. "It's weird."

"What's that?"

"Everything that's happened today. It's a lot to process."

"I imagine."

"Plus . . . Nicole, I still have feelings for Braden, even after everything."

"How long were you two together?"

She paused for a moment. "Three or four months? I know it's not long, but . . ."

"It takes time," Nicole said softly. She remembered her conclusion that Kira likely needed a friend. "But it's not weird. I think it's normal what you're feeling."

"I hope so. At least this is taking my mind off it. Hard to concentrate surrounded by all this stuff."

There was indeed a lot of stuff, every imaginable knickknack or souvenir was on display, most with "Wall Drug" stamped on the front, or a picture of Mount Rushmore, or a jackalope. That was one thing Nicole didn't get the allure of, the fabled rabbit/antelope combo. Then again, some people didn't get the allure of shrimp and grits either.

"Maybe Jimmy should get this hat instead," Kira said a minute later, holding up a baseball cap with the brim and front panel both made to resemble the face of a bison, while two "horns" flapped out from the side.

"I will pay for your bus fare if you get him to buy that," Nicole said.

Kira didn't take the bet and put the hat back on the shelf. Nicole wandered over to the row of mugs, and found several that would be good for her dad, assuming she had a way to get one to him. She heard Kira ask someone, presumably one of the many Wall Drug employees on hand, if the Christmas trees were up year-round. There were a lot of Christmas trees, displaying the vast array of Wall Drug ornaments, and hearing Kira mention them made Nicole stop and wonder how long it had been since the entire Turner family had been together for Christmas. Too long.

"You like these?" Kira asked a few minutes later, holding up a pair of drop earrings that looked like dreamcatchers.

Nicole nodded.

"Are you getting anything?"

She'd promised the friend she and Jimmy had stayed with the night before a souvenir of some sort, and figured this might be as good of a place as any to find a T-shirt. So she said she was going to peruse the apparel in the next store over.

"I'm going to hang out here a little while longer," Kira said, "then make my way over to Jimmy." She winked. "I want to see how he looks in a cowboy hat."

"I'll meet you over by the fudge shop."

Kira nodded, and Nicole turned for the door, worried about Jimmy again. That cowboy hat better be at least a ten-gallon the way his head would puff up with a little flattery from Kira. There had been trouble like that before . . .

*   *   *

Jimmy had taken his time, meandering through a couple other shops before making his way to the Buckboard Clothing Store and the Boots and Western Clothing Store at the far corner of Wall Drug. He searched for boots first, figuring his first pair shouldn't be overly ostentatious. He found a pair of dark brown boots with no frills that weren't *too* uncomfortable, or *too* expensive. He lived frugally, and had been planning on this trip for a while, so a little splurging was in order.

Next he moved to cowboy hats. He knew nothing about them, other than white hats were for the good guys and black hats for the bad guys. He tried on three or four styles in several colors, checking each in a mirror, before narrowing it down to a black "gambler" hat or a dark brown "cutter." He tried each on several times, trying to picture them with various shirts he wore—or would buy.

He heard jingling, and turned to see Kira and her bangles standing beside him. She held her thumb up, her forefinger pointed at him. "Stick 'em up, Tex."

"Hey," he said, facing her, "which one is better?" He placed the brown cutter on his head, then removed it and replaced it with the black gambler.

"Turn to profile," Kira said.

He did.

She reached up and took the hat from his head. She placed it over her hair and then took the brown one from Jimmy's hand and fit it onto his head. "That one," she said with one eye closed.

"You sure?"

"Yeah."

"They have ladies hats," he said, grinning at her with hair cascading from under the gambler hat, which wasn't quite the right fit for her. "You know, in case you want to blend in."

"Yeah," she said.

"Hey, I didn't mean to bring that up and bum you out."

"You didn't."

"Can I ask you something?"

She removed the hat and handed it to him. "Sure."

He took a few steps to replace it, then said, "Do you have a plan? I mean, beyond catch a bus? Nicole is always getting on me for acting without thinking and flying by the seat of my pants, so it's a shame she's not here to hear me ask this. But . . . once you get on that bus and get a few states away, what's next?"

Kira ran her hand through her hair, bangles clanking away. "I don't know. Unless I'm totally barking up the wrong tree about Braden's family, they won't just let me get away."

"Why not?"

"I know things about them."

"Like what?"

"Names, faces, the layout of the property—I mean, that's always a big thing when the FBI invades some nutjob's compound, isn't it, knowing where stuff is beyond what satellite shows?"

Jimmy shrugged.

"And I know all about their guns—firepower, in FBI terms. Braden and his cousins loved to show them off. And I've heard them say stuff, political comments, stuff you wouldn't say in public, stuff that could be pretty condemning if the feds start looking for indictments."

"You think the FBI is coming after them?"

"I don't have anything concrete, but, you know how sometimes you just sense something is off?"

He nodded.

"Well, my meter was off the charts."

"Then that's another reason to get you a hat."

She narrowed her gaze. "My intuition that the FBI is coming after them?"

"No. Well, yeah, because the Gardiners would have a reason to come after you, in theory."

"What's the other reason?"

Jimmy smirked. "Because it would look good on you."

"Thanks, but I'm kind of watching my spending now that I'm unemployed."

"Well, want to tag along while I look for flannel?"

"It's a hundred degrees out."

"Yes, but winter comes early to northern Wisconsin."

They browsed for a few more minutes, during which Jimmy found a two-for-one sale on "cowboy" shirts, albeit not flannels. He bought them, the hat, and the boots, and as the cashier was ringing them up, he asked, "Nicole say where she would meet us?"

"Um, said something about fudge."

"Okay good. That'll take her forever so she can't complain about my time in here."

They made their way back to the main hallway, then turned toward the back of the complex and the store selling fudge. Nicole was not there, and Jimmy turned to look and see if they'd missed her. Then Kira tugged his arm.

"What?"

"They have a back yard."

"I saw."

"Let's go take your picture."

"My picture?"

"In your new gear."

Now he narrowed a gaze at her.

"We've got time to kill," she said, then leaned toward him. "And I think cowboys are cute."

"You can call me handsome, you can call me a stud, you can call me good-looking, but don't you dare call me cute."

Kira's face went blank.

"John Wayne in *Big Jake*. Sort of. Without the cussing."

"Who and who?"

Jimmy turned around in mock disbelief.

She pulled his arm again. "Come on, John." She led him out into the open-air Wall Drug Back Yard, where the western theme continued. The back yard contained a splash pad for kids, a mini-mold of Mount Rushmore, a Conestoga wagon hitched to porcelain horses, and a huge jackalope suitable for mounting to pose for a picture. Jimmy could be moved by a pretty face, but not onto a jackalope the size of an elephant. So Kira had him pose by the Conestoga wagon, after changing into his new boots and donning his hat. She snapped several pictures, then joined him for a couple selfies, including one in which she stole his hat and wore it herself. He didn't mind a bit.

"Wanna see what's back there?" Kira asked when she'd snapped enough pictures. Beyond the back yard was another building containing another snack shop, an arcade, and a much-hyped T-Rex.

"Sure, unless . . ."

His phone had just vibrated.

"Nicole?" she asked.

Jimmy swiped his phone to see the text. "Trouble."

"What?"

He turned the phone to her. "I don't know," he said, showing her the single word texted to him by his sister:

trouble

CHAPTER FIVE

Nicole selected a T-shirt with the words "Where the Heck is Wall Drug?" stamped on it for her friend, figuring it was her sort of humor. She also picked out a few postcards for various people. Knowing Jimmy's tendency to dawdle in those rare moments when he was shopping for something, she didn't rush to the checkout. When she finally did pay, she checked her watch and saw that it had been more than twenty minutes since they'd split up after coffee and donuts. Even with the time change, it was getting late in the afternoon. So she passed on fudge for the time being, figuring she could grab some on the way out while Jimmy went to gulp down more coffee or have his picture taken with Wild Bill Hickok.

She walked back through the various shops, then cut through a small hall with a stagecoach over the doorway and emerged back into the mall. She allowed herself to be diverted by the Hole in the Wall Bookstore (clever, she thought) for a few minutes, then turned her attention to the western wear stores. There were boots, hats, shirts, belts, purses, moccasins and more. But there was not a would-be Highwayman and his would-be girlfriend.

She checked a second time, just to be sure, then exited to the mall. She stood there for a moment, trying to recall if she'd said something that he or Kira had interpreted other than that she would find them here. She sighed. One of the reasons she and Jimmy had drifted apart in high school was talking past each other, so there was no reason to think that had ceased in the last five years.

When Nicole looked up, two guys in leather were approaching her. To be fair, they were wearing much more than leather, but it stood out. So did matching patches over the left breast, black shields with red and gold trim and a red BH and gold G interwoven in the center. One guy was white, thick and muscular, the white T-shirt under his vest stretched at the seams, myriad tattoos showing on his arms beneath it. Black wraparound sunglasses were stuck in short-buzzed blond hair. A thick goatee hung several inches below his chin. The other man was darker-skinned, Native American it appeared, and wore a black, long-sleeved shirt under his leather vest. His hair was jet black, tinged with white, and wavy to his shoulders. They looked like a dozen other bikers Nicole had seen since arriving at Wall Drug, and yet they looked very different. And they were homing in on her.

"Excuse me," Wavy Hair said. "Do you have a second, ma'am?"

Nicole swallowed. "Uh . . . yeah," she said without thinking.

Goatee held up a smartphone and showed her the screen.

"Have you seen this woman?" Wavy Hair asked as Nicole studied the screen, hoping her eyes didn't literally bug out of her skull. The photo had been cropped, showing a woman leaning on the shoulder of a man in a leather jacket. She too wore a leather jacket, a little short on the sleeves and torso, over a red V-neck shirt. She was smiling coyly at the camera, hair draped over a third of her face, which was highlighted with blush and dark mascara. She looked different, but there was no mistaking Kira.

"Ma'am?" Wavy Hair asked again.

Nicole looked up. "Yeah." She swallowed to allow her time to construct a story. "Yeah, I passed her on my way in, about ten minutes ago. Maybe fifteen," she added quickly, realizing she was carrying a bag with her purchases, meaning she had spent time inside.

"You saw her?" Goatee asked. "You're sure?"

She looked at the image again, trying to think. She managed a nod.

"As you were coming in?" Wavy Hair said. "Was she headed out?"

"Yeah. I stopped on the sidewalk to check my phone, in the shade. I heard a load roar and turned and saw her get on a bike with a guy."

"You're sure it was her?"

Nicole nodded. "I recognize that hair. And she had an . . . I don't know, sort of strange look on her face. Like she was scared."

"Did you get a look at this guy?"

"No, not really. He was wearing a leather jacket. Dark hair, I think. Sorry."

"Did you see them leave?" Goatee asked.

"I heard the bike start, like I said, which is what made me see her again. And then I heard it idle a little and take off, but I wasn't paying attention which way it went." She shrugged. "Sorry."

"You've helped us a lot," Wavy Hair said. "Ten or fifteen minutes ago?"

"I'd say more like fifteen. I bought a couple things," she said, lifting the bag slightly.

"Can you tell us anything about the bike?" Goatee asked. "A Harley?"

"Lots of chrome," Nicole said with a wince. "It caught the sunlight. I really only glanced when I heard the noise, just enough to see it was the same girl who'd passed me."

"Anything else you can think of?" Wavy Hair asked. "It's urgent we find her."

"Sorry. I wasn't thinking anything of it at the time."

"Of course. Thank you," he said, and the duo turned to exit the building. Goatee was already dialing on his phone.

Nicole turned around, then joined an old prospector on the bench as her legs threatened to give out. She replayed the conversation in her head, wondering if she had screwed up or given something away. She had been desperately trying to think as fast as she was talking, while fighting off questions in her head. How had the Gardiners found them at Wall Drug? Were they canvassing the entire state of South Dakota? Why had they picked Nicole of all people, because she was standing right by the entrance or because someone at the gas station had given them a description? And did they believe her or were they hiding that they suspected her?

She forced herself to her feet and walked to the front door, sidestepping a family that entered, and then peering outside. After a few seconds, she spotted the duo, now joined by two others in similar attire.

They stood in the middle row of parking spaces, not far from Jimmy's Jeep. Nicole at first feared they somehow knew which vehicle was theirs, but then saw them getting astride their Harley Davidson motorcycles. She watched until they backed out and rode off, then she returned to the bench. She withdrew her phone and texted Jimmy:

trouble

She forced a few deep breaths, then sent:

where r u?

His reply came a minute later:

bakcyard whas wrong

don't move. coming to you

She took a few more deep breaths, stood, and took a look out the window to confirm Wavy Hair, Goatee, and their pals were gone, and then headed down the hall to the Wall Drug Back Yard.

*   *   *

"She didn't say what it is?" Kira asked.

Jimmy shook his head. He and Kira had moved to the shade of a pavilion covering a walkway leading across the backyard.

"You think it's them?"

He looked right at her. "Nicole likes to worry sometimes, but she doesn't panic. This sounded urgent."

Kira turned one way then the other, searching the back yard. Jimmy did too with his eyes. There were a couple dozen people milling about—posing on the jackalope, going between buildings, resting on a bench, looking at a map. None that looked like a vengeful motorcycle gang, and none that were paying either of them any attention.

Nicole's garnet shirt and white shorts appeared around a trio of people waiting in line for pictures on the jackalope. Jimmy tapped Kira's arm and they met her in front of two bears carved out of logs and next to a one-ton petrified log. "What's up?" Jimmy asked. "Everything okay?"

"Yeah," she said, then raised her eyes to his head.

He took off his cowboy hat and tousled his hair.

"What's going on?" Kira asked.

"I came to find you all by the western wear store, and you weren't there."

"Yeah, we were taking pictures of my new hat," Jimmy said sheepishly.

Nicole didn't seem to mind. "I came out of the store and two guys approached me and asked if I'd seen you," she said, her eyes on Kira.

"Me?"

"They had your picture on a phone."

"What'd you say?"

"I said I'd seen you coming out of the store while I was coming in fifteen minutes ago. I said you got on a bike with some guy and rode off."

"Did they buy it?"

"I think so."

"You think so?"

"I was lying faster than I could think, Kira, but they left and met up with two other guys, and they rode away too."

"Oh man," she said, putting a hand on her forehead. "Oh man."

"But they're gone, right?" Jimmy said, touching Kira's arm for reassurance.

"They left," Nicole said. "Four of them. I replayed everything I said, and I don't think there's anything there to throw them. I mean, to make them doubt I was telling the truth."

"I just can't believe they found me here," Kira said.

"And picked you to question," Jimmy said to Nicole.

"I was standing twenty feet from the front door, so maybe I was the first person to ask."

Kira exhaled. "We should get out of here."

"Actually, I don't think so," Jimmy said.

"Why not?"

"Nicole said they left, and four of them?"

"One of them was calling as they left me, and I saw two other guys meet them at their bikes. Four."

"Sounds like they were calling off the search," he said. "Meaning they bought her story that you hopped on a hog with some guy and took off. So this is the *last* place they'll think you are now."

"So we should stay?" Kira said.

"Yeah. Let them ride on ahead. They'll probably figure you're headed for Rapid City, so we don't exactly want to roll into town an hour from now and risk running into them at the bus station or a restaurant."

Kira bit her lip. "I guess that makes sense."

"So what do we do?" Nicole asked.

"Besides drink more five-cent coffee?"

"Jimmy."

"Just to be extra careful, we should lay low for a little while. How about Kira and I go hang out in the arcade, in the back corner." He donned his cutter cowboy hat. "I'll practice my six-shootin' while she clutches my arm."

"Jimmy."

"Just stereotyping," he said to Kira, who didn't seem to mind. "Just in case there happens to be any other bikers strolling around, we'll be mostly out of sight and not where they'd expect anyhow."

"And what should I do, wander around to head off any others that might show up?"

"Too many guys in leather for that."

"I got a couple postcards. I could sit out on the front porch and write notes and keep an eye out?"

"That's a good idea." .

"And what do we do if they come back?" Kira asked.

"They won't," Jimmy said. "These are just precautions."

"But if they do?"

"She can warn us, and we'll be in a crowd of people. They won't try anything here."

Kira bit her lip.

"Besides," he growled, tugging his hat a little lower, "I've asked myself the question, and I feel lucky."

"Clint Eastwood, right?"

He pointed at her and clicked with his mouth.

Nicole rolled her eyes. "I'll text you," she said and walked off.

Kira, beaming from ear to ear, leaned in and grabbed Jimmy's arm. "I am definitely lucky that I found the two of you."

CHAPTER SIX

By now, Nicole was growing familiar with various stores, hallways, and alcoves of Wall Drug. Not counting entrances to the back yard via an alley that ran between it and the main store and that ended at 5th Avenue on the north side of the compound, there were four means of egress to or from the store. All faced Main Street on the West. One was the door they had used to enter originally, and inside of which Nicole had met Wavy Hair and Goatee. A second led into the main souvenir store and passed Ted Hustead's Cowboy Orchestra, a glass-enclosed set of mechanized figurines that played instruments and sang to passing customers. A third led to the drug counter, and the fourth was on the northwest corner and opened to the Emporium, with more gifts and an assortment of taffy. Nicole bought a small bag and wandered back through the store keeping an eye out for anyone in leather. She spotted a few people, but dismissed them as regular bikers. None of them had the BHG patch she'd spotted on Wavy Hair and Goatee or seemed intent on doing anything but browsing.

Nicole returned to the fudge store and picked out a small sampling— small being half a pound. With her taffy and fudge in tow, and content that no one affiliated with the Gardiner family was still searching for Kira at Wall Drug, she headed out to the front porch and took a seat on a bench halfway between the two middle doors. Hitching posts with bronze horses' heads atop them were interspersed with log support columns for the canopy over her, which still kept the bench in shade. The faintest of breezes at least offset the late afternoon heat, and Nicole took a few minutes to compose herself. She'd replayed events with Wavy Hair and Goatee half a dozen times and had yet to find a mistake they could use to determine Kira's true location.

Still keeping an eye out, she dug a pair of postcards out of her bag and then found a pen in her purse. On the backside of a picture of Mount Rushmore, she wrote a quick note to her college roommate. They had kept in touch over the summer, and Tabitha was one of the few people who understood Nicole's plight. She'd majored in English at South Carolina, with minors in education and journalism, opening doors in several directions. She'd interned and worked part-time in various professions over the summers and during the school year, and had landed a two-month contract as an assistant editor with a women's fashion magazine in Minneapolis upon graduation. It had been okay, but hadn't settled Nicole's mind as to whether to pursue a career in journalism, take her love for kids and combine it with her degree to become a teacher, or pursue further education. That had been part of the reason for this vacation, to clear her head and think.

The note to Tabitha complete, Nicole scanned the street again, then switched to the second postcard. It had "WALL DRUG" emblazoned on it in large letters, each filled with a different scene from the store. It was a little kitschy, but her parents would appreciate it. If she could get it to them. Wes and Karen Turner had been working as missionaries in the Philippines for the last three years, after Wes had served a long tenure as a pastor in Eau Claire. They helped run a girls' school in Manila, which pulled on Nicole's heart too when it came to a profession.

Thinking of her parents, thinking of the distance, thinking of the lack of contact choked Nicole up, but she kept the note light and festive. That meant omitting mention of Jimmy and Kira. She sighed, shaking the pen back and forth between her fingers. Their little touches, their smiles, their compliments—it all told a story that he liked her and she liked him. That was understandable—Kira was cute and pleasant, and Jimmy was decent-looking and fun. But he had something of a track record with girls—both in high school and since, from the little Nicole had heard of the latter. He either fell for a girl who didn't reciprocate his feelings or for one who did and got hurt when Jimmy moved on shortly thereafter. To Nicole's knowledge, he'd never gotten serious with a girl, but the cycle was taking a toll on him—even if he didn't let on. And there wasn't much chance of him and Kira having more than a whirlwind "romance," if flirting at Wall Drug could even be called romance.

Nicole sighed. Jimmy was twenty-four, and while he had typical male immaturities, he was a responsible adult. He didn't need his kid sister managing his life. She'd confided such things in Tabitha too, as soulmates did, and her roommate's advice had been simple: pray for him. Nicole had been muttering fragments and run-on prayers in her head since spotting Wavy Hair and Goatee, and she took a minute now to pray something a little more coherent, both for the group's safety, and for wisdom for Jimmy.

She finished the note to her parents and decided to figure out how to send a postcard around the world later. She put both postcards back into her bag of purchases and checked her phone. No word from Jimmy, which wasn't a surprise. It was after five-thirty, meaning a good forty-five minutes to an hour since her interaction with Wavy Hair and Goatee. The coast was clear. It was also getting late if they wanted to get to Rapid City, drop off Kira at the bus station, and get to their hotel and find dinner before it got really late.

So she stood and headed back through the mall one more time, through the back yard, and to the arcade. She found Jimmy, still in his boots, taking aim with a rifle in the shooting gallery. Animatronic targets popped up in an old west vignette, and he blasted away with a laser gun. Kira stood beside him, wearing his cowboy hat, firing a pistol herself. As Nicole approached, they seemed to be playfully arguing over who had taken out the latest target. It ended with him good-naturedly poking off her hat, and her giving him a shove that caused him to miss the next target.

Forget worrying about Jimmy falling for Kira.

He had fallen.

*   *   *

"Jim-my!" Kira squealed, giving him a shove. He had just blasted a skeleton head that popped up on her side of the shooting gallery, and winked at her as he took a step back. Out the corner of his eye, he spotted Nicole, and turned her way.

"Hey, everything okay?"

"Fine," she said in a way that made him think it wasn't.

"No sign of the Gardiners?" Kira asked.

Nicole shook her head. "Are you all ready to head out?"

"What time is it?" Kira asked.

"Twenty 'til six," Nicole answered.

"Wow."

"Time flies when you're having fun."

"I think we're set," Jimmy said. "Did you need to stop for fudge?"

Nicole held up a small paper bag.

"Okay then." He and Kira placed their guns on the counter and turned to leave. "You okay?" he asked Nicole, noting her arms folded as she leaned backward a touch.

"Fine," she said again, again lacking conviction.

They turned and exited to the back yard, the shadows beginning to grow across the pavement. The temperature was still hot, but a little more bearable than an hour ago. Figuring "When in Rome," Jimmy stopped at one of the ice water wells to get a free paper cup of ice water. Nicole continued walking, while Kira hung back for him. When Nicole reached the door leading inside and turned around, she sighed to see they weren't behind her.

"You sure you're okay?" Jimmy asked as she held the door for them.

"Just tired."

"Uh-huh," he said with an eyebrow raise as he walked past her.

"Jimmy."

He turned around. "Yeah?"

"Where are your shoes?"

He looked down at his boots, which he'd been wearing since he and Kira had taken pictures by the Conestoga wagon. "Hmm."

"Did you leave them at the shooting gallery?" Kira asked.

He snapped. He'd set them down to shoot and forgotten about them. "Two seconds," he said, then hurried back—as fast as his growingly sore feet would allow—to the shooting gallery and retrieved his shoes from beside a teenage boy getting his Billy the Kid on. Jimmy stepped aside, changed footwear, and carried his boots back to the mall where Nicole and Kira were waiting quietly.

"How far is it to Rapid City?" Kira asked as they started walking again.

"Forty-five minutes." Jimmy answered. "Maybe a little more to downtown."

"Are we going downtown?"

"I assume that's where the bus station is."

She nodded.

"Something wrong?" Nicole asked.

"I'm afraid they'll be watching the bus station."

"We'll be careful."

Jimmy cast her a glance, which she returned behind Kira's back with a practical glare.

They emerged onto the sidewalk, then out into the sun as they crossed the northbound lane of Main Street to the Jeep. He'd forgotten to crack the windows, and was sure the interior would be a sauna. So when Nicole asked him to open the back, he held up a finger. "I'm gonna get the windows down first."

He handed his boots to Kira, who also still wore his cowboy hat. He nearly burned his hand on the door handle as he fished his keys from his pocket, then leaned in to crank the engine.

Nothing happened.

Jimmy withdrew the key and climbed onto the seat. He reinserted the key and turned the ignition. No clicking, no grinding, nothing. He withdrew the key again, stared at it for a second, and determined it was in fact the right key. He took a breath and tried again, getting the same result.

With a sigh, he climbed down and walked back to where Nicole and Kira stood. His sister raised her eyebrows at him.

"It's dead," he answered.

CHAPTER SEVEN

"What do you mean it's dead?" Nicole asked.

"Not living," Jimmy said. "It won't start."

"Dead battery?"

He shrugged.

"Let me try," she said, extending a hand for the key.

He tossed his key ring to her and stepped back so she could get around to the driver's side door. He turned to Kira. "You should have maybe held out for a duo with a more modern vehicle."

"I chose well," she said.

He nodded.

"How old is your battery?" Nicole asked as she came back around the back of the Jeep.

"I don't know, a couple years. Hasn't given me any trouble."

"Do you have roadside assistance on your insurance?"

He shrugged again.

"Jimmy."

"What? I drive from my house to Red Robin and Cabela's. I don't think a lot about breakdowns."

She sighed and reached for her purse.

"Here," Jimmy said, taking her bags from her, then his boots back from Kira. Nicole found her wallet, then a card inside it, and proceeded to call the number on the card. "You might as well wait in the shade," Jimmy said to Kira.

"Actually, I could use the restroom." She took off the cowboy hat and placed it on his head. "I'll meet you back here."

He nodded and watched her off.

"Where's she going?" Nicole asked, lowering her phone.

"Get rid of her coffee," he said. "Any luck?"

"Holding."

"It's Sunday," Jimmy said.

"I know that."

"I mean, nothing's going to be open as far as a mechanic."

"Super."

"Does roadside assistance replace a battery?"

"Sometimes."

"I don't think it's a battery," he said.

"Why not?"

"Dead batteries usually click or rev or something. Don't they?"

"Not if they're totally dead."

"Which doesn't make sense, since it's been fine all day."

"Yes, hello," Nicole said back into the phone, and turned to pace away from Jimmy. He lifted his hat and wiped the sweat off his brow and onto his sleeve, then replaced the hat. He watched his sister, wondering why she had a bee in her bonnet. It was more than the Jeep not starting, because she'd been cranky before that, and it wasn't just picking up Kira—he didn't think. Whatever the case, he figured it was best not to exacerbate it. So he dug out his phone and began looking for a towing service in the area, just in case Nicole's insurance carrier's roadside assistance wasn't readily available in Wall, South Dakota.

It wasn't. Nicole reported a minute later that it would be a couple of hours before someone could come. Jimmy held up his phone, showing the number of a local towing service.

"Where are we going to have it towed?"

"I saw a garage when we were turning onto Main Street, just down the way."

"It won't be open tonight, like you said."

"I know."

"That means spending the night."

"I saw several hotels."

Nicole sighed. "We should wait for roadside assistance."

"Odds are, we'll still need it towed. I don't think it's the battery."

"Then what?"

He shrugged.

She sighed again.

"Let's ask her," he said as Kira emerged from the darkness of the porch and started across the street. When she rejoined them, Jimmy explained the situation.

"So we're stuck here overnight?"

"Unless you want to try to hitch a ride with someone else," Jimmy said.

Kira winced.

"Call the towing service," Nicole said. "See if they can get here any sooner."

He nodded.

"I'll start checking hotels in case. I hope you're okay with budget accommodations," she said to Kira.

"I'd prefer it," she said. "I'm not exactly flush."

"We'll pay," Jimmy said, pausing from dialing. He looked at Kira but spoke to Nicole as much as to her. "We'd be getting two rooms anyhow, whether you were with us or not."

Kira's smile was worth whatever smoke was coming from Nicole's ears, so he finished placing his call. It was answered promptly, by a man named Brett who ran a one-man towing service in eastern Pennington County. He promised to be there in fifteen minutes, and the trio adjourned to a bench in the shade to wait.

Jimmy expected a rig like Larry the Cable Guy's character in *Cars*, and impressed Kira with various impersonations of Owen Wilson, Cheech Marin, and John Ratzenberger while they waited. But he was surprised when a new, bright blue truck quietly coasted down Main Street. "Brett's Badlands Towing" was scrawled in cursive along the side, and someone had hand-painted buttes and gorges beneath the text on the door and wispy clouds above the text. Brett was the opposite of Larry the Cable Guy in appearance too, tall and thin, but with a firm handshake and a friendly smile. He had a portable battery charger, and before loading the Jeep onto his rig, attempted to jump the battery. After a few minutes, he and Jimmy confirmed that was not the issue, and made towing arrangements. Brett recommended Wall Auto Helpers, the place Jimmy had seen on the way into town. He knew the owner, which figured in a small town, and offered to call him that night to alert him of the Jeep's arrival and make sure it got on the docket for the morning. Then he asked if they had a place to stay.

Jimmy gestured at Nicole and Kira, still waiting in the shade, and said they were looking for places.

"Hole-in-the-Wall Inn doesn't sound like much," Brett said, "but they've got clean rooms, cable, and a discount if you mention our name. Plus the café serves the best pie west of the Missouri, and it's walking distance from Wall Auto Helpers."

"We'll check it out."

"How many of there are you?"

"Three."

"I can squeeze you all in the cab if you want. Not sure if you've got luggage or anything, but I can drop you there or wherever on the way."

"Give me a sec to check with them?"

"I'll get it loaded."

Jimmy thanked him and trudged over to Nicole and Kira, where he laid out the situation.

"I was actually looking at the Hole-in-the-Wall," Nicole said. "Rooms are only fifty-nine per night, and the pictures make it look clean."

"He can give us a ride over," Jimmy said. "Drop off our luggage, then find some dinner?"

Nicole nodded.

"Works for me," Kira said.

It only took Brett a few minutes to get the Jeep loaded onto the back of his truck, and then the trio crammed into the clean cab. Because of the angled parking, Brett had backed his tow truck down northbound Main Street, blocking traffic. With everyone inside, he proceeded south to 6th

Avenue, where he maneuvered over to the proper lane and continued south. When he reached the boulevard they had come in on, he turned west and made a loop around to the eastbound lane, driving past Wall Auto Helpers and pulling into the parking lot of the Hole-in-the-Wall Inn.

A vaulted roof marked the office and the Hole-in-the-Wall Café, while a pair of wings stretched out south and east, each containing six rooms with doors facing the parking lot or a surprisingly clean pool and surrounding patio. The trio quickly unloaded their luggage and anything they wanted from the Jeep. Then Jimmy gave Brett the keys. Brett promised again to reach out to Keith, the owner of Wall Auto Helpers, and they shook hands before he drove off.

It took only a few minutes to procure (at a ten-percent discount) a pair of side-by-side rooms facing South Boulevard. Jimmy quickly dropped his duffel and purchases on his bed, then opted to keep the cowboy hat on. He locked his door and leaned on a pillar supporting a small porch over the sidewalk while waiting for Nicole and Kira. His sister emerged first, mumbling about the hassle of canceling the first night of their reservation in Rapid City.

"You okay?" Jimmy asked when she was done.

"Are you going to keep asking me that?"

"Until you give me an answer I believe."

Nicole sighed. "It's been a long, weird day. There's a lot to process."

He nodded.

"And I'm a little concerned that you seem less interested in processing and more interested in—"

The door opened and Kira stepped out, causing Nicole to stop mid-sentence. But Jimmy didn't need her to finish. He may not have been an expert at reading women's looks—even his sister's—but he could tell she wasn't wild about Kira, or about him and Kira having a good time, despite the circumstances. He lifted his hat a little, the way cowboys in Westerns often did, and decided he wasn't going to let his sister's mood impact his.

Kira looked the same as she had earlier in the day, which was just fine by him. Nicole had swapped her flip-flops for tennis shoes, now that they were on foot for the rest of the evening, and bound her hair into a ponytail. She swiped a loose strand away from a pair of brown, oversized sunglasses. "Where to?" she asked.

"Those hot beef sandwiches looked pretty good at Wall Drug," Jimmy answered.

"In this heat?"

"Otherwise, we passed the 3 Amigos Cantina. But I doubt they have anything besides Mexican food." He looked at her for a minute. "Chevy Chase? Spilling the taco?"

"I got it, Jimmy." She turned. "Kira?"

She shrugged. "Whichever."

Nicole looked to Jimmy.

"You decide," he said.

"Mexican food sounds good, but only if you promise not to sing 'Blue Shadows on the Trail' all night."

"I will do my best."

CHAPTER EIGHT

Nicole trailed Jimmy and Kira as they walked a few blocks to 3 Amigos Cantina, located across Main Street from the Harley Davidson dealer and a block south of Wall Drug. The sign hanging over the sidewalk featured a silhouette of a man in a mariachi costume, just like the ones worn by Steve Martin, Chevy Chase, and Martin Short in ¡*Three Amigos!* The trio was seated at a bistro table with swivel chairs in an airy dining room that resembled an urban loft more than a cantina. But out of the heat and with food for her rumbling stomach imminent, Nicole wasn't about to complain.

They took a few minutes to study the menu, which also featured the mariachi silhouette, and to attack endless chips and salsa. After they had placed orders, Kira leaned forward. "I just want to thank you both again for everything you've done for me. I can't believe where today ended after how it started."

"You're welcome," Nicole said.

"It's actually been kind of fun," Jimmy said.

"Fun?" Nicole asked.

"I always dreamt of being a spy."

"You tried on hats while I lied to two guys showing me Kira's picture. Not exactly James Bond."

He shrugged. "Gotta start somewhere."

"And I'm sorry if I've caused any stress," Kira said.

"None," Jimmy said as he reached for a chip and plunged it into the salsa.

"You haven't," Nicole said, which earned her a sweet smile, that kind that could make her forget the misgivings she still had about Kira. It was the same smile she'd seen on a lot of girls at South Carolina, the kind that could charm guys to do almost anything. Thinking of that made Nicole's misgivings return.

"You know," Jimmy said, pausing to lick a crumb off his lip, "this car breakdown may turn out to be a good thing."

"How so?" Kira asked.

"Well, figure Braden's family followed Nicole's fib and headed to Rapid City. They'll watch the bus station, probably ask at hotels and gas stations. If we had gone on, there's a chance they'd stumble onto somebody who had seen us. Slim chance, but a chance," he said, reaching for another chip. "But like I said before, there's no way they'd think you got on some guy's bike and rode with him a block south to have tacos or three blocks to spend the night at the Hole-in-the-Wall Inn."

"Meaning this is the last place they'd think to look for you," Nicole said.

Kira reached for a chip. "What about tomorrow, when we *do* get to Rapid City?"

"They can't chase you forever," Nicole said. "And, like I said before, we'll be careful. But once you're on a bus, you could be anywhere. They can't have the manpower to chase you all across the country. I'm surprised they came this far."

"I don't know. The Gardiners can be obsessive."

"That reminds me," Nicole said. "The two guys I ran into both had patches that said 'BHG' on them. Something-Something-Gardiner?"

Kira frowned. "I don't know. Probably. They were big on their family identity. Big Hog Gardiners, maybe. Big Hairy Gardiners, more like it."

"Booger-Headed Gardiners," Jimmy chimed in.

"How mature," Nicole said as Kira snickered.

"Bike-Hoarding Gardiners," Jimmy said.

"Black-Hearted Gardiners," Kira said

"Their senior members are Blue-Haired Gardiners," Jimmy said.

44

"I'm back in first grade," Nicole muttered.

"Come on, Nic, we aren't holding a coming-out party in Mother and Dad's plantation parlor."

She frowned.

"Lighten up."

She nodded and took a sip through her straw of her sweet tea. She exhaled. "Blonde-Hunting Gardiners."

They all laughed, but it was cut short when two guys in leather jackets walked in the front door. They were followed a minute later by two women in leather. Several furtive glances from Kira eased her mind that they weren't part of the Gardiner family, and when they were shown to a table across the restaurant, she took a deep breath. She fiddled with a chip, then looked up at Nicole. "What did the guys look like?"

"That asked about you?"

She nodded.

"One was white, big, buzz cut, a long goatee," she said stroking an imaginary beard. "Tattoos."

"Blond hair?"

"Yeah."

"Sounds like Frank. Braden's uncle."

"The other was a Native American, wavy black hair starting to gray."

"Johnny. Works with Braden."

"I didn't get a look at the two they met up with outside."

"But?" Jimmy said, noticing the hesitation in her voice.

"It struck me as odd, how friendly they were."

"Friendly?" he asked.

"Called me 'ma'am,' were hurried but still polite, things like that."

"They put on a good front," Kira said. "And, they're generally pleasant people, until you get on their bad side. Braden . . . could be the sweetest guy in the world, the total opposite of what you'd expect from a tough, gun-toting, Harley-riding guy in leather. But . . . the way he looked at me when he threatened me . . ." She shook her head.

There wasn't much more to be gained by discussing the past, Nicole figured, and Jimmy apparently concurred. They turned the conversation to their vacation plans and the differences between life in northern

Wisconsin and South Carolina. The only interruption during dinner of shrimp tacos, a steak quesadilla, and a taco salad was a call from Keith, the owner of Wall Auto Helpers. After taking the call outside, Jimmy came back and reported that Keith guessed—based on his conversation with Jimmy—that the problem with the Jeep was either the solenoid or starter motor. Either way, he promised to get after it when he opened at eight the following morning.

They finished their meals and exited the cantina full and festive less than an hour after entering it. The sun was low and the shadows cast by building façades and decorative lampposts were long.

Jimmy checked his phone. "Quarter to eight."

"Meaning the sidewalks roll up in fifteen minutes," Kira said.

"I think so," Nicole agreed.

"Take advantage while they're out," Jimmy said, nodding north.

"I'm Wall Drugged out, Jimmy."

"It's only open 'til eight too. But it's a beautiful evening, we're in a heartland town straight out of central casting, and I could stand to work off that last quesadilla wedge."

"Me too," Kira said, putting a hand on a stomach that was flat as the Minnesota interstate. But the evening was perfect, so Nicole agreed, and the trio strolled up the east side of Main Street to the corner of 5th Avenue, stopping across from a bank on the east side of the street and a building housing the county sheriff, highway patrol, and the satellite office of South Dakota Game, Fish & Parks on the west. They crossed the street and turned south.

"You ever ride a bike?" Jimmy asked Kira.

"You mean like a pedal bike?" she replied.

"I mean like that," he said, nodding at a Harley parked in front of one of the jewelry stores on their right.

"With Braden a bunch, but never my own."

"I had a dirt bike in high school."

"I'd pay to see you on that now," Nicole said, "with that hat."

"I always thought a real bike, a hog, would be terrifying."

"Why's that?" Kira asked.

"You fall on a dirt bike, you'll get a little banged up," Jimmy said. "You fall on a Harley, it'll crush you."

"Pretty sure falling isn't all that common," Nicole said.

He shrugged.

"Don't worry, I'm sure teenage you was very cute on your dirt bike," Kira said with extra pouty lips and a smirk that came out in a giggle.

Jimmy winced, and Nicole couldn't contain a grin either.

They stopped at the corner of South Boulevard, just as the sun was setting almost directly down its northwestern track. The afternoon clouds had dissipated, leaving just a few wisps in the sky to catch the sunlight. Out in the wide-open space, it was beautiful.

Jimmy nodded his head left. "Anybody have room for ice cream?"

Nicole followed his gaze a block up the street to the glowing red sign of a Dairy Queen.

"My treat," he said.

"That sounds good," Kira said.

"I was actually thinking that pool at the motel seems inviting," Nicole said.

"That a no?"

"No, ice cream sounds inviting too. Especially if this is one of those rare moments where you're buying."

CHAPTER NINE

This was the life, Jimmy realized. He sat sprawled on a chaise lounge lawn chair on the patio circling the Hole-in the-Wall Inn's small pool. The sky above was a million shades of pink, magenta, and purple as it reflected the last vestiges of daylight. The air was still warm, borderline hot, but comfortably so, especially since he held a Dairy Queen Blizzard in his hand, slowly spooning chocolate ice cream with hunks of cookie dough into his mouth. He was on vacation with his sister, who, despite their distance the last few years and her somewhat cranky mood that afternoon, was his oldest friend. And they'd met Kira, helped her out of a jam, gotten to know her. And now, thanks to a car breakdown, they had more time with her.

The two women sat with their feet dangling in the pool, which they'd found both clean and warm. Now and then a car went by on South Boulevard, or a person crossed the parking lot to or from the café, a motel room, or just because it was on their path. And traffic on I-90 a few hundred yards away was constant. But for all intents and purposes, they had the world to themselves.

Jimmy stirred the contents of his cup, blending the melted parts with the solid ice cream below, then took another bite. He looked at Kira, who, like his sister, licked an ice cream cone as she swished her feet back and forth in the pool. There was something about her—a . . . sweetness that came out through her vulnerability, through her trust in him and Nicole, through her ability to have a good time trying on cowboy gear or playing like kids at the shooting gallery or enjoying the simple pleasures of ice cream and a swimming pool in spite of recent danger—that he found alluring. It worked with her natural good looks to make her beautiful, and while Jimmy knew their time together was fleeting and there was no future beyond delivering her to Rapid City tomorrow, that didn't mean he couldn't thoroughly enjoy the moment. No matter what Nicole might think or say.

Jimmy noticed the two of them giggling, and turned a wary eye toward them, staring at Nicole until she cracked. "We were just wondering if you were going to sleep in your new hat."

He looked up at the brim of his cowboy hat, which had become so light on his head he didn't even notice it. "Well, I didn't buy it just for the photo op," he said, adjusting it slightly. He frowned, wondering why that statement suddenly bothered him. He shrugged it off; this was no time for worrying. "I mean, if you can bring back a Brett Butler accent and an SEC attitude from a few years at Carolina. . ."

"What? Brett Butler?"

"The lady from *Gone With the Wind*. Well, I declare," he said in falsetto, "I do believe you Notheners have underestimated the value of mediocre Southeastern Conference football."

Nicole's look was somewhere between incredulity and amusement. "Brett Butler . . ." she finally said through a laugh, "is the lady from *Grace Under Fire*. And *Rhett* Butler was the leading *man* in *Gone With the Wind*."

He frowned.

"You have me confused with Scarlett O'Hara, and I do not have a Southern accent. And if I did, it would not sound like that."

"Why would an Irish girl have a Southern accent?"

"What?"

"O'Hara. That's Irish. Or Scottish." He shook his head. "Not Southern genteel."

"What?" Nicole asked again, barely able to keep in her laughter.

"And you can argue you all you want, but when you call people 'honey' and 'sugar' and ask for sweet tea with your tacos, you're Southern. And remember when you practically started a fight with Tyler a few Christmases back over who stole whose logo, the Packers or Georgia?"

Nicole started to reply, then stopped when she saw Kira doubling over in silent laughter. She fell to her side, then shrieked as she nearly fell into the pool, then shrieked again when half of her ice cream did fall off the cone and into the pool. Nicole had reached out to catch her, lost her balance, and nearly fell in as well, flailing to stay on the ledge and in the process dropping her cone with a splat on the patio.

Jimmy shook his head, then sang a high-pitched version of Toby Keith's "I Can't Take You Anywhere."

Nicole stood, retrieved the remnants of her ice cream cone, and tossed it in a garbage can. "You come at me for being Southern, while you dress and sing like you're auditioning for an all-female musical remake of a John Ford classic."

"I have . . . no idea what that even means," he said, huffing out a laugh. "But you're going to make our guest fall into the pool yet," he said, nodding at Kira who lay back on the patio, her diaphragm bouncing as she laughed, one hand over her face.

"I'm going to get the fudge I bought, seeing as how my dessert has gone by the wayside." Nicole placed a hand on Jimmy's shoulder in passing. "Behave yourself while I'm gone."

He tipped the brim of his cap in concession, then spooned some more of his fast-melting Blizzard.

*   *   *

When Nicole returned with both fudge and taffy, she and Kira joined Jimmy at a mesh table off the corner of the pool. A gentle breeze had kicked up, bringing warm air across the badlands, and Jimmy watched it play with wisps of Kira's hair. A low, mournful wail announced the arrival of an eastbound freight train, just before the locomotive's headlight pierced a path through the darkness. Once again, Jimmy felt as if he, Nicole, and Kira were the only three people on the planet.

"I could get used to this," Kira said after a few minutes of silence, other than for the clackety-clack-clack of a hundred hopper cars following the locomotives through town.

"What's that?" Nicole asked through a mouthful of taffy. "Vacation?"

"No, being free," she said, turning her face into the breeze and closing her eyes. "Not having a care in the world."

"Amen to that, pilgrim," Jimmy said in his best John Wayne accent with another tip of his cap.

Nicole shook her head and rolled her eyes at him.

"The last few weeks with Braden and his family, and especially running today . . ." Kira shook her head. "I'd forgotten what this was like." Her eyes now open, she swept them across the darkening panorama. "I'd forgotten why I originally came to South Dakota."

"Wasn't that for work?" Nicole asked.

"Well, yes, but also because I wanted to see the world, experience the vastness. Somehow it makes you feel smaller, the way looking at the stars or standing on a butte looking at the Mississippi River does, and that feeling of smallness makes you feel bigger inside."

Jimmy frowned. He didn't quite know what she was saying, but somehow he knew what she meant.

"What's CoMo like?" Nicole asked.

"CoMo?" Kira asked.

"George Clooney's lake in Italy?" Jimmy asked.

"Columbia, Missouri," Nicole said. "You said you looked for work there, and I assumed you had grown up there."

"Oh, yeah. I just haven't heard it called CoMo before," she said.

"Must be an SEC thing," Jimmy said.

"Missouri is in the SEC," Nicole said. "It's how everyone at South Carolina referred to Columbia, Missouri, as opposed to Columbia, South Carolina."

"Clever. So CoMo and CoSC?"

She plonked a piece of taffy off his forehead.

"Columbia is a nice college town," Kira said. "Fastest growing in the state, a hip vibe. But it's . . . crowded, and not just with people. There's trees everywhere, hills and forests outside town. Somehow it makes you feel . . . stuck."

"You're not stuck out here," Jimmy said. "I've seen three trees since lunch."

"You think you'll ever go back there?" Nicole asked.

"To visit, maybe. My mom and grandma both live in Columbia. But, no. I felt the same way when I left Columbia—left Missouri, in fact—that I felt when I left Pierre today. I had no idea what would happen or if I'd be able to actually get away, but I felt like a bird with wings that had been unpinned." She sighed.

"Something wrong?" Nicole asked.

"That carefree vibe is having trouble staying," Kira said. "I can't help thinking that Braden's family is going to find me, that this won't be a happy ending."

"You really think they'll go to the ends of the earth to find you?"

"I don't know."

"I mean, don't take this wrong, but you weren't an insider, one of their ranks who broke away from the cult or turned on their plan. You said it yourself, you don't know *what* they're planning."

"I know," Kira said, twisting an empty taffy wrapper in her fingers. "I don't have anything on these guys, nothing that should make me a target. But all they have to do is think that I know something."

"Why would they think that?"

"Maybe I *should* know something, based on what I've seen and heard. Or what if I *do* know something but don't know that I know it?"

Jimmy dipped into his cup, which was empty of ice cream but still contained a few balls of cookie dough that he'd saved. He lifted one to his mouth, and kept the spoon there to hide a frown. Kira had told him, while browsing for hats, that she knew names, faces, property layout, a gun count, and incriminating comments the Gardiners had made. Now she claimed not to know anything. Did she mean "knowing something" differently than she had meant "knowing things" earlier? Was her afternoon comment a "fog of war" moment? Or was one or the other statement a mistruth, a sign that she was hiding something?

"That's a lot of ifs and maybes," Nicole said.

"I know," Kira answered. "But until I'm truly gone, far away from here forever . . . I don't know that I'll be able to really feel safe."

Even that was somewhat contradictory to what she'd said just a few minutes ago, about not having a care in the world. Maybe she was just confused, carried back and forth with her emotions.

"Well, you're safe for now anyhow," Nicole said. "Nobody knows where we are, and Braden and his family certainly aren't going to look for you poolside at the Hole-in-the-Wall Inn eating taffy and dropping ice cream into the pool."

Kira giggled, and for no reason, it spawned into another fit of laughter. Even Jimmy couldn't help chuckling. He thought of Kira stealing his hat at the shooting gallery, of her laughing uncontrollably by the pool, of that sweetness he'd seen several times before and now again in her features as the moonlight cast them in its pale glow. He wasn't going to hold a few passing remarks in the heat of the moment against her, or, for that matter, fret about eluding the Gardiners at the Rapid City bus station or stress over saying goodbye. Tomorrow, they could deal with all that.

Tonight was too fun for such concerns.

CHAPTER TEN

Something caused Nicole to stir, and she turned over to look at the clock on the nightstand between the two twin beds in her and Kira's room. Red numbers were fuzzy without her contact lenses, and she squinted to make them out. 12:21. She sighed and started to roll back over, then stopped. She looked at Kira's bed, and in the faint glow from the clock numbers, a smoke detector on the ceiling, and ambient light peeking in through a crease in the curtains, she saw that it was empty.

Nicole propped herself up on her elbows and blinked a few times. The bed was definitely empty, the covers pulled back. Kira was not in the lone armchair in the corner, nor standing by the window. No light streamed under the bathroom door.

Nicole tousled her hair. After hanging by the pool until almost ten, the trio had called it a long, busy day and split into their rooms. Jimmy had no doubt stayed up late watching reruns of some adventure TV show—*Leverage* or *Burn Notice* or *Covert Affairs*—but Nicole and Kira had both done their nightly routines and gone straight to bed. In Nicole's case, at least, sleep had come easily. It would have come easily again now, and she was tempted to lie back down. But something about Kira's absence bugged her. She doubted Braden's family had circled back to Wall, started questioning hotel clerks, and somehow lured Kira out of bed without waking Nicole. She also doubted she was next door watching TV with Jimmy—he was too smart for that. A late-night walk, however? Thinking by moonlight by the pool?

Nicole dropped her head back on the pillow, trying to still the analytical part of her mind, the part that said she should investigate. She gave it a few minutes, and when she was certain Kira wasn't using the bathroom without a light, she sighed and sat up, swinging her legs off the bed. She reached for the lamp over the nightstand and flicked it on, flooding the room with its yellow light. It did not illuminate Kira with knees tucked to her chest in the corner brooding.

Nicole stood, looking down at her legs. She was a cold sleeper, no matter the climate, and wore cotton pajama pants with an oversized, extra-comfy gray sweatshirt with a navy blue palmetto tree and crescent moon—icons from the South Carolina state flag—stamped on the front. She deemed this to be acceptable attire for midnight, and padded into the bathroom where she'd left her glasses. She donned them, tousled her hair again, and ducked back out into the room. She stabbed her feet into her flip-flops, then remembered a room key at the last moment.

It was gone.

Nicole sighed. Kira had left, taking the only key—an actual key, not a keycard, attached to a plastic fob with the room number engraved on it. That was considerate, at least, meaning she could let herself in quietly. But it also meant that if Nicole left the room, she'd be stuck.

There was nowhere for Kira to have gone, other than a walk, and if worst came to worst, Nicole could wake Jimmy and crash in his room. So she slipped from the room and onto the porch. The parking lot was lit by the moon, half full and high in the sky, and a pair of pale lights on top of rickety poles. Beyond the lot, the city of Wall seemed asleep. Streetlamps lit a vacant boulevard. To the right, hotel and gas station signs imbued the sky with red and blue hues. Nicole cast her eyes right and left and saw no signs of Kira out for a midnight stroll.

She turned toward Jimmy's room and saw no signs of activity there—no lights on, no glow from a TV. She debated not waking him, but reasoned he would want her to, especially if Kira's absence was anything other than innocent. Hoping she didn't disturb any other patrons, she rapped softly on his door. She waited nearly a minute, then tightened her fist and knocked a little harder. When a third knock a minute later produced no result, she thought about calling his cell. It was fifty-fifty he'd left it on, but she had left her phone in her room. Her room she was now locked out of.

Yet again, Nicole sighed, then turned toward the lobby of the hotel and, on the far side of it, the pool. Her relief at not finding Jimmy and Kira cuddled up streaming *Almost Paradise* would be temporary if she found them swimming together in the middle of the night. But as she rounded the corner, she could see the pool and the patio around it were empty. If she found them holding hands in the bleachers of the rodeo grounds between the motel and the interstate . . .

She turned and looked through the lobby, and spotted movement in the café beyond it. Shocked that it would be open 24/7, she figured it was worth a try and pulled the glass door to the lobby. The front desk was unmanned, while a fat TV in the corner silently played The Weather Channel. She passed a rack containing half a hundred brochures for area attractions and pushed through another door with "Hole-in-the-Wall Café – Open All Night" stenciled on the glass. There was a serving counter to the left, with six barstools facing it. Straight ahead was an old jukebox beneath a window. To the right were three booths—each with their own window. Jimmy, wearing his cowboy hat, sat in the last booth, his back to the door. Kira, her hair in a messy bun, sat opposite him. It was better than the bleachers . . .

"Hiya, hon," a woman behind the counter said. She had bright pink, spiky hair and studs through her ears, eyebrows, and chin, and Nicole figured it was the only type of person who would work solo in a diner at this hour. At least her smile was genuine.

"I'm with them," Nicole said.

"Can I get you anything?"

"No, I'm fine. Thanks."

The woman nodded and resumed wiping down the surface of the counter. Nicole trudged over to Jimmy and Kira. Both had coffee mugs and pie plates—the pie half eaten—in front of them.

"Not interrupting, am I?" Nicole asked as she slid in beside Kira.

"No, of course not," Kira answered.

"Nic, you want some pie?" Jimmy asked. "Peach is delicious."

She observed that his pie was served à la mode, and raised her eyes to his cowboy hat. It did not match a Green Bay Packers T-shirt that she knew, from past experiences, had served as sleepwear for him for years. Somehow, the combination looked utterly ridiculous, or maybe that was just the hour.

"What are you all doing here?"

"Eating pie."

"I mean why?"

"I couldn't sleep," Kira said. "I didn't wake you, did I?"

"No."

"I thought I'd go for a walk, then saw the TV on in Jimmy's room." She shrugged. "I knocked, and he suggested pie."

"Seriously, Nic, try th—"

She cut him off with a look, then softened it when she realized their coffee and pie date was harmless. "Was he wearing the hat when you knocked?" she asked.

"No," Kira said with a laugh.

Jimmy made a show of doffing the cap, revealing thoroughly disheveled hair. He ran a hand roughly over it, then put the hat back on.

"Good choice," Nicole said.

"We were actually talking about tomorrow," Kira said.

Jimmy took a slug of coffee. "We figure we're stuck here 'til at least noon."

"And possibly longer," Kira said. "Depending on what's wrong, what parts they might need, and the odds of having them on hand."

"In case you didn't notice, there's not a Napa or AutoZone just down the street," Jimmy said.

"Great," Nicole said. She pushed the sleeves on her sweatshirt up to the elbow. "So you all figure out what to do with the morning?"

"Checkout time is noon," Jimmy said, "so sleeping in, for starters."

"Well, when you have a second dessert at midnight . . ."

"Third, if you count the taffy and fudge."

Kira giggled.

"Then, this place actually has a pretty appealing breakfast menu."

"I can't believe they get enough business," Nicole muttered, making sure Pink Hair wasn't around.

Jimmy shrugged. "You're a trucker on the lonely highway, want to take a load off and have a slice of pie and a second slice of Americana with it . . ."

Nicole shook her head and looked at Kira. "Would you believe he's a romantic? This guy?" she said, pointing.

"Well, he did invite me to pie."

"I'm drawn by the open road," Jimmy said with another shrug. "Nothing romantic about it." He slugged more coffee.

"Okay, so after we sleep in and have breakfast," Nicole said. "What then, especially if it is going to take most of the day?"

"We'll have to see if we need to get another night. If not, I can drink a good quarter's worth of coffee at Wall Drug and browse. I could use a belt buckle."

She rolled her eyes, then leaned on the edge of the table. "We are on a time limit. This is already cutting one day in Rapid City."

He shrugged. "Not like there's much we can do about it. Even if tomorrow's shot, we still have a day for the badlands and a day for Mount Rushmore. And if worst comes to worst, we could do the badlands day after tomorrow on our way in to Rapid City."

"You forget, we have to take Kira to the bus station."

"She is willing to hike with us first, *if* it comes to that."

"They surely won't come looking for me on a hiking trail," Kira said.

"No, I suppose not."

"It'll work out somehow," Jimmy said, cutting off a wedge of pie, then stabbing his fork into the ice cream to get a little of it too. The bite was huge, and barely fit into his mouth. He swallowed, rinsed with coffee, and caught Pink Hair's eye at the right moment for a refill. When she was gone, he said, "The big question is, what's after you get on that bus?"

Kira looked down. "I still don't know."

"Have you figured out where you'll go, in the interim?" Nicole asked. "You have to get a ticket for somewhere."

"I've been thinking Denver," she said. "From there I can go south to Texas or New Mexico, west, or even back north. And I ought to be able to get lost in Denver."

"Plus, you don't want to keep heading west on 90," Jimmy said. "In theory, that's where they'd look for you."

"Why's that?" Nicole asked.

"Because people running tend to run in a straight line."

"This from watching all those episodes of *NCIS* that one Christmas?"

"This is from running away from Mike Peabody on the middle school playground," he said with a grin.

"But as far as what's after Denver," Kira said, "I don't know. I guess I'll go where there's work, maybe find a town where there's enough people to blend in but not so many that anyone would think to look for me there. Then, try to start life over."

"You should come to Eau Claire," Jimmy said, and if Nicole had been wearing closed-toe shoes, she would have drilled his shin.

"It's a city, but nobody knows anything about it. Most people, present company included," he said with a playful grin at Kira, "couldn't find it on a map. And it's east, not west. They'd never find you there."

Nicole tore her eyes away from Jimmy to Kira, hoping she'd shoot him down. About next, he'd suggest she forget the bus station and just come home with them.

"Maybe someday," Kira said, and Nicole exhaled. "But for now, I need the wide-open spaces. I'm thinking Arizona. I hear Sedona is beautiful."

Jimmy began singing Jamie O'Neal's "There is No Arizona," and—closed-toe shoe or not—Nicole found his shin and kicked it mid-chorus.

CHAPTER ELEVEN

Monday dawned warm and sticky, and also quite early. The combination made the prospects of a morning run unpleasant for Nicole, but after the way she'd been packing in sweets—a Snickers bar, a donut at Wall Drug, part of a Dairy Queen cone, and several pieces of fudge and taffy—the day before, it was necessary. She and Kira had left Jimmy with the last half of his cup of coffee around one a.m., and when Nicole had awakened, Kira had still been sound asleep. She'd donned a pair of running shorts and a tank top and exited to the yellowish haze post sunrise.

A dirt trail led past the Wall Rodeo Arena and passed under the interstate next to the railroad tracks. Wary of rattlesnakes or other wilderness creatures, Nicole followed the trail to a small service road that ran along the interstate and also curved to head due south through a small, somewhat wooded neighborhood. She followed it to a highway identified as Golf Course Road, by which time she was sweating profusely. But this was nothing compared to summer mornings in South Carolina.

Running typically gave Nicole a chance to think and pray, and this was no exception as she headed east. She thought about Jimmy and Kira, about Jimmy and her, about their futures. Jimmy seemed content to drift through life, and that was his prerogative. But Nicole wanted more. She wanted a career, a family someday, and that necessitated a husband. When she'd gone off to South Carolina, she'd dreamt about finding it all there—

a godly Southern man with the desire to raise a big family, a degree that would transition to a career, and because of those two, a settled future. She'd left as single as she'd arrived and with a degree that gave her options but predestined none of them.

She had hoped, somewhere during the car rides and nature hikes and slow dinners at relaxing restaurants to talk to Jimmy about this. For all his quirks and smart-aleck comments and despite the fact that they hadn't been as close in recent years—and even though he was a guy—there was nobody on earth she trusted more. At least, no one on this hemisphere of earth.

But now he was preoccupied with Kira, and probably would be for a while. He'd come home from summer camp one year obsessed with a girl he'd met there, thinking about her, talking about her, writing letters to her—only to never see her again. This smacked of that, only on a larger, more mature scale. Nicole was worried about his reaction to however things with Kira ultimately ended.

So was it concern for Jimmy that made Nicole wary of Kira or jealousy because she was taking up time with Jimmy that Nicole craved? Or was it something in her story that, although Nicole still couldn't put a finger on it, bugged her?

She had jogged back north past dozens of rentable frontier cabins, a cemetery, and more Wall Drug billboards while posing the question to herself, and as she crossed beneath I-90 and into Wall, she still didn't have an answer.

Cutting down a side street past several chain hotels and past the Wall Food Center, Nicole returned to the Hole-in-the-Wall Inn and slowed to a walk as she crossed the parking lot. Needing to cool down, she walked over toward the pool as breakfast aromas wafted from the café and made her mouth water. So much for sleeping in, Jimmy was sitting in the same chaise lounge lawn chair, a mug of coffee on the table beside him. Mercifully, he was not wearing his cowboy hat.

Nicole pulled out a chair and sat down opposite him. He looked up, at the same time reaching for his mug. "Hey." His eyes widened. "Hey. You shower with your clothes on?"

"I went . . . for a run," Nicole panted.

He nodded, sipped his coffee, and set the mug down.

"Can I . . . talk to you for a minute?"

"One sec," he said, then lowered his eyes to his lap, where Nicole realized a Bible was open. For some reason, that surprised her. She'd never questioned Jimmy's faith, but had trouble picturing him having morning "quiet time."

She waited a minute, listening to birds chirping and the never-ceasing hum of interstate traffic.

"I have a theory," Jimmy said.

"What's that?"

"I'm reading Ezekiel, and—"

"You're reading Ezekiel?"

"I'm doing a Bible in a year plan."

"And you're only in Ezekiel?"

"I shouldn't actually be there until later this month, but I got bored one rainy day in July and pounded through a few books."

She nodded. "This theory?"

"Ezekiel is one of those books that you can't gain much from just reading. Winged animals passing fire back and forth, wheels with eyeballs. You have to study it like you're writing a seminary paper. Not that I know anything about that."

Nicole sighed.

"Sorry, you wanted to talk to me."

She looked at him as he set his closed Bible on the table and took the mug back. He raised an eyebrow, waiting.

"Jimmy, don't take this the wrong way, but—"

"Uh-oh," he said over his mug before taking another drink.

She exhaled. "I just want to make sure you don't get hurt."

"First sip was a little hot, but—"

"Jimmy."

"Hurt how?"

"With Kira."

He shook his head. "Why would I get hurt with Kira?"

"Because unless I'm totally daft, you and her . . ."

"Like each other?"

She nodded.

"You're not daft. At least as far as I'm concerned."

"And you are aware that we're going to drop her at a bus station today and you'll probably never see her again?"

He nodded. "That's why I'm trying to enjoy the time with her as much as I can."

"But are you going to be okay with her being gone?"

"It is what it is," he said with a shrug.

"That's not an answer."

He leaned forward and set his mug next to his Bible. "Someday, I'm going to meet the future Mrs. Turner—I can say that, can't I, that's not misogynistic or something?"

Nicole slowly shook her head.

"Anyhow, I'll meet her, we'll fall in love, and be happy forever. Until then, any girl I meet is just a good time. And I don't mean that the way the world means it. I mean, there's no future in it, so why act like there is? If we both accept that it's just a good time—no emotional or psychological or physical commitment—what's the harm?"

Nicole cocked her head. "Jimmy, I'm not sure if that's incredibly mature or incredibly immature."

"Neither am I."

She let out a thin smile.

"But I appreciate you checking in. Where would I be without my older little sister?"

"I just want you to know that . . . if you did get hurt, you have someone to talk to."

"Thanks, Nic," he said with a smile. "Now, go hit the showers. It smells like roadkill around here."

With a sigh, Nicole stood, figuring she should appreciate what sincerity she did get from her brother.

CHAPTER TWELVE

Jimmy had already heard from Keith at Wall Auto Helpers by the time he met Nicole and Kira for breakfast at the Hole-in-the-Wall Café. Rita, the pink-haired waitress from the night before, had been replaced by Darrel, a beefy guy with a stained shirt with sleeves cut off to reveal tatted arms. He served as waiter and cook, and made a mean omelet. While they ate—fruit and whole wheat toast for Nicole and a waffle for Kira—Jimmy updated them on the status of the Jeep.

"Keith said we need a new solenoid."

"A what?" Kira asked.

"Something-something-something with the starter," he said, taking a bite of his toast. He reached for his third mug of coffee of the day. "Sounds like a pretty easy repair, but he'll have to order the part from Rapid City."

"Oh great," Nicole said. She had changed from her sweaty running clothes to a blue blouse with flared sleeves, and seemed in a better mood after their morning talk. Or had until he'd mentioned ordering a new solenoid.

"Said it should be here by ten, and expects to be done with the car by noon. He offered we could keep our luggage there if we need to check out before then."

"I guess that's not too bad. We can have you in Rapid City mid-afternoon," she said to Kira.

She nodded. Her hair was in a loose ponytail today, with several wisps hanging beside her face. It looked good with a lavender V-neck and a pair of silver hoop earrings. She exhaled. "I guess that means we have a morning to kill."

"I'm going back to Wall Drug," Jimmy said, scooping hash browns onto his fork. "I'm serious about that belt buckle, and maybe some Dr. Scholl's for those boots. Maybe another donut."

"How do you stay so thin?" Kira asked. "I feel like I put on five pounds just last night."

"Clean living, I guess," Jimmy said as he cut into his omelet. "Lots of coffee."

"How does that help?"

"Gives you energy, burns off the weight. Speaking of, I could use another few cups of that five-cent brew."

"We're going to have to stop to pee three times between here and Rapid City," Nicole said.

"I don't think there are three places between here and Rapid City. But noted."

"Mind if I tag along?" Kira asked.

"Not at all. Nic?"

"I think I might get some sun by the pool," she said, lifting a white arm. "Too much time indoors this summer."

They finished eating, then split up. Nicole headed for her room to change, and Jimmy and Kira set out on foot for Wall Drug. It was already hot, with not a breath of wind. Jimmy had checked the five-day forecast on Saturday, and it had called for typical summer conditions in Rapid City—heat, chance of afternoon storms. He had not expected this sort of heat, but then again, maybe Wall was different than Rapid City. Mountains altered weather patterns. Did the Black Hills count as mountains?

"I don't think your sister likes me very much," Kira said as they walked. They were on the sidewalk on the east side of Main Street, in front of a brown, multi-ridged building that was the National Grasslands Visitor Center. Jimmy had been wondering what constituted a national grassland as opposed to regular old grass until Kira spoke. Then he stopped walking.

"Why's that?" he asked.

"Little things."

"Like?"

She dragged the toe of her tennis shoe on the pavement. "For starters, I get the feeling you had to talk her into even taking me along yesterday."

"Why do you say that?"

"Call it feminine intuition, one woman's take on another."

"Nicole's very analytical, likes to think things through before making a decision. That's all it was."

Kira nodded, and they resumed walking.

"Not convinced?"

"I don't know. The way she looks at me, like she's suspicious of me, for example. And she seems impatient or upset when we're flirting with each other."

"I don't think you need to worry," Jimmy said. "Like I said, Nicole's analytical. And careful."

"Careful of what?"

"You are—were—a stranger. That makes her nervous."

"I see."

"Nervous is the wrong word. She's wary, and not because she's afraid you're some serial killer psycho we picked up. It's . . . because of me."

"Because of you?"

"She's afraid you're going to break my heart."

Kira slowed and looked at him, her eyes full of mischief. "Am I?"

"We'll cross that bridge when we come to it," Jimmy said. "For now, let's just enjoy the moment."

She smiled. "Fair enough."

*   *   *

Nicole debated whether or not she wanted to bother changing into her swimsuit or not. She felt kind of odd laying out in what was essentially the parking lot. Plus swimsuits were no fun to pack up when wet. But while the pool wasn't big enough for more than a stroke or two, she really did feel like a quick, refreshing dip. And how was a parking lot any different than a beach? So she changed, grabbed sunscreen, sunglasses, a bottle of water, her phone, a towel, and a Terri Blackstock novel, and headed out to the pool.

She was relieved to find it empty, and spent a quick ten minutes cooling off in the water. Then she dried off, wrung out her hair, and stretched out on a chaise lounge. After applying sunscreen, she quickly lost herself in the novel. She didn't worry about Jimmy and Kira, or the Gardiner family hunting her down, or her future, or the cost of repairs to the Jeep. The pages, and the minutes, flew by, and she barely thought to turn over after a couple chapters.

The third was long, and when it was done, she picked her phone up from her towel and checked the time. She deemed she had time for one more chapter and plowed ahead, again losing herself in the plot. So much so that she didn't notice anyone approaching until the metal gate around the patio creaked.

Nicole looked up from her book and turned her head, expecting to see Jimmy and Kira. Instead it was a man in dark slacks and a light blue dress shirt. He was maybe thirty, with short brown hair and a clean-shaven face. Nicole regarded him without moving, figuring he was just out to see the pool or maybe to sit and enjoy the morning. Then he set his eyes on her and walked over.

"Hello," he said.

Nicole closed her book on her finger and sat up. "Hello."

The man stopped six feet from her, close enough to be in her personal space but not so close that she felt intimidated. Even so, her senses were on high alert. Her peripheral vision saw no one else, although there had to be motorists or pedestrians around. The man was tall, at least six-one or six-two, and carried himself with composure, relaxed it seemed. His shoes were polished, his shirt shiny. Its sleeves were rolled to below the elbow, and the top two buttons were open, either for style or temperature. He looked like a businessman after a Saturday morning of work, a federal agent or cop post-shift, or a young professional on the prowl at a singles bar. None of those things belonged at the Hole-in-the-Wall Inn's pool patio at quarter after ten on a Monday morning.

"I wonder if you could help me," he said in an even, non-accented voice.

"How so?"

"I'm looking for a young woman named Kira Angel."

CHAPTER THIRTEEN

Nicole frowned, thankful that because the sun had been reflecting off the white pages of her book, she'd kept her sunglasses on despite lying on her stomach. They shielded her eyes from the man and, hopefully, kept her surprise at bay. She also covered by reaching down for her towel and her phone. "Kira Angel," she repeated as she stood, draping the towel around her waist, holding it with one hand while the other clutched her phone. "And you're just asking random strangers?" she added, then padded over to a chair at the table. She hoped the man would take the queue and sit down, putting a table between them and disarming him a little.

He ambled after her, but stood behind the chair instead of sitting. He smiled with lips closed. "I don't think you're random."

Nicole frowned again, hoping to convey total confusion without outright lying. For one thing, she believed it was wrong, even if she had stone-face lied to Frank/Goatee and Johnny/Wavy Hair yesterday. And she didn't want to make a habit of it, of trying to keep stories straight, especially since, for some reason, she had a feeling with this stranger it might come back to bite her. Better to play it coy. So she shook her head and said, "Who's Kira Angel? I don't know anyone by that name," she added, concluding that wasn't really a lie. They'd never learned Kira's last name.

The man smiled as if he saw right through her, and Nicole knew it wasn't the heat making sweat appear on her brow.

"Maybe we should start with introductions," the man said, still grinning crookedly. He pulled out the chair and sat down. He pressed out a wrinkle on his slacks, and Nicole couldn't shake the thought that he looked like he'd stepped out of a catalog for gentlemen's business leisure wear. "My name is Travis."

"Nicole."

"It's nice to meet you, Nicole. What brings you to Wall?"

She tried to hide the frown this time, because she didn't want to keep scowling at the guy. But she felt the same way she'd felt during last year's South Carolina-Clemson game when the Clemson quarterback had thrown a slightly backward pass to the wide receiver. It was similar to a play they'd run half a dozen times earlier in the game, and it sucked the defense up to make the tackle. Only that time, the receiver hadn't run the ball but taken a step back and thrown a backbreaking touchdown pass to another, now uncovered, wide receiver. High up in the stands at Williams-Brice Stadium, Nicole had seen it all unfolding and known a trick was coming. Focusing her eyes on Travis now, she tried not to get sucked in.

"I'm on vacation."

"If you don't mind me saying, you've picked an odd destination."

"To be candid with you, Travis, I don't really care what you think about my leisure choices."

He chuckled, and this time it seemed genuine. "Fair enough."

"Why are you looking for this Kira person?"

"That's a rather confidential matter."

"I see." Nicole shook her head. "And why again are you asking sunbathers at such an 'odd destination'?"

"Miss Angel was seen in your company yesterday."

"Mine?"

"That's correct. And your brother's. Jimmy, is it?"

Nicole couldn't help startling at the fact that this man knew her and her brother. She swallowed, buying time. It was hard to think on your feet when you were off balance on your heels. She decided offense was the best defense—something South Carolina's now-embattled football coach would have done well to realize.

"Travis, I get the feeling you're not telling me something."

He leaned forward. "I am somewhat limited in what I can divulge," he said. "Confidential," he added at the same time Nicole said the same word. It caused him to chuckle again.

"Where were we seen together?"

He lifted an arm and pointed over her shoulder. "Just down the way, at Wall Drug."

Nicole nodded. She was being goaded. He clearly knew the answers to the questions he was asking, and was waiting for her to cross the line and lie. Then he'd either whip handcuffs out of his pocket and announce she was under arrest for hindering an investigation or whistle for a limo with his mob associates to whisk up and drive her off somewhere. She took a breath, felt the sun on her flushed face, heard the distant sounds of birds, a lawnmower, and interstate traffic. They grounded her.

They also clarified her thinking. Kira was not who she claimed, not if she had both Braden's family and Travis asking questions. And Travis was the antithesis of everything Kira had told them about the Gardiners, and even what Nicole had observed the other day. The Gardiners were bikers—they looked and dressed like the stereotype; Travis fit the stereotype of a TV fibbie. The Gardiners had been urgent and insistent; Travis seemed like he enjoyed the game. And whereas Travis played nice, the Gardiners' politeness had seemed genuine, a fact that registered more with Nicole now than it ever had. She had no idea what Travis was after, who Kira Angel was, or why so many people wanted to find her, but something clearly was going on. And until she knew what, she wasn't telling anyone anything.

"Who saw us?" she asked. "There were quite a few people at Wall Drug yesterday afternoon."

"My . . . associate," Travis answered, although Nicole was sure a P-word had been about to come from his lips—a P-word like "partner," as in fellow agent? And yet, if Travis were a fed, why hadn't he led with the badge and a few more "ma'am's"?

"She described it as if you were more than fellow tourists looking at the same rack of souvenir keychains."

"I'm sorry, but I can't help you."

Travis nodded, that same thin smile still on his face. "Can't," he said, "or won't?"

"You know, you're the second person to ask me about a girl," she said, trying that offense over defense thing again. It worked, as Travis's expression flinched for just a second. Nicole kept going. "Two men stopped me yesterday, as I was leaving Wall Drug, asked if I had seen a girl. Showed me her picture on their phone. Pretty, young—maybe twenty—long blondish-brown hair?"

Travis nodded along.

"I wasn't able to help them either," she said. "But it's odd, you know? They didn't tell me her name, but it makes me wonder if you're not looking for the same woman."

"What did these two men look like?" Travis asked.

"Bikers. One was big, buzz cut, a goatee, lots of tattoos. The other was Native-American or Hispanic, wavy black hair. Both wore leather vests, had a BHG patch on the breast."

"BHG?"

"That mean something to you?"

Travis shook his head, but now Nicole was sure *he* was lying.

"What'd you tell these guys?"

Nicole stared him in the eye through her sunglasses and lied. "That I hadn't seen her."

Travis nodded. He dropped his leg, which had been crossed over the other at the knee, to the pavement. "Nicole, thank you for your time."

She was a little startled, and was slow to extend her hand when Travis stood and reached his to her. She half expected him to pull her close and tell her he knew she was lying. But he didn't. He merely shook her hand, smiled a little wider, and turned and walked away.

Nicole watched as he strode to the far end of the parking lot and got into an innocuous sedan. She pretended to be looking at her phone, waiting for him to drive away. But he didn't. He merely sat behind the wheel, hidden from her view by the glare of the windshield. When it became apparent he wasn't leaving, it confirmed Nicole's suspicions as to his sudden departure. He hadn't ended the conversation because she had convinced him she didn't know Kira, but because she had convinced him she wasn't going to divulge anything. So Travis was going to stake her out and wait to see who came to her or where she went.

She quickly collected her things and walked back to her room, acting as if she didn't have a care in the world, but not relaxing until she was safely in her room with the door locked, bolted, and chained.

CHAPTER FOURTEEN

Jimmy sat back, the ankle of one leg balanced on the knee of the other, his second mug of five-cent coffee in his hand. The first had been consumed with another donut, this time in the shadow of a woodcarving of Paul Newman and Robert Redford's characters in *Butch Cassidy and the Sundance Kid*. Kira had passed on more sweets, imbibing only in the coffee, and, while Jimmy had eaten, she had divulged that her father had died when she was sixteen. It had left her world shattered, especially when it turned her mom into an alcoholic and forced Kira to live part-time with her grandma. She didn't have to say it, but it was obvious her family situation was part of the reason she'd left Columbia and ultimately Missouri, and why she wasn't looking for a bus back to the Show Me State.

Jimmy was amazed at her openness with a stranger. But then, as he sipped his coffee and looked into her blue eyes, he realized they weren't really strangers anymore. After the last twenty hours or so, and after what they had dealt with together, he wasn't ready to say they were soulmates, but neither were they strangers. Which was why, when she turned the question on him and asked about his parents, he had no problems being open with her.

"Dad was a pastor at this small church for most of my life," he said. "But it wasn't growing, and the leadership of the church more or less told him it was time to move on. He and mom and been talking about missions work, and—"

"Missions?" Kira asked.

He frowned for a second, realizing that standard evangelical Christian parlance might not be standard for most people. "Yeah. Um, it encompasses everything from charity work to straight-up evangelism, typically overseas," he finished with a frown, realizing "evangelism" might be more Christian jargon.

"Proselytizing," Kira said.

He shrugged. "Less about converting people to one religion over another and more about sharing the truth of the Bible with them."

"And that's what your parents do?"

"They run a girl's school in the Philippines, so they fall somewhere in the middle of charity and evangelism."

"Is it hard being away from them?"

"It's always hard to be away from someone you care about."

Kira looked at him over her mug, then took a drink. When she lowered it, she was grinning. "Are we still talking about your parents in the Philippines?"

He grinned back.

"Before she turned to alcohol, my mom tried to comfort me after my dad died. She said when you hold someone close in your heart, they can never truly be far away."

Jimmy nodded.

She tipped her head to the side. "It always sounded a little trite to me, but I don't know, maybe it's true."

Jimmy's grin returned. "Are we still talking about our parents?"

"Apply it however you want," she said.

He looked at her for a moment, then down as he reached for his coffee.

She reached a hand out to him, placing it on his wrist. He raised his eyes to hers again.

"What are you thinking?" she asked.

He turned his head slightly.

"Something's on your mind."

"You're not going to like it."

She withdrew her hand. "Why not?"

"Because it isn't romantic."

"What are you thinking?"

He nodded at the statue. Paul Newman was facing their way. "You ever see the movie?"

She followed his gaze. "What movie?"

"*Butch Cassidy and the Sundance Kid.*"

Kira shook her head.

"It's a classic. Butch and Sundance—Newman and Redford—originally part of the Hole-in-the-Wall gang . . ."

"The Hole-in-the-Wall gang? Like the motel?"

He nodded. "Yeah. They end up on the run after robbing banks and a train, and Butch—Newman—talks the Kid and his girl into going to Bolivia."

"Okay."

He set his mug down and leaned forward. "Kira, there's a part of me that wants to run off to Bolivia with you, and Sundance if she'd go with us."

"Nicole?"

"She's actually more of the Butch of the group and I'm Sundance, but this metaphor is stretched as it is."

Kira too leaned forward. "So what's stopping you?"

"I don't speak Spanish, for one. And practicality, for the big one."

She pursed her lips. "Yeah."

"There's one other thing."

"What's that?"

"Butch and Sundance died in Bolivia."

Her eyebrows went up.

"Shot to pieces by the Bolivian Army."

"You're right." She shook her head. "That's not very romantic."

*   *   *

"Jimmy!" Nicole screamed, tossing her phone onto the bed.

He had not answered when she'd called immediately after returning to the room, nor five minutes later when her furtive peeks through the sheer curtains revealed that Travis's sedan was right where he'd left it. Watching her? Waiting for Kira to show up? Waiting for his female p—associate to arrive from skulking around the woodcarvings and year-round Christmas trees at Wall Drug? Wondering who he was and what he was doing had only caused Nicole's brain to invent new and worse theories, so she'd double-checked the door locks and taken her second shower of the morning, rinsing off the chlorine and sweat. She'd put on the same clothes as before, blow-dried her hair, and checked the parking lot again: sedan still there. She'd checked the clock: 10:46. She'd called Jimmy again: no answer again, causing her to throw her phone. He'd either let the battery run down or was too busy flirting with Kira about belt buckles and accessories to bother answering her call.

Unable to reach Jimmy, Nicole concentrated on Kira. She ran her story through her head again—falling for Braden, discovering his family was a motorcycle gang scheming up something, feeling threatened, running, being pursued across the Dakota plains. It made sense. There were no obvious holes. Frank and Johnny showing up at Wall Drug to ask about her validated the story, didn't it? And what of Travis? Who was he and what did he want Kira for? Was he the clean-cut, well-dressed "white sheep" of the family, the way Alan was to Jase, Willie, and Jep Robertson, coming at the problem from a different angle? If so, that would mean the Gardiners had homed in on Wall as Kira's location. Was he a fed who'd forgotten his badge? Was there some other aspect of Kira's story that led to a third-party being involved? If so, what?

Nicole went to the window again. The sedan was there. Jimmy and Kira were not. Nicole turned to Kira's backpack on her bed. It would take them at least five minutes to walk back to the motel, and Nicole had the key so Kira would need to knock to get it in. Hating herself for it, Nicole walked over to the backpack. She paused for a minute, then convinced herself it was for her and Jimmy's own good and unzipped it.

In addition to the leather jacket Kira had tossed on the chair, a small pouch of personal items on the bathroom counter, and the clothes on her back, Kira's belongings amounted to the American flag tank top she'd worn the day before, a black T-shirt with a yellow and white Tiger on it—the University of Missouri's logo—a pair of blue jeans, a pair of ankle socks, a few changes of underwear, and an extra-large St. Louis Blues T-shirt that Nicole knew served as Kira's pajamas. A side pocket had a small pouch with a few items of jewelry and a small bottle of hand lotion. A small front pocket was locked by a tiny padlock, and felt as if it contained another pouch. No journal pouring out her heart or divulging secrets, no wallet with credit cards or other forms of ID, but she could have that on her. Nicole didn't recall her carrying a purse, but she could have a pocket on that denim skirt for a small wallet or a clip of cash. She had paid cash for her dinner and breakfast—insisting on it—and clearly had money or a credit card for a bus ticket and more clothes.

Nicole thought of the locked pocket again, and searched the jewelry pouch for a key. Not there. She searched the backpack again for any other pockets. Nothing. She peeked out the window again, didn't spot Jimmy or Kira, and went to the bathroom. She carefully went through Kira's toiletries and found no key there either. In a skirt pocket? Tucked into her shoe? Left behind in Pierre?

Nicole checked that everything was as she'd found it, then collapsed on her bed with a sigh. She'd learned nothing from her invasion of privacy. Other than the jewelry pouch, there was nothing to suggest that Kira hadn't quickly crammed a few necessities into a backpack and run away like she claimed.

With another sigh, Nicole looked down at her phone and mumbled her brother's name again.

*　　　　　*　　　　　*

None of the belt buckles spoke to Jimmy, and he always reasoned he and Nicole could stop on the way home (say, for a coffee break) if he changed his mind. So he and Kira exited Wall Drug emptyhanded and crossed at 5th Avenue after Kira expressed a desire to browse a few of the shops on the west side of the street. He figured they had time, since the Jeep wasn't done yet and they had over an hour before checkout at the Hole-in-the-Wall Inn.

They hit a jewelry store and a couple trading-post-style gift shops, doing little more than browsing and enjoying being together. Nicole's words that morning about him never seeing Kira again were starting to reverberate in his head, as was Kira's euphemistic statement about holding people close in your heart. Sounded trite to him too. He thought about how they could keep in touch, but realized it would be mostly empty, like the unreturned letters he'd sent to that cute little redhead from summer camp . . .

They emerged from an air-conditioned gift shop into the heat, albeit shaded by an awning, and from Billy Currington and Miranda Lambert on the radio to the revving of motorcycles on Main Street. Jimmy was about to reach for his phone to check the time when Kira suddenly grabbed his arm and pulled him to the right.

"Wha—"

She crouched behind a cab-covered pickup truck, and he instinctively imitated her. Before he could ask another question, she peeked up and over the bed of the truck.

"Kira?"

She reached for his hand and stood, pulling him down the sidewalk.

"What's going on?"

She didn't answer, her head on a swivel. She darted between another pickup on the left and a sports car on the right, crouching down and then lifting her head over the bed of the truck. Still holding his hand, she led him across the southbound lane of Main Street. They weaved between two more parked cars, then waited in a stoop as several northbound cars breezed past. A dark blue hatchback saw them and stopped, letting them cross, which they did still hand-in-hand, Kira's ponytail flopping back and forth as she looked to the north, then toward the entrance to Wall Drug, and back. Jimmy's eyes, having barely adjusted to the sunlight and practically been blinded by rays glinting off windshields, now had to adjust to the shade of the Wall Drug awning, then the interior of the main mall as Kira led him inside.

She still held his hand, and he pulled to stop her. Her head whipped around.

"Kira, what's going on?"

"Those motorcycles that were going past as we came out? They were the Gardiners!"

CHAPTER FIFTEEN

It was eleven o'clock. Checkout at the Hole-in-the-Wall Inn was in one hour, and Nicole didn't know if Jimmy and Kira were eating homemade ice cream at Wall Drug's soda fountain or being sweated in the back of a federal agent's Crown Vic. Three calls and a text to Jimmy had gone unanswered, so she scrawled a quick note on the motel's stationery and slipped it under his door. Then, cognizant that Travis was still sitting in his sedan, she laced up her tennis shoes and set out walking.

She thought about waving at Travis, but instead ignored him. She figured she had time to walk to Wall Drug, scout around, and still get back well before noon. In addition to hopefully finding Jimmy and wringing his neck, she could determine if Travis was sitting on her or the hotel.

The heat was stifling, and there still wasn't a whisper of breeze. The sky above was tinged with haze, and the horizon was fuzzy and gray. By the time Nicole passed 3 Amigos Cantina and crossed 6th Avenue, she was sweating and ready to throw Jimmy's boots in the pool. But at least there was no sign that Travis was following her, via car or on foot.

She entered Wall Drug through the same door they'd used the day before, arriving in the mall. She scanned for Jimmy's white Kwik Trip T-shirt or Kira's lavender blouse. Not spotting either in the mall, she "browsed" through the Western wear stores, then made a systematic search through various shops and stores, followed by the dining rooms. After that, she checked the back yard and arcade, coming up empty on all fronts. Knowing she could have easily missed them, she decided to make another pass and increase the odds that, if they were there, she'd spot one of them.

Then her phone vibrated in her back pocket.

*   *   *

"Are you sure?" Jimmy asked.

Kira's eyes were wide. "I saw the BHG emblem on the back of one of their vests. And Lance, Braden's uncle, has a distinctive bike. It's them."

"What are they doing here?" he asked himself as much as her. "They must be backtracking."

"We need to get out of here," she said, tugging him down the hall. But he hesitated. "Jimmy."

"Why not run back to the motel?"

"Because we'd be out in the open. They looked like they were rounding at the end of the block, and I was afraid they'd see us. We can disappear in here."

"To what end? They'll come in or be waiting when we come out."

"Not if we go out the back way."

"Yeah, I guess." He nodded but pulled her back again. "Walk normal. If they come in and start asking around, we don't want a bunch of people to have seen us run helter-skelter through here."

She nodded, dropped his hand, and walked briskly but reasonably through the mall. Jimmy followed, glancing around and back several times. His mind was racing, wondering how and why the Gardiners were back at Wall Drug. There was no way they picked it as a random place to re-search, was there? Were they also at the motel? Was Nicole in danger?

He thought about calling her, but as they exited to the back yard, he grabbed Kira's arm again.

"What?"

"This way," he said, guiding her south down the alley, remembering that the back yard was enclosed. The alley emptied to a gravel parking lot with a garage, a dumpster, and—coincidentally enough—a Coca-Cola truck. They didn't try to hitch a ride. Beyond the parking lot was a small house and, beyond it, the next street. The street was wide open, with a church and another parking lot in front of a large corrugated building on the far side. South one block, a residential neighborhood contained more trees and parked cars. Without Jimmy's urging, Kira turned south.

They quickly crossed 6th Avenue, looking west for signs of motorcycles or leather-clad men. They continued south, with Jimmy reminding Kira to walk at a normal pace. "Just imagine we're two people out for a late-morning walk."

"It's a hundred degrees, Jimmy."

"All the more reason not to run."

"How did they find us?"

"I don't know. But I should call Nicole." He drew out his phone, seeing he'd missed several calls and a text. All from Nicole. He didn't bother to check any of them, but dialed her number. "Come on . . ." he said as it rang several times. He and Kira were halfway down the block, her momentarily walking backward to look behind them.

"Jimmy!" Nicole shouted into the phone.

"Hey. Where are you?"

"In the back yard."

"Wall Drug?"

"Yeah."

"What are you doing there?"

"Looking for you all! Somebody came to see me at the hotel, looking for Kira."

"What?"

Kira sensed the distress in his tone and stopped. So did he.

"I was at the pool and he came up asking for Kira Angel. He wasn't like the others—well-dressed, clean-shaven. He said his reason was confidential, but thought I knew her."

"What'd you tell him?"

"Nothing."

"Did he buy it?"

"I don't think so. He sat in a car in the parking lot until I left."

"Why'd you leave?"

"Because you don't answer your phone!"

"Sorry. Did he follow you?"

"No. Where are you?"

"On the run," he said.

"What?"

"Kira spotted a couple Gardiners. We snuck out the back way."

"Where are you going?"

"Not back to the motel," he said.

Kira's eyes bored into him.

"What do we do, Jimmy?" Nicole asked.

"I don't know. We need to find a place to lay low, to think."

"Want me to come to you?"

"No. Stay there. See if you see any Gardiners."

"What do I do if I do?"

"Text me."

She huffed.

"I'll pay attention."

"What if I run into the same two guys?"

"Tell them your car broke down and you're stuck in Wall."

"Where are you all going?"

"I'll call you."

"Okay. Be careful."

"You too." He ended he call and took Kira's arm to start her walking. As they did, he updated her.

"Who would be asking about me?"

"I don't know. Doesn't sound like a Gardiner."

"What are we going to do?"

Jimmy turned them left on 7th Avenue, away from Main Street. He repeated what he'd told Nicole, that they needed to lay low and think. "I remember seeing hotel signs when we were coming into town. I've got enough cash to get a room, I think. We can hide out there."

"What about Nicole?"

"I don't know. I'm thinking about that."

At Glenn Street, they turned south, walking on the sidewalk on the west side of the street. They passed a few houses before a Super 8 and an EconoLodge appeared on the right, offset by a Best Western on the left. Jimmy scouted them quickly, dismissing the Super 8 because it had internal corridors. The EconoLodge lobby had worse views of the most number of doors, so he pointed to the right.

"Hang outside," he said. "I'll get a room and that way if anyone should happen to start questioning hotel clerks, none of them will have seen you."

She nodded.

Jimmy instructed her to wait on the sidewalk, hidden by the pool house from the lobby, while he went inside. He tried to negotiate an hourly rate, which got him a dirty look. He settled for one night, for a room for one adult, and even though he paid cash, he had to provide an ID. He was given a room for that night on the second floor, far end of the building, and returned to Kira on the sidewalk. Watching to make sure no one was looking, they crossed the parking lot. He gave her the keycard, and while she opened the door, he stood watch again. Spying no one, he slipped in behind her and locked the door while she closed the blinds.

Then she threw herself into his arms.

CHAPTER SIXTEEN

Nicole roamed through Wall Drug again, spotting a couple bikers, but with no way to tell that they were or weren't members of the Gardiner gang—not without being obvious about trying to identify patches on their vests. And with the size and sprawling nature of the building, there was no telling how many bikers she had missed. She emerged into the mall beside Buffalo Bill at 11:38, twelve minutes after ending the call with Jimmy. She debated calling him again as her phone vibrated in her hand.

"Jimmy?"

"Where are you?" he asked.

"Still at Wall Drug."

"Any sign of you know who?"

"No."

"Okay. You should head back to the motel. I'll meet you there."

"Just you?"

"Kira's staying here, in another motel room for the time being, until we can make sure no one's following us."

"Okay."

"Call me when you get to the room, let me know if that guy you saw is still sitting out front in his car."

"Okay." She turned and started walking. "Jimmy?"

"Yeah?"

"You hear about the Jeep yet?"

"No. I'll call him. It is almost noon. Call me when you're back."

"I will." She ended the call and stepped outside, sweeping her eyes right and left. Sun glinted off the chrome of half a dozen motorcycles, and her eyes picked up a man and woman in leather and tattoos walking north on her side of the sidewalk. She realized it was silly, thinking that because Frank and Johnny had worn leather and been inked, and because a lot of bikers did and were, that anyone who was a threat would look the same. Travis had resembled a salesman showing up to the middle innings of his kid's Little League game, and he was looking for Kira too. Every face and every vehicle was a potential threat.

Time was of the essence, so she walked briskly back toward the Hole-in-the-Wall Inn. She kept her eyes peeled for anything overtly suspicious, and saw nothing. It took only five minutes, and when she crossed South Boulevard, she saw Travis's sedan no longer in the parking lot. She wasn't convinced she wasn't still being watched from somewhere or by someone, and suddenly couldn't remember how to walk naturally. She let herself back into the room, which seemed cold with the air conditioner rattling. She locked the door, then before calling Jimmy, called the front desk to see if they could get an extension on checkout time. The answer was no. They had thirteen minutes, so she headed into the bathroom to pack while dialing.

*   *   *

"You think I'll be safe here?" Kira asked.

"No one knows you're here. Keep the door locked and bolted until I come back. You'll be safe."

She took a deep breath and nodded.

"We'll figure a way out of this, Kira. I'm not going to let anything happen to you."

She forced a smile and took his hand as he turned to leave. "Be careful, Jimmy."

He smiled.

"What?"

"I was going to give you Paul Newman's last line to Robert Redford in *Butch and Sundance*, but you haven't seen it and my Paul Newman is average at best."

She squeezed his hand and smiled.

"I'll be careful," he said. "Locked and bolted," he added as he opened the door, then slipped out.

The coast, as expected, was clear, and he set out for the Hole-in-the-Wall Inn. Nicole had reported that the guy watching the room was gone, and he'd told her that Keith, owing to a delayed part delivery from Rapid City, now promised the Jeep by one o'clock. He worked up a sweat in the short walk back, and rapped on Nicole and Kira's door before opening his. Nicole peeked her head out.

"You could have stood by the peephole," she said.

"I have four minutes to pack."

"Did it take you any longer before we left?"

He clicked and pointed a finger and thumb gun at her. She followed him out of her room and into his, Kira's backpack over a shoulder and her rolling suitcase behind her. He held his door, then closed it behind her.

"Jimmy, what in the world have we gotten ourselves into?"

"I don't know," he said, scrambling to pick up a few loose clothes and toss them in his duffel bag. "But we owe it to Kira to get her out of it."

"We owe it? We didn't start any of this."

He stopped, his hand on the bathroom doorpost. "You accusing her?"

"No, I'm just saying this isn't our fault."

"Oh." He scraped his deodorant, body spray, toothbrush, and toothpaste into his toiletry bag, then plucked a small travel container of body wash from the shower.

"But Jimmy, something's off."

"What kind of something?" he asked, emerging from the bathroom.

"Why are so many people looking for her?"

"I don't know. What exactly did this guy of yours say?"

"He said he was looking for Kira Angel, and had reason—" She stopped.

"What?" he asked.

"You have a dumb look on your face."

He shrugged.

"Is it because I said Kira's last name was Angel?"

"No idea what you mean." He tossed the toiletry bag into his duffel, then looked around the room once before zipping it. He'd left his boots in the Jeep, and his cowboy hat was by the door. He'd grab it on the way out. "You cleared out of your room?"

"Yeah. Where are we going?"

"To get our car. Keith said we could hang out there. Have your key?"

She held it up. "What about Kira?"

"She has cable."

Nicole frowned.

"If anyone is watching us, I don't want them to see hide nor hair of Kira. We'll pick up the Jeep, head out of town, and make sure we don't have a tail. Then, if the coast is clear, we'll drive back and get her."

"And if it's not clear?"

He shrugged again, donned his hat, and opened the door.

"Jimmy," she said, following.

"Yeah?"

"Travis, the guy in the sedan, said he had a female partner."

"Lucky him."

"He said that she saw Kira with me in Wall Drug. Whoever he is, he knows."

"But he didn't do anything about it?"

"No."

"This is weird."

"Very."

He ducked inside the lobby with both their keys to check out, then rejoined Nicole in the sun. "You said he was sharp-dressed, clean-cut?" he asked.

She nodded.

"No leather?"

"No. He looked like a Saturday afternoon fed."

"A fed? He show you a badge?"

"No."

"Weird," he said and started walking.

"Very," she said again.

He stopped. "What's a Saturday afternoon fed?"

"More casual. And—I don't know—something about him was . . . He was like a cat playing with its food. He was smug, glib, didn't seem all that upset that I was dodging his questions but he obviously knew I was."

He shook his head. "Weird."

"Very."

CHAPTER SEVENTEEN

The TV in the very small waiting room of Wall Auto Helpers showed a hunting show with a lot of whispering and very little shooting. But the mountainous scenery—somewhere in Wyoming—distracted Nicole from all that was going on. Her mind was spinning, trying to process Kira's story, the Gardiners, their re-arrival in Wall, Travis and his surveillance. Jimmy had his sneakers propped up on her suitcase and didn't seem concerned, but Nicole knew him well enough to know he was.

Just after twelve-thirty, Keith—who seemed to be not only the owner but also the sole mechanic at Wall Auto Helpers—announced that the Jeep was fixed. The total was less than Nicole expected, under two hundred dollars, and she promised to settle with Jimmy later while he charged the repairs. It was his Jeep, he argued, so why should she have to pay for repairs. She didn't argue, what with other things on her mind.

They loaded their luggage into it, including Kira's backpack. They saw no signs that anyone was surveilling the garage. Jimmy turned east on South Boulevard, then swung into the Exxon station on the corner. He didn't need gas, but said it would make it harder for a potential tail to stay hidden. While he topped off the tank, Nicole kept her eyes peeled and saw nothing.

They headed south on Glenn Street, under the interstate, where it turned into Highway 240.

"Not getting on 90?"

"It'll be easier to spot a tail on this," Jimmy said as he checked the rearview mirror.

"See anything?"

"No."

They drove past the Frontier Cabins, on the same road Nicole had jogged that morning—eons ago. The two-lane highway was also known as the Badlands Loop, and ran straight south for about eight miles before beginning to wind through the park's features. As such, it no doubt got a fair amount of traffic, so Nicole wasn't sure how Jimmy would differentiate a tail from a tourist, but she was more than happy to let him take the lead. Plotting and planning ahead of time—that was her strength. Making decisions as fast as they came at you—that was his.

"It's fifty-five," she said a minute later, noticing that Jimmy was still crawling. "Everything okay with the Jeep?"

"Just making sure . . ." He paused as an SUV zipped past them. "A tail would hang back. An angry bunch of tourists from Illinois, on the other hand . . ."

"There's a method to your madness."

He sped up to the speed limit and drove for a mile or two before turning around in a gravel drive that encircled a steel-roofed Quonset hut. A couple more southbound vehicles zipped on by toward the badlands.

"Satisfied?" Jimmy asked.

"I guess so."

"Let's go get Kira."

Nicole nodded.

"You want to call her?"

"She doesn't have her phone, remember?"

Jimmy frowned.

"What is it?"

He shook his head. "Call the EconoLodge."

"You know the number?"

"No, but I'll bet ol' Google does."

She found the number while he waited for northbound traffic and finally turned back onto the highway. She dialed and asked for Kira's room number. It rang and rang. "She's not answering," Nicole announced.

"Leave a message if it will let you. Tell her you're going to call back in five minutes."

"What if she does—Kira, it's Nicole. We have the Jeep and no tail. We'll call back in five minutes." She tapped to end the call and looked at Jimmy.

"This is kind of fun," he said. "You know what we should do?"

"What?"

He winked. "Put on some Outlaw Country."

Nicole rolled her eyes.

They killed five minutes making a lap around Nicole's jogging route that morning, then she called Kira again. This time she answered, and when Jimmy snapped his fingers, Nicole handed him the phone.

"We're about two minutes out," he said. "I'll park right by the staircase. You should be able to see the Jeep from your window. If it's all clear, Nicole will roll down her window and drape her arm out. . . . No," he said with a grin. "Two minutes." He handed the phone back to Nicole, who saw the call had ended.

"What's 'No'?" she asked.

"She asked if this was a trick from *Butch and Sundance*."

"I was wondering where you picked up this spycraft."

"Making it up as I go."

All signs were clear, as far as they could tell, as they arrived back in town, through the intersection with South Boulevard, and into the parking lot of the EconoLodge. Jimmy said what Nicole was thinking—that Travis or Lance Gardiner or Michael Westen could be watching from an unknown vehicle and they'd never know it—but also that they couldn't become paranoid. So he coasted to a stop in a vacant space beside an extension from the second-story corridor. It sheltered a staircase connecting the two levels.

"All right, Fiona, flutter your fingers in the breeze."

Nicole obeyed, and both cast their eyes to Kira's room. Thirty seconds later, she emerged through the door. She cast a glance at the parking lot, then hurried along the corridor. She disappeared into the stairwell, then reappeared and that quickly was at the back door of the Jeep. She climbed in, and Jimmy put the gearshift in reverse. Before backing out, he looked back at Kira. "All good?"

"In a manner of speaking," she said.

"Yeah."

Jimmy exited the parking lot onto Glenn Street and headed south again, and again under the interstate. Nicole looked at him but said nothing, figuring he again had a plan. This time, instead of continuing on the Badlands Loop, he took the ramp to I-90 East.

"Where are we going?" Kira asked.

"Checking for a tail," he said.

She turned around.

"Nobody followed Nic and I when we left the garage, but I'd rather be safe than sorry."

"How did they find us?"

"Technically, they didn't," Nicole said.

"But they were looking again, and in the right place."

"They were."

"And what about the guy who visited you?"

Jimmy had to merge slowly behind a semi, then swerved into the left lane and stomped on the gas.

Nicole turned around in her seat once he slowed to a moderate eighty miles per hour, and described Travis's appearance.

Kira shook her head. "Doesn't sound familiar."

Still looking at Kira, Nicole said, "He struck me as a fed."

"A fed? A federal agent?"

Nicole nodded.

"Did he say he was, or show a badge?"

"No."

"Then why did you . . ."

"The way he looked, talked, acted. Actually, he struck me more as someone pretending to be a federal agent."

"And not wanting to get busted for impersonating one," Jimmy said.

"So the question is," Nicole said, "why would a federal agent—" She turned her attention to Jimmy "—or a pretend one, want to find you?"

She finished by looking back at Kira, who had given nothing away with her expression. Say, if she was hiding a secret that would explain Travis, and possibly the Gardiners too, displaying such urgency in finding her. Now, in answer to Nicole's question, she gave nothing away either, merely shaking her head.

"I don't know," she finally said. "I really don't."

Jimmy kept his eyes on the mirrors, speeding up to ninety and slowing down to seventy. He'd passed an exit a mile east of Wall, where Highway 14 diverged from the interstate and headed due east, whereas 90 curved southeast. The next exit was five miles away, leading to a country road in the middle of nowhere. When they reached it, he announced that he'd seen no signs of a tail or anything suspicious, and signaled for the exit ramp.

"So now what?" Kira asked.

"Braden's family is back in Wall, but we don't know if it's because they have some reason to think you stayed there or because they're desperate and looking anywhere they can think to look. And Nicole's guy Travis, while he believed you were here and with us, has disappeared. And none of them know where we are now unless they've got a drone up overhead or snuck into the garage and put a tracker under our bumper."

"Meaning?"

He'd turned and now passed under the interstate. "Unless either of you disagree, we stick to the original plan and head for Rapid City."

"Nicole, what do you think?" Kira asked as Jimmy turned onto the I-90 Westbound ramp.

"We'll have to be careful, because we have no idea where they might be looking for us. But if anything, it seems like they've backtracked." She nodded for confirmation. "I agree with Jimmy."

"Then it's unanimous," Kira said. "On to Rapid City."

As if to emphasize the decision, Jimmy accelerated up the onramp and over the rise. Then he turned to Nicole, and, in what was a pretty good impersonation of Johnny Depp as Captain Jack Sparrow, said, "Bring me that horizon, matey."

CHAPTER EIGHTEEN

The trio covered the fifty-five miles to Rapid City in forty-five minutes. There wasn't a lot of non-semi traffic, and Jimmy saw nothing in his mirrors to indicate anyone was following them. As they climbed out of the Cheyenne River valley and settled onto flat plains, his eyes and attention focused on the horizon, where hazy ridges took shape, the first indication that they were approaching the Black Hills.

Kira had actually dozed in the backseat, and Nicole had been mostly silent after they passed Wall with no Harley Davidsons or non-descript government cars sliding in behind them. But they were both alert and awake as the outskirts of civilization and dozens of billboards announced their arrival in the Gateway to the Black Hills. All hungry, they decided to find somewhere to grab a late lunch. Jimmy took the second exit into town and suggested they find a place a little off the main path. Just in case someone came looking, it might be best not to be in the first McDonald's or Taco Bell that came along. That was fine, Nicole said. She wanted *food* anyhow.

They chose an On the Border a mile south of the interstate and off the main drag, situated at the top of a valley in which the majority of Rapid City was nestled. Beyond it, rows of green ridges grew fainter and fainter until they disappeared into the haze. Wearing his cowboy hat to look less like a tourist—although Nicole argued the Kwik Trip shirt killed that vibe, not to mention his cowboy vibe—Jimmy led them inside, where they were seated in a booth by the window and promptly plied with chips and salsa.

Their departure from Wall had been anticlimactic, and the adrenaline ebbed over mesquite-flavored fajitas and brisket tacos. Jimmy enjoyed what were likely some of his final moments with Kira, as they still planned to deliver her to the Greyhound Bus station downtown after lunch. Even Nicole, who'd been wound a little tight the last twenty-four hours, loosened up when Jimmy mimicked their waiter, whose accent was somewhere between Mexican bandit, Texas rancher, and stoned surfer.

They lingered over the meal, as if the restaurant was a safe haven from the real world. As Nicole dug into her purse for a credit card to pay the bill, Jimmy tipped his hat up and leaned back in the booth. "How do we play this?"

Kira, who sat beside him, said, "How do you mean?"

"I mean, I don't think we should just drive down to the station, shake your hand, and say goodbye."

"I was hoping for more than a handshake."

Jimmy grinned at her and avoided his sister's gaze. "We know that the Gardiners headed west looking for you, or they wouldn't have shown up in Wall, and it presumes that—although some of them ended up back in Wall—they continued west after talking to Nicole because they wouldn't have expected you to turn around and head back east. And since there's nothing between Wall and here but three shrubs and a bush, it stands to reason that they had a presence in Rapid City, and still have a presence, and that would likely include truck stops, restaurant clusters, and the bus station."

"So you think they'll be watching the station."

"I think it's a possibility."

"Me too. But what do we do?"

Jimmy looked to Nicole.

She raised an eyebrow. "You've been doing well so far."

He nodded. "For starters, we should call ahead, see when the bus to wherever you're going leaves, and not get there any too early."

Kira nodded. The waiter stopped by to pick up Nicole's credit card. Then Jimmy said, "Nicole can drop us off."

"You two?" she asked.

"They'll be looking for Kira alone, or Kira with both of us, or Kira with you if this Travis guy is involved."

"Okay."

Jimmy looked at Kira's hair. It was thick—full-bodied, he thought they called it on shampoo commercials. "You ever wear a ball cap?"

"Once or twice."

"I've got one you can borrow. Stuff your hair under it, or put it in a bun behind it, anything to keep it from flowing behind you. Wear your shades, maybe a change of clothes they wouldn't expect. I'll hang with you until you board the bus, then keep an eye out until after it leaves to see if there's anyone lurking around." He shrugged. "I'm not sure what else we could do."

"I am," Nicole said. "Pray."

*   *   *

Jimmy and Kira got out of the Jeep in the parking lot of a Mexican restaurant just north of the Milo Barber Trolley Station, which also housed Rapid City's Greyhound Bus stop. The late afternoon air was hot and stifling, and tinged yellowish orange by haze. But that was of little concern, other than for making a sticky situation stickier.

The only bus leaving Rapid City and going directly to Denver departed at quarter after five. So after finishing their late lunch, the trio had driven to a nearby strip mall where, on Jimmy's suggestion, Kira had purchased a Denver Broncos T-shirt at SCHEELS. It went against her upbringing in a Kansas City Chiefs household, but would enable her to blend in once in the Mile High City, and would look natural at the bus station.

Kira had changed into the T-shirt—as well as her pair of jeans, which would be less conspicuous than her skirt—in the store's bathroom. Then, on the ride downtown, she had threaded her hair through the back of Jimmy's camouflage Cabela's cap and tied it into a bun. With a new pair of cheap sunglasses also purchased at SCHEELS, she'd at least require a double take before being recognized.

For his part, Jimmy wore his cowboy hat and sunglasses, and had changed shirts since the morning. And before Nicole had dropped them off, she'd circled the entire block. They'd spotted one motorcycle parked on the block, albeit not in front of the trolley station. The coast was clear, at least as far as they could tell.

Nicole remained in the Jeep, waiting for a call from Jimmy. He and Kira walked to the trolley station's front entrance, both of their heads on a swivel. He carried her backpack, one less marker the Gardiners could home in on. Together they approached the ticket counter, and Kira purchased a one-way ticket to Denver, which would take her south through Hot Springs, and from there south and west into Wyoming to I-25, which led to Denver via Cheyenne. She was due to arrive around midnight.

They had ten minutes before boarding, and Kira asked Jimmy to hold her backpack while she used the restroom. He wandered around the small terminal, observing other passengers. Yet again, he saw nothing suspicious, which made him suspicious. Could this really be a clean getaway?

Kira rejoined him with a wan smile on her face. "I guess this is goodbye," she said, nodding at the clock on the wall.

"I guess," Jimmy said. "I'll hang around until the bus heads out."

"I'll give you my number," she said, "in case you see something. It'll be good to know."

"Okay. And let me know when you get to . . . wherever it is you ultimately go. Let me know that things turn out all right."

"I will," she said, and they quickly exchanged numbers. Something was bugging him as they did, but he ignored it, not wanting to spoil the moment.

"Thank you, Jimmy, for everything you did," Kira said with a beautiful smile.

"You're welcome."

"Thank Nicole too."

"I will."

She reached up and touched his cheek, then leaned in and brushed his other cheek with a soft kiss. Her thin smile as she stepped back had a dimple in it, and was as cute as you please. He returned it, then shrugged off her backpack. "Here you go."

"Thanks." She took a deep breath. "Goodbye, Jimmy."

"Goodbye, Kira."

She turned for the door to the loading dock, stopping just before passing through. She looked back, smiled, and offered a wiggling of her fingers wave. He held up a stationary hand in return. Then she turned again, passed through the doors, and was gone.

CHAPTER NINETEEN

Nicole held up her bottle of water to examine the contents. Approximately one-third of its sixteen ounces remained, and, instead of chugging it, she took off her sunglasses and then dumped the water on top of her head. As it splattered onto her shoulders and rolled down the sides of her face and her neck, it provided only minimal and temporary respite from surging morning heat. At least now that they had emerged from the canyon, there was a little breeze, and even that she could have done without as it caused tiny bits of sand, dirt, and grit to stick to her sweaty face and arms. Geographic features took a backseat when it came to the reason this place was called the badlands.

Jimmy had observed nobody suspicious boarding Kira's bus the night before, nor any signs that anyone was watching her or him. So he'd texted Nicole to pick him up, then guided her on what she deemed an unnecessarily obtuse route to their hotel, a Cambria Suites just off Rapid City's easternmost exit from I-90. They had checked in a day late, having determined on the drive to continue with the rest of their vacation. Repairs to the Jeep, rooms at the Hole-in-the-Wall Inn, a room at the EconoLodge, and a few of Kira's meals had added to their budget. But they could save a few dollars here and there, bite the bullet for extra expenses, and make the most of the time that was left. They'd grabbed dinner at a burger joint named Sickies Garage, just a walk across the parking lot from their hotel, and laid out the rest of the trip. The forecast had called for more heat each of the next two days, so they'd opted for the badlands on Tuesday and Mount Rushmore on Wednesday.

Worn out from the day's craziness, they had turned in early and been up early. Jimmy had gotten a text from Kira, announcing she'd reached Denver safely. He seemed to be handling the "breakup" pretty well, from Nicole's perspective. To save money and time, they'd passed on breakfast out and grabbed something from the hotel. They had not passed on coffees (a Smores espresso in Nicole's case) from Black Hills Blend, a place she had scouted ahead of time and refused to sacrifice. They'd left Rapid City before nine and headed via Highway 44 to the Ben Reifel Visitor Center on the far eastern corner of Badlands National Park. They had talked trails and weather conditions with a cute, square-jawed park ranger, and determined it was best to do their hiking before it got too hot.

That ship had sailed. It was noon, and already the heat was oppressive, and no amount of water or orange slices could keep Nicole from feeling its effects. As she sat on a rock, looking down the slope at the end of the canyon at a grove of juniper trees and then endless prairie broken by eroded stone formations, she couldn't understand how Jimmy was surviving. She wore cotton shorts and a white Gamecocks racerback tank top. He wore jeans with a dark, plaid, button-down shirt and his new cowboy hat. He stood, hands on his hips a dozen feet away, staring out at the expanse.

"Beautiful, isn't it?" he asked.

"Yeah."

"Can you imagine this view at sunset . . . or sunrise, with the shadows and the contrast?"

Nicole retrieved another bottle of water from her rucksack, which she had volunteered to carry for the first half of the hike, now sitting on the ground beside the rock. She stood, unscrewed the cap, took a healthy swig, then extended it to Jimmy. "Thanks," he said with a smile, then took a moderate sip.

"That it?"

"Uh-huh."

"You should hydrate."

"Thing is, I got distracted by that 3-D relief map at the visitor center and didn't use the restroom. And I did get a large coffee at that place."

"You're a guy. Isn't this nature's restroom?"

"I'm afraid I'll erode a feature. I'm fine."

She shook her head.

"What?"

"How are you not passing out?"

He lifted his eyes. "I don't think cowboys wore these originally to create a style, Nic. Keeps the sun off my face. Keeps me from getting flushed," he said, nodding at her.

"And the jeans?"

He shrugged.

"In fact, I don't think I've seen you wear shorts all summer. It's like a hundred degrees. Why don't you wear shorts?"

Jimmy looked at her for a moment, then reached down and pulled his left pants leg up to the knee. He stuck his leg toward her. "Do you like the look of this?"

"What?"

"Is this appealing, something that gives you pleasure?"

She frowned at him.

"Well, is it?"

"Not especially, no."

He released his pants leg. "Me either. Or anybody else, for that matter."

"You are a strange man, James David Turner."

"Besides, I've always thought shorts are kind of for boys."

"Aren't you the *man* who bragged to me last month about winning an eBay bid for an Atari?"

Jimmy winced, then looked away as he removed his hat and wiped his brow on his sleeve. Nicole was relieved to see sweaty circles under his arms—he was in fact not a cyborg. When he turned back, he was grinning. "Are you hot?"

She sighed.

"I'll take that for a yes. What are shorts doing for you?"

Nicole bit her tongue, pleading for her brain to think of a retort to Jimmy's absurd logic. But none came. In fact, she found herself fighting a grin at his way of thinking and his dumb smirk. But she wouldn't give him that satisfaction. Instead, she reached for the water bottle, and he handed it back. She took another long gulp before turning her eyes back to the panorama spreading seemingly to the Nebraska border. Then again, maybe it did in fact.

"You ready to head back?" Jimmy asked a minute later.

Nicole nodded.

He squinted. "You mad?"

"No."

He nodded and started trudging back through the canyon. Technically, it was the Notch Trail, a two-thirds of a mile long winding path through hoodoos and buttes and across some grasslands. It might as well have been a dry gulch at this point, marked only by white-topped stakes. Pristine Florida beaches and snow-capped granite mountaintops had their allure, sure, but so did a languid swamp rimmed by moss-covered oaks or an eroded wasteland like this, at least in Nicole's mind. And yet, one could only look at so many identical features without losing interest. Then again, maybe it was the heat index, which had to be in the triple digits.

The canyon widened, and they had to walk single file along a cliff's edge. Focused on their footing, they didn't talk until they stopped at dual stakes marking the top of a fifty-rung rope ladder that led down into the canyon again. A couple was climbing the ladder, so they took a break to rest, drink more water, and wipe sweat from their brows.

"You okay?" Jimmy asked as Nicole wiped her forehead with a towel from her backpack.

"You want an energy bar?" she asked in return, sticking the towel back into the backpack as she spoke.

"Do you think this place floods a lot?"

She frowned.

"Sorry, we're not just doing random questions?"

She huffed out his name.

"Seriously, something's eating you."

She shook him off as the couple reached the top of the ladder, and they stepped aside to let them pass.

"You first," Nicole said.

He nodded, looking down the steep hillside. He looked at her. "Forward or back down it? Backing down seems kind of girly, no offense, but I'd hate to roll down to the bottom."

"Forward but lean backward as you walk."

He pointed at her, then started down, but with a look in his eye that told her the conversation wasn't over.

CHAPTER TWENTY

Nicole followed Jimmy down the ladder, focused on each wrung—wood beams, connected to the others by cables. The rungs were solid, but one wrong step could be treacherous. Which is why she was annoyed when, a third of the way down, Jimmy decided to resume talking. "If this were a movie, I'd stop here and confront you."

She said nothing.

"You know, have the pivotal discussion in the most dangerous spot. Like Orlando Bloom and Keira Knightley getting married during a battle and a hurricane in *Pirates of the Caribbean*. Or every episode of *24*."

She stared at him before asking, "What pivotal discussion?"

"Something is bothering you, and it's not my choice of apparel."

"Just keep going," she said.

He did, but stopped when they were at the bottom again. He looked at her, clearly not ready to let it go. So she sighed and dug for water again. "It's Kira."

"You miss her too? The sister you never had and now don't again?"

"No. Something doesn't sit right with me."

"Like what?"

"Jimmy, ever since we picked her up, something in her story hasn't made sense."

"Like what?" he repeated.

"That's just it, I can't put my finger on it. But little things keep nagging at me."

He waited instead of asking again.

She took a drink before answering. "For starters, why would her ex-boyfriend's family chase her across the Dakotas when all she knows about them is a vague sense that they're up to something? I mean, loving motorcycles, tattoos, and guns doesn't make a person a criminal. And then Travis, the aesthetic antithesis of the Gardiners, mysteriously shows up and intimates that we're connected to her. But he doesn't threaten me, doesn't bribe me, and doesn't bother to do more than sit outside our hotel for an hour in his car."

"That's easy. He melted."

"Can you be serious with me for a minute?"

"Sorry, Nic." He nodded down the trail, and they trudged side-by-side slowly. "She did know things, by the way."

"Things?"

"That could make her a danger to them. Names and faces, the layout of their compound, their firepower, comments she'd overheard."

"How do you know?"

"She told me."

"When?"

"When we were shopping for hats."

"Then why did she say she didn't know anything? Remember by the pool, she said maybe she knew something but didn't know she knew it?"

He nodded and hung back, allowing her to lead through a narrower portion of the trail. When they were again side by side, he had a frown. It disappeared with a shrug. "I don't know. I'll grant you she doesn't seem to have a smoking gun, but if they are up to something nefarious, her knowing anything could be a danger to them."

"And who's Travis?"

"Beats me. An undercover fed trying to take them down?"

They took a few steps. "I went through her backpack, Jimmy."

He turned his head.

"When you all were at Wall Drug yesterday morning, after Travis showed up. I wanted to know what she was hiding."

He nodded.

"I found nothing. A few changes of clothes. No money. But she did have a locked pocket."

"So?"

"So, she clearly was hiding something."

"For good reason, it would seem."

Nicole sighed. "What about her not knowing what CoMo was?"

"I didn't know what CoMo was."

"You're not from CoMo, Jimmy!"

"Are you jealous?"

"Jealous?"

"This was supposed to be Nic and Jimmy time, catching up, bonding, etcetera, and instead I spent twenty-four hours fawning over Kira? Fawning? That seems a little much. I wouldn't call it fawning. Would you? Anyhow, you get the idea."

Nicole didn't answer right away, in part because the path narrowed and they had to go single file again, her in front. Was she jealous? She'd wondered the same thing, but didn't think that was it. Truth was, Kira brought out something in Jimmy, made him more—alive was such a cliché, but an accurate one. Kira took a guy whose personality sometimes faded into black and white and made it vibrant.

At a widening of the path, Nicole stopped. "I'm not jealous, Jimmy, I don't think. Like I told you the other morning, I was concerned about you, unfounded, it seems, because you're fine apparently. But . . . I don't know. All I can say is something seemed off with her."

"Why are you worried about it now?" he asked.

"I don't know."

"I mean, she's in Denver. It's not like we can go get her."

"I know."

"We could stop at Wall Drug on the way back, hope to run into one of those guys with a BHG patch, and rat her out."

"Of course not."

He shrugged. "Fair disclosure, I had questions about her a few times too."

"And that didn't bother you?"

"No. Take her phone for example. She told us she left it in the diner."

"But she had one."

"Yeah. Took selfies with me after I bought my hat."

"And that didn't send up a red flag?"

"It bugged my subconscious, but I didn't realize why until she texted me this morning. Could be she thought she had left it there, or didn't want us to worry that she was being tracked. Who knows, maybe she's duplicitous and has two cell phones, and is one day going to start wearing pant suits and running for president." He waved his hands. "What difference does it make?"

"Really, you're giving me Hillary Clinton right now?"

"I thought that'd resonate with you. Isn't she from South Carolina?"

"New York."

He frowned.

"Bill was from Little Rock, which is in Arkansas, not South Carolina. And I've been a Republican since I was like four. Why would that resonate with me?"

He shrugged.

"Forget it, Jimmy. Like you said, she's gone."

She resumed walking, but wasn't able to forget it. She felt like the gears were tumbling in the back of her brain, only something was out of whack and wouldn't let them fall into place.

They were almost back to the trailhead, now out of a canyon and in a plain of prairie grass broken by more features. Prairie dogs popped up here and there, then ducked back into their holes before she could get a good look at them. She slowed to swig the water bottle she'd been holding in her hand, and Jimmy said, "You remember Carlin?"

"Who is Carlin?" she asked, extending the bottle to him.

He took it. "Perky blond girl I dated for about a half hour my senior year."

She shook her head.

He took a drink, half of which coursed down his chin, and he wiped it off with his wrist. "She was one of those Pentecostals who heard God speak aloud every morning, telling her what to have for breakfast."

Nicole raised an eyebrow.

"Not quite, but she was out there. Anyhow, I misjudged her terribly."

She nodded, waiting for the point.

"Other than that, I think I've been a pretty good judge of character. And Kira . . . graded out okay."

"Just okay?"

"I mean good. Well. Well? Graded good? Graded well."

Nicole sighed. "And not just because she was cute and flirted with you?"

"It's not entirely about that," he said in a fairly good George Clooney, and Nicole had to grin. But it faded when she remembered what Kira had told her at Wall Drug while they had been browsing for souvenirs. Jimmy apparently saw her expression change and nodded at her. "What?"

"Something else she said."

"What?"

"She said she still had feelings for Braden."

"Okay."

"I asked how long they had been together, and she said three or four months."

"Is this the long way of telling me that I was her rebound one-day boyfriend?"

"Jimmy, she clearly liked this guy, at least before she found out he was crazy, and then even a little bit after."

He nodded slowly.

"And yet she didn't know how long they'd been together? 'Three or four months'? Trust me, a girl would know, down to the hour."

He nodded again but said nothing, and Nicole resumed walking, eager to get back to the Jeep and cold water in their small travel cooler. She had to look back to see if Jimmy was following, and he was, several paces behind. She sighed to herself, wondering if she had pushed too far for no reason and upset him. Maybe she was obsessing over this, over-analyzing things that weren't really there. It wouldn't have been the first time . . .

"Were you in a serious relationship?" Jimmy asked when they were just yards from the trailhead parking lot.

Nicole turned around. "Excuse me?"

"Junior year, I didn't hear from you for a whole semester, and you barely found time to FaceTime me over Christmas break, much less come home."

Nicole opened her mouth but nothing came out.

"By spring, you were your old self, and now you're sensitive about the length of Kira's relationship." He shrugged. "Just doing the math. You tell me if it adds up."

Nicole said nothing as Jimmy shrugged again and walked past her. She watched him go, suddenly feeling the heat with a new intensity and finding it hard to even breathe.

CHAPTER TWENTY-ONE

Waylon Jennings was singing about Hank Williams as the South Dakota terrain passed by at eighty miles per hour. When Jimmy had asked, after fifteen minutes of silence, if he could play some music, Nicole had acquiesced with a soft, "Fine." She hadn't spoken in multiple syllables since they'd finished their hike.

They had eaten some fruit, downed some water, and changed shirts—in Nicole's case in the pit latrine in the middle of the lot. Then they'd driven the meandering Badlands Loop State Scenic Byway, which wound first beneath, then up, then alongside the main ridge running through the park. Jimmy pulled over at several picturesque vantage points, but when Nicole remained in the air-conditioned Jeep a second time, he got the hint and continued out of the park, settling for a few more glimpses out his window and a view of some wild bison in the prairie north of the park. He hadn't even joked about stopping at Wall Drug when they swung through town to get back on the interstate.

They crested a small hill, and the Black Hills emerged on the horizon, barely distinguishable in the haze. The day was just as hot and sticky as the day before—maybe more so—but now accompanied by a breeze that, when he'd stood on an exposed platform at Conata Basin Overlook, had felt tinged with something. He knew plenty of old farmers who could feel the weather in their bones or the breeze or whatever, and Jimmy didn't have the gift. But he sensed a change in weather was in the air, or that a storm was brewing. He looked over at his sister, her elbow on the rim of the door, her palm propping up her head as she looked listlessly through the windshield. Two storms in one day.

He decided to wade into the water. "Look, Nic."

She turned her eyes, not her head.

"Nicole. Clearly I stepped in it back there." He shook his head and glanced her way. "I didn't mean to upset you. I shouldn't have poked—I should have left things alone."

Now she slowly turned her head. "It's okay, Jimmy."

"Is it?"

She shifted in her seat and sat up. She licked her lips. "His name was Paul. We had a class together sophomore year, but didn't really know each other."

"You don't *have* to tell me about it if you don't want."

She swallowed. "We were both at the same party, and it got wild and we left at the same time, ended up walking to The Creamery to get ice cream, and we talked for hours. Over the next few months, we became really good friends, and then something more." She'd resumed looking out the windshield, but now turned and looked Jimmy in the eye. "I thought he was the one."

"What happened?" he asked softly.

"The week before Christmas break, he told me that he wasn't into me romantically, that he really liked me as a friend, but didn't think . . ." She swallowed. "That he could ever be in love with me." Her voice was almost a whisper as she said, "I thought he already was."

Willie Nelson was singing "My Life's Been a Pleasure," and the mood wasn't what they needed, so Jimmy punched it off.

"I was a mess for Christmas, which is why all I could muster was a quick video chat. I was heartbroken, not to mention trying to figure out what was wrong with me, why a guy like that wouldn't—no, *couldn't* be in love with me."

"There's nothing wrong with you, Nic."

She smiled. "I know that, now. But it took a while—and a couple good friends—to figure it out."

Jimmy said nothing.

"It's kind of like that passage in the Bible about when a demon leaves a place, then comes back with seven others and finds the place empty, and inhabits it again and makes it worse? Here I am with no boyfriend—and only one or two dates—since then, and I'm not sure if I want to be a career woman or a wife and mother who works on the side like the Proverbs 31 woman, and which one will appeal to the right guy, and have I mentioned I haven't found him yet?" She sighed. "My old demons start coming back."

Jimmy wanted to speak, but couldn't figure out what to say.

"And sometimes still, when I see someone like my brother seemingly having it *so* easy to start falling for someone, those old feelings of inadequacy surface."

"I had no idea," Jimmy said finally, as out the window the miles blurred past.

"Of course you didn't," she said with a shrug. "I didn't tell you."

Jimmy stared through the windshield, trying to gather his thoughts so they wouldn't come out wrong. "You know," he finally said, looking back her way, "I'm pretty sure the 'right guy' isn't going to pass you over because you do or don't have a career ambition. He's going to love you for who you are. And if he doesn't, that's his loss more than yours."

"Thank you, Jimmy. Tell me, when did you become so mature?"

"As we speak."

She grinned. "Thanks for listening." She exhaled. "It feels good to be able to unburden this to someone who really matters. But," she added, sitting up in her seat, "I don't want a pity party. I'm doing pretty well, most of the time. And I don't want to spend the rest of our trip sulking, or worrying about Kira or the past."

"Good for you."

"I want to go for a swim, then find a nice place for dinner, and kick my feet up for the night."

"Got a place in mind, for dinner?"

"What about Firehouse, the place all the trucks were advertising?"

Jimmy nodded. Interspersed with Wall Drug billboards along I-90 West were numerous fire trucks-turned-advertisements and billboards for Firehouse Brewing Company in Rapid City.

"I checked out the menu, and it looks good."

He nodded. "Fine with me."

"I thought we could go a little early," she said, glancing at her watch, "maybe browse some of the downtown shops?"

Jimmy grinned as he looked over at Nicole's hopeful and a little sheepish look. "That's fine. You know, while you swim, I think I'm going to check out Cabela's."

"Jimmy, you work at Cabela's."

He nodded.

"Aren't they all the same?"

"I'll find out. Besides, I need to replace my cap." He found himself thinking of Kira and her thin-lipped smile as they'd said goodbye. He only wished her hair hadn't been tucked up under his—now her—camouflage Cabela's baseball cap.

*   *   *

There were no parking spots in the shade at Cambria Suites, so Jimmy settled for a spot as close to the nearest entrance to their rooms as possible. It was actually closer to the neighboring hotel, which would probably give it shade about the time they planned to leave for dinner. He backed in for what it was worth, then looked at his sister. "How far did we hike today?"

"Mile and a half, maybe."

"Feels like more."

"It's not the mileage, honey," she said in a deep voice.

"Reverse Indiana Jones, very good," he said.

"Sorry, I must be tired."

They got out and trudged across the grass and through an opening in an iron fence that surrounded Cambria Suites' courtyard. With several patio tables and a fire pit, the courtyard wrapped around the enclosed pool area and connected the parking lot to a rear and side entrance to the hotel. Jimmy swiped his card to open the door, then followed Nicole up three flights of stairs to their side-by-side rooms.

"How long you figure you'll swim?" he asked as they exited the stairwell.

"Half hour maybe."

"Plus a shower, do your hair, yada, yada, yada." He waved a hand. "I'll be back before you're done. Give me a call when you're ready to head out."

"Okay. Uh, Jimmy." She had stopped whereas he kept walking.

"Gonna get some ice."

"In what, your hat?"

He stopped, looked up at its brim, then at his grinning sister as she retrieved her key from her backpack and opened her door.

"Must be heat stroke," Jimmy said, striding back. "Maybe you had a point about not wearing shor—"

Nicole's scream interrupted him.

CHAPTER TWENTY-TWO

Nicole had never been given to dramatic responses—whether it was getting the Barbie Dreamhouse she desperately wanted one Christmas, attempts by her older brother and his friends to startle her, or a fourth-quarter touchdown by the Gamecocks. She was measured, at most eliciting an intake of breath that could be called a gasp. But when she opened her hotel door, she let out a full-blown scream, somewhere between a dignified Southern woman's cry of alarm and a blood-curdling step-on-a-Lego barefoot howl.

Jimmy arrived so fast he almost knocked her over. "What is—"

He stopped and stood beside her in the doorway, looking at the mess. The contents of her suitcase had been strewn all over the floor in the "living room" of her suite. Shirts, shorts, swimwear, underwear—clean and dirty—covered the floor. Her Bible, the novel she'd been reading, and her journal were beside them, having all clearly been rifled through. Her purse was on the desk, upside down, its contents spread out as if to be cataloged. In the bathroom to her left, someone had emptied her travel bag and laid out deodorant (with the lid off), as well as shampoo and conditioner and body wash (caps all unscrewed). Her jewelry box had even been ransacked.

It didn't stop with her belongings. The furniture had been moved, the cushions of the chair and couch tossed aside. The bedding on her king bed had been stripped to the mattress and piled in the corner. The lampshades were askew and the paintings on the wall crooked or sitting on the floor beneath their previous hanging spots.

Nicole dropped her backpack from her hands. Beside her, Jimmy stroked his hand over his mouth and jaw. She found her voice first. "What . . . in the world, Jimmy?"

"I'm going to check my room," he said, then backed out of the doorway. Nicole surveyed the room again, noticing other objects that had clearly been moved and items of hers that had been exposed. She heard nothing from next door, and stepped out of her room and to Jimmy's doorway. He stood in the middle of his room, which looked exactly like hers, only with a few less possessions scattered around the room.

"Jimmy," she said softly.

"No, I did not leave it this way."

"What happened?"

"I don't know."

"I mean, I know what happened, but . . . why?"

"I don't know."

"We should alert the hotel."

"Let's see if anything's missing first. It doesn't look like it."

"Don't touch anything though."

He nodded, and they each spent a few minutes looking over their respective rooms. Whoever had ransacked them had been methodical, and Nicole's memory was good enough that she could account for everything. She'd taken her wallet with her money and credit cards with her in her backpack, but none of her jewelry—of marginal worth—nor her laptop computer had been taken. The laptop had been removed from its case, which had also been emptied, and had been booted up, but was unharmed.

"The Gardiners?" Jimmy asked, startling a gasp out of Nicole.

"Don't do that."

"Sorry. Else your boy Travis?"

"It seems too coincidental not to be related to them or Kira, but why?"

"I don't know. You want to go get the hotel dick or should I?"

"I don't care," Nicole said.

"Why don't you go."

"Are you being gallant, in case they come back?"

"No. I'm going to text Kira while you're gone and let her know to be careful. This is clearly bigger than we thought."

*   *   *

The manager of the hotel seemed more alarmed by the ransacking of their rooms than did Jimmy and Nicole. She apologized profusely, numerous times, and insisted that the police be called. Under the circumstances, they didn't argue with her.

When the officers arrived, they took statements from Jimmy and Nicole and commended them for not touching anything or altering the rooms as they'd been found. They asked expected questions, first of the manager, such as had there been reports of any other break-ins, any history of such activity, any disgruntled or suspicious employees, any guests that had drawn negative attention? All were answered in the negative.

Then they focused on Jimmy and Nicole, asking who they were, where they were from, why they were in Rapid City, where they had been during the day, and, lastly, if they had any reason to suspect anyone or had any idea why they had been targeted.

Jimmy looked at Nicole, and she at him.

The two officers, a heavyset white man and a woman with darker skin and a braid, waited.

"We met a girl at a gas station halfway across the state," Jimmy said. "She said she was on the run from her ex-boyfriend and his somewhat crazy family, and we gave her a lift to Rapid City where she caught a bus to Denver."

"Did you encounter her ex or his family?" Heavyset/Officer Fenton asked. He was taking notes, on an actual notepad and not a tablet or phone.

"She did," Jimmy said.

"We were at Wall Drug," Nicole said, "and a couple of stereotypical bikers showed me her picture on a phone and asked if I'd seen her. I said I'd seen her leave town and they believed me."

"That's all?"

"Yeah," Jimmy said.

"What was this girl's name?" Braid/Officer Hardy asked.

"Kira Angel."

"When you say 'girl,' about how old are we talking? A minor?"

"No. Well, I don't think so. I didn't card her. She looked about our age. Said she'd dropped out of college, and we didn't question it."

"She said the guys who talked to me, when I described them, were Johnny and Frank, if that helps," Nicole said.

"Last names?" Fenton asked.

"Gardiner, possibly. She also mentioned a Lance Gardiner, and her ex Braden."

He jotted down the names.

"But the truth is," Jimmy said, "we have no reason to think it's them other than the odds of this being a coincidence."

"Did Miss Angel give either of you anything?" Hardy asked.

Jimmy shook his head. Nicole took a beat longer, before saying, "No."

"Did she seem to be hiding or concealing anything, or talk about having an item she was hiding?"

"No," Jimmy said. "Not that I recall. Nic?"

"No," she said again.

"Is there anything else about her, about your interactions with her, that you think might be pertinent?"

"No," Jimmy said. "We dropped her at the bus station yesterday, and we thought that was the end of it. Like we said, we spent the day hiking in the badlands."

"Have you been in contact with her?" Fenton asked.

"She texted me that she'd arrived in Denver last night, and I texted her when we saw our rooms. I haven't heard back from her."

"Could you give us her number?"

"Sure."

Jimmy fished out his phone and accessed Kira's number. As he did, and as he showed it to Fenton, Hardy said, "From the look of things, whoever did this was searching very carefully for something particular, and it doesn't appear they found it. If they were looking for high-value objects or drugs, they would have been much quicker and less thorough. And if they were just looking for any items of value, some of your jewelry and certainly electronics would have been nabbed."

"So what do we do?" Nicole asked.

"A couple options," she continued. "We can bring in our CSTs and dust for fingerprints, look for any other items. Even if they wore gloves, which is probable given their thoroughness, it's likely they left something in the way of DNA. But that doesn't mean we'll get a match unless they're in our system, and it would require you to leave everything as it is while that takes place. Or, since nothing appears to be taken, we can file a report and follow up on what you've given us, but likely—and I'm just being honest with you—not make much progress. We'll get a copy of the hotel's security cameras, which don't cover this hallway, but might enable us to piece together some faces of who could have been in the area. But that won't be conclusive. All that said, it is up to you."

Jimmy looked at Nicole.

"What are the odds you all catch them if you all do a full exam?" she asked.

"Depends on if they're in the system. If so, we likely find a DNA match. But that takes time, and there's as good a chance as not that they're not still in the area."

"Do you think we're in danger?"

"They were very thorough, which means they took a lot of time and risk that you would come back and interrupt them. That tells me they're brash, but also that they *didn't* want to harm you, or they would have waited for you to return."

"It also suggests," Fenton said, looking up finally from his notes, "that they might have known your plans, known you'd be gone most of the day. That means they've had a pretty close eye on you, which sounds scary, but again suggests they've had opportunity to harm you if they wanted to."

"We can't say for sure," Hardy said, "but this doesn't seem like someone interested in hurting anyone."

Fenton nodded along.

"But criminals are unpredictable. If you choose to stay, you should be careful."

CHAPTER TWENTY-THREE

There weren't as many shops to browse in downtown Rapid City as Nicole had thought. She and Jimmy still wandered for several blocks, ducking in and out of a few places, trying to guess the president by his full-sized statue on each street corner, and enjoying what had turned into a reasonably nice evening. The heat of the day had started to abate, a hazy layer of clouds had moved in to turn the sky faded orange, and a steady breeze kept the humidity down. Even so, Nicole envied the kids dancing in the splash park at the Main Street Square while their parents watched, chatted, or studied their phones. After all, she had been denied her swim.

She and Jimmy had talked it over and decided to stay in Rapid City— at least for the time being. They'd also decided not to bother with having the police dust for prints or DNA in their rooms. Both were confident whoever had ransacked them had done so carefully and with minimal evidence left behind. And neither wanted to stay in their sweat-soaked hiking clothes any longer than necessary. So they had thanked Officers Fenton and Hardy and exchanged information in case anything else came to light. Then they had packed up their possessions, auditing as they went, finding absolutely nothing missing. The manager of the hotel had apologized again, several times, and provided them new rooms on the fourth floor and the other end of the hotel, comping their entire stay.

They had locked and bolted their respective doors, then showered and freshened up. By that time, it had been quarter after four, and they'd agreed to stick to their original plan of heading downtown for shopping and dinner.

Nicole's eyes followed toddlers, boy and girl twins, chasing each other through the dancing fountains of water. She turned her eyes back to Jimmy, who leaned against a slab of granite, checking his phone.

"You hear from her?" Nicole asked.

He looked up. "No."

"Sorry."

"It's fine," he said, pocketing the phone. "I'm not lovesick; just want to make sure she's okay."

Nicole nodded, not sure if she believed him or not.

"Say, I've been thinking," he said.

"About?"

"Who, why, and how."

She had been enjoying the evening thus far, not thinking about the break-in at their rooms—or what was happening to their new rooms now. But it was best to let Jimmy express himself instead of forcing him to keep it bottled in. So she looked at him and waited.

"You can't pick a hotel door—at least, not a hotel like this. The Hole-in-the-Wall Inn, sure. But here you'd need a keycard or something out of a spy movie to 'pick' the lock."

"Are you suggesting it was an inside job?"

"No. Just considering options. We can assume nobody pulled the old 'I lost my room key' at the front desk, or Aliana would have said something. I assume they have records."

"Liana."

"What?"

"Her name was Liana, not Aliana."

"Are you sure?"

Nicole nodded.

"Liana. Liana? Aliana?" He frowned. "Whomever. That means they either snuck behind the desk and made themselves a key—"

"Unlikely."

"I agree. Or they could have cobbed one off a hospitality cart, or bribed-slash-threatened a maid to let them in."

"In the latter case, there should be someone to identify them."

"Yeah, but I doubt it's that."

"So they lifted a key."

"That's my guess."

"Okay, that's the how. The who is the Gardiners?"

"That's also my guess. Or Travis."

"Why didn't you mention him to the cops?"

"Why didn't you?" he asked.

"I got the feeling you didn't want me to."

He nodded. "They'll follow up with Kira, but I hate to jam her up, create any more of a trail than there is to her. And we don't know anything about Travis, if that's his real name, which I doubt."

"Still, we did technically withhold information."

"Technically, we withheld lots of details."

Nicole sighed. "Keep walk—" She suddenly turned back toward the splash pad.

"Something wrong?"

"Speak of the devil," she said.

"Who?"

"Travis."

"Where?"

"Halfway down the block, looking in the window of that toy store."

"Are you sure?"

"No. But I think so. I don't want to stare."

"Maybe we should," Jimmy said. "What if I turn around and yell, 'Hey, Travis, whassup, bro?'"

"Will you stop it?"

"Just trying to lighten things up."

"I don't want to be light right now; I want to be nervous."

"You could have fooled me," he muttered.

She snuck a glance, but now there were pedestrians in the way.

"Didn't you say he played coy with you?" Jimmy asked.

"Yeah."

"Maybe we should give him the opposite treatment. Maybe we should confront him."

"Or maybe we should run."

"Like literally, into traffic?"

"Like try to lose him."

"To what end? We clearly are the two most easy people to locate on planet earth."

"Easiest," she said.

He raised his eyebrows.

"Sorry."

"You want to run? Go back to the car, scrap Firehouse for Popeye's, and be back across the Big Muddy by dark?"

"No," Nicole said. "No, I don't want to run away. I don't want to be reckless, but I don't want to run either."

He shrugged. "Then what? Wait here to see if he moves first?"

"Let's go eat," she said.

Jimmy squinted.

"Let's go have dinner, act like we haven't seen him, act like nothing's up."

"Okay . . ."

"If we're trying to keep heat off Kira, then we make him think nothing's up. We're not running from him, we're not confronting him, we're going on with our vacation because we have nothing to hide."

"I like it," Jimmy said.

"For real?"

"For real. And I'm starving too. Let's eat."

"Okay," Nicole said with a genuine smile. She turned west, away from Travis or his lookalike, and they started walking.

"But say the word," Jimmy said as he fell in beside her and winked, "and we'll split up and meet at the safe house in half an hour."

*   *   *

"We never finished our conversation," Nicole said after their waitress left, having taken their orders. They were seated in an open-air enclave on the ground level of Firehouse Brewing Company. Ceiling fans hanging above stringed lights augmented a breeze blowing in through an open garage door from the street, which kept them cool. So did iced tea that both of them had been guzzling since the waitress had dropped it off. The stage behind them was empty, but a large family at a table at its base made up for it. Their lively conversation and screams from young kids mixed with the sounds of the city coming in off the street and created a din of background noise that actually made it convenient for Jimmy and Nicole to chat at their table in the middle of the room. Unfortunately, the why was the one aspect of this all that Jimmy didn't want to address.

"We didn't," he said, lifting his glass again.

Nicole shook her head, waves of hair tumbling across her shoulders. "Why would anyone break into our rooms?"

"No idea."

"You think it was random?"

"No. They just happened to hit our side-by-side rooms and no others? No way."

"So we were targeted," she said, looking past Jimmy, toward the street.

"You see him again?"

"No," she said. "Just thinking."

They had walked a block from Main Street Square to the restaurant, entered the front door, and been guided to an outdoor table in the garage. They hadn't looked, but they hadn't seen Travis following them at any point, nor since they'd arrived. Maybe he was parked in a car across the street, maybe he'd given up like in Wall, or maybe he was having a craft beer upstairs.

"I know you told the cops no," Nicole said, "but she didn't give you anything, did she? Kira, I mean."

"A kiss on the cheek and warm feelings in my soul," Jimmy said.

"I mean it."

"No," he said, shaking his head.

"Me either."

"I take it back. She gave me five bucks for pie. I tried to resist, but she insisted. You think she stumbled into a counterfeit ring?"

"It's not the most ridiculous theory."

"Really, it's not? A bunch of bikers in Nowhere, South Dakota, are printing and passing out fake Lincolns, and now are chasing Kira across the state and broke into our room because she stole their printing plate and hid it in your drawers?"

"When you put it like that . . ."

"If Kira's involved in something hinky, and I'm sure you're sure she is by now, I have *no* idea what it is."

"I'm not *sure* she's involved in anything. I just think the more coincidences we have, the less likely it is something big *isn't* going on."

Their waitress returned with Fire Caps, mushrooms stuffed with crab and cheese. They were delicious, and required more tea for each of them. Out of theories as to why they had been targeted or for what, and determined to go forward with their vacation, they discussed plans for the following day. Mount Rushmore was on the agenda, along with a drive on the Needles Highway and to Black Elk Peak. Figuring an early start was again prudent, they kicked around options for the rest of the night. Jimmy's weather app said a line of storms was brewing, and he suggested they drive to the top of Skyline Drive to get views of Rapid City and watch the storms roll in. After finding Ronald Reagan's statue on the downtown street corner, Nicole said.

Entrées were a buffalo burger for Jimmy and a half rack of ribs for Nicole. When they arrived, along with a tea refill for him, they gave up talking for eating. The baby of the family by the stage was in meltdown mode, and a trio of young women recently seated at the next table over were talking extra loud and cackling at every other sentence, so it would have been hard to carry on much of a conversation anyhow.

"How is the buffalo?" Nicole asked when Jimmy sat back with a sigh.

"Good. Dry, but good."

"You full?"

He shook the ice in the bottom of his glass. "Need more tea."

"You're going to get up tonight more times than Grandpa," Nicole said.

"Well worth it," he said, trailing off as his phone vibrated. He pulled it from his pocket, then frowned at an unknown number. He showed it to Nicole, who shook her head. "Area 605, that's here, right?"

"Yeah."

He swiped to answer. "Hello?"

"Is this Jimmy?" asked a deep, gruff voice.

"Yeah. Who's this?"

"We want the flash drive. Give it to us, and nothing will happen to the girl."

CHAPTER TWENTY-FOUR

Nicole watched over a fork with a tendril of meat on it as the blood drained from Jimmy's face. She set down her fork. "What is it?"

"I don't know what you're talking about," Jimmy said.

She waited, pleading with her ears to hear something on the phone, which was absurd, because she could barely hear Jimmy.

"Kira?"

"It's Kira?" Nicole asked.

He shook his head, then pushed back from the table. He held up a finger, indicating Nicole should wait, and was saying something she couldn't hear as he turned and walked toward the street. Nicole exhaled, then reached for her sweet tea. With her eyes, she followed Jimmy until he turned the corner on the sidewalk. She sighed, then figured she might as well eat as sit there and wonder. Especially as good as the ribs were.

The women at the adjacent table were talking about the crowds at Mount Rushmore, and to take her mind off speculating, Nicole tried to eavesdrop and pick up any potential tips for her and Jimmy's visit. She covered by taking another drink of tea, and when she set down her glass, a shadow covered the table. She looked up to see Travis.

Her eyes widened, then narrowed in a frown. "What are you doing here?"

He was dressed in a checked button-down shirt, sleeves again rolled up, this time with khakis. He had the same smirk as before. "Mind if I join you?"

"Yes, I mind," she said.

He sat down anyhow.

"What are you doing here? Did you call Jimmy?"

"No."

"Did your partner?"

"No."

"Then what do you want?"

"Where's Kira?"

"I have no idea."

He looked at the table. "Two plates. She wasn't with you earlier. Staying at your hotel?"

"Did you break into our hotel?"

Travis frowned, legitimately, Nicole thought. "No."

"You say that a lot," she said, leaning back.

"It's the truth."

She huffed.

"I'm not the one telling lies."

"Neither am I. I have no idea where Kira is."

"But you do know Kira. You're admitting that this time."

"I'm not admitting anything. Who are you, Travis?"

"That's beyond your need to know."

"My brother's a black belt, so you'd better not be here when he gets back."

Travis smirked. "I doubt that."

Nicole exhaled. "I don't know where Kira is. I wouldn't tell you if I did. Now will you please leave?"

Instead of getting up, he leaned forward. "It is in your best interest, and hers, that you cooperate."

"Why?"

"I can't—"

Nicole had had enough. "Get out!" she yelled, loudly enough for others to hear. Intentionally. Travis hesitated, and Nicole flung her sweet tea at him. "Leave me alone!" She screamed it this time, allowing her voice to pierce. Peripherally, she noticed multiple heads turned her way, and a waiter stepped over as Travis stood.

"Is there a problem?" he asked.

"I was just leaving," Travis said.

"Ma'am?"

"No problem, as long he doesn't bother me anymore."

The waiter turned to address Travis, but he had already started for the exit.

"Is there anything I can get you?" the waiter asked.

Nicole didn't need to force herself to blush, knowing most of the other patrons were still watching her. "No, thank you."

"I'll get you another tea," he said.

Nicole avoided eye contact with anyone, instead picking at her plate—her appetite gone—with her head down as she waited for Jimmy to return.

*   *   *

"I don't know what you're talking about," Jimmy said, staring straight through Nicole.

"The drive for the girl," the voice repeated.

"Kira?"

He had trouble hearing the man's response, and Nicole asked him something lost in the babble around them. So he stood, held a finger up to hopefully mollify his sister, and turned for the street. "Say again," he said.

"We have Kira," the man answered. "You give us the drive, we'll let her go."

Jimmy walked on autopilot, weaving around tables and servers until he was on the patio. He pushed through an iron gate to the sidewalk and turned west. "Who are you?" he asked.

"That doesn't matter."

"What have you done to Kira?"

"Nothing. And it will stay that way if you give us the drive."

"I don't know what you're talking about," Jimmy said, fighting not to shout as he walked past more outdoor tables in front of a building also labeled as Firehouse. "Winery," "Tasting Room," "Souvenir," and "Gifts" were labeled on the windows. Beyond the building was a parking lot for the next building, a bank. After closing time, the parking lot and sidewalk were empty, and Jimmy stopped when he reached the bank. "I don't have any drive, and you should know that after digging through our rooms."

The voice on the other end was silent, which Jimmy took for a confession.

"I don't have any drive. I don't even know what kind of drive you're talking about. But I do have a couple of cops on speed dial who would probably like to talk to you. How about I give them your number?"

"Leave the cops out of this," the voice said sternly.

"Let me talk to Kira. Let me know she's okay."

"She is fine. And you can talk to her when you give us what she gave you."

Jimmy was about to insist that she hadn't given them anything, but realized that if they had Kira, she might have said that she had to buy herself some time. And time was what he needed. "I can't give you something if I don't know who you are."

"We'll text you a meeting location. We can be in Rapid City in six hours."

Jimmy said nothing.

"You there?" the voice asked after ten seconds of silence that felt like hours.

"—dying," Jimmy said.

"What?"

"My battery is dying. I'll have to call you back. Do not hurt her," he added before punching the call off. Then he powered off his phone and, for the first time since receiving the call, paid serious attention to his surroundings. He was alone. Vehicle and pedestrian traffic was flowing as normal. No one seemed to be paying him any attention, and if anyone was watching from a parked car or building window, they were doing so inconspicuously.

Jimmy stuffed the phone into his pocket and hurried back to Nicole. They needed to put their heads together and figure out what to do next.

CHAPTER TWENTY-FIVE

Nicole finally grabbed Jimmy's arm and forced him to stop walking. They were on the sidewalk, across Main Street from Firehouse Brewing Company, a block east of the Jeep. Jimmy had returned to the table, getting the attention of their waitress on the way, and told Nicole they needed to leave right away. He'd brushed off questions or given partial answers, throwing cash on the table to cover their bill as soon as the waitress brought the check and leaving their unfinished entrées behind. He'd again ignored Nicole's questions as they'd meandered back through the restaurant and out to the street, during which time Nicole's roving eyes had not spotted Travis. Now, as they started walking west, she reached out for her brother.

"Jimmy, what is going on?"

"They have Kira."

"What? Who?"

He shook his head. "I don't know. He sounded like a Gardiner," he said, then started walking.

Nicole hurried beside him. "What do you mean, sounded like a Gardiner?"

"Gruff, husky voice. I could picture him on a Harley."

"And they have Kira?"

"They said they wanted the drive—"

"What drive?"

"I don't know. But they said if we gave it to them, she'd be okay."

"Jimmy . . . what do we do?"

"I don't know."

"What did they say to do, where to meet or exchange or whatever?"

"They didn't. I said my battery was dying and I'd call them back."

She ran her hand through her hair, looking around again. Everyone else on the sidewalks and street seemed to be having a perfectly normal, enjoyable summer evening. How had she and Jimmy gotten thrust into this mess? And it was a mess. She had never considered, back at Wall Drug or when Travis had showed up at the Hole-in-the-Wall Inn, or even when their rooms had been ransacked, that they would find themselves in such a desperate situation. Yet here they were.

They reached the Jeep and got in. It was stifling, and Jimmy started the engine and lowered the windows.

"Now what?" Nicole asked.

"I don't know."

"When are you going to call them back?"

"As soon as I figure out what to say."

"They didn't say what kind of drive they were looking for? A flash drive, a hard drive, is their some other kind?" she asked as Jimmy kept shaking his head. "And you're sure Kira didn't give you anything?"

"No. If she had, they'd have found it when they went through our rooms. I had my keys, wallet, and the clothes on my back when we left this morning."

"I had my backpack," Nicole said.

"Was she ever alone with it?"

"I guess so. I mean, it was in my suitcase until yesterday, but she could have gone through my stuff while I was in the shower and put something in it that I didn't notice. But why?"

Jimmy shook his head again.

"If she did take something of theirs, it means she's been lying to us from the jump."

"Can we not do this now, Nic?"

"When's a better time. It kind of impacts what we do next."

"Does it? Are you really willing to walk away and let them do . . . whatever to her?"

Nicole sighed as she looked away. "I didn't say walk away."

"We need to call them back," he said, "try to get more info."

Nicole nodded.

Jimmy adjusted the A/C, then rolled up the windows for privacy. He dug out his phone and called the previous number back, on speaker.

"That was fast," said a voice that was in fact gruff and husky. It wasn't Frank or Johnny, for what it mattered.

"Car charger," Jimmy said. "I want to talk to Kira."

"She's unavailable at the minute."

"What does that mean?"

"Means just what it sounds like. You give us the drive, you can not only talk to her, you can have her."

"I'm telling you, man, I don't have any drive. I don't know what you're talking about. And neither does my sister, who's sitting right beside me."

"She said she gave it to you, and we're inclined to believe her. We're on our way to Rapid City. You have until we get there."

"We're not in Rapid City anymore," Jimmy said, looking at Nicole. He shrugged.

"Where are you?"

"Like I'd tell you."

"How soon can you be in Rapid City?"

"I'll have to check a map."

"I think you're stalling."

"Desperately, because I don't know what you want! What drive?"

"Call when you get to Rapid City. And no cops."

"Don't hurt . . ."

The phone clicked from a disconnection before he could finish.

*   *   *

"Where are we going?" Nicole asked when Jimmy turned north off Main Street.

"The hotel."

"And . . . ?"

"I don't know, Nic. I don't know what to do, other than go search your backpack and strip the Jeep down to the hubcaps. But she wasn't ever alone to hide anything in the Jeep." He looked her way. "And why would she?"

"Why would she tell them she had if she hadn't?"

"Self-preservation?"

"At our expense?"

He shrugged. They were on 190, a spur into town from I-90. Jimmy's mind was reeling, spinning, trying to process and plan. Gruff Voice hadn't called his bluff when he said they weren't in Rapid City, but had called him out when he thought he was lying about the drive. It was logical, having had their rooms ransacked, that they might have left town, and that was several hours ago, so it bought them at least several more hours. But if there wasn't a flash drive or a small hard drive hidden in Nicole's backpack . . .

"There's something else to consider," Nicole said.

"What's that?"

"As soon as you left to take the call, Travis walked in and sat down."

"What?"

"He was the same as before, asking where Kira was, being coy . . . He gave me a 'no need to know' line. That's not civilian talk."

"What else did he say?"

"Not much." She shook her head. "I asked him if he broke into our rooms, and he looked sincerely confused."

"I think it's safe to say that was the Gardiners. What made him leave?"

"I made a scene and threw my tea at him."

Even given the circumstances, Jimmy couldn't help but smile. He took the curving exit to I-90 East and merged with a steady flow of traffic. "So what are our options?" he asked.

"You're asking me?"

"Brainstorming. Asking both of us."

"We call the cops," she said.

"I knew that would be your first answer."

"Bad guys on TV always say not to go to the cops because it's the best option for people in our situation."

"But it's risky."

"If they're monitoring us."

"Our ransacked rooms would suggest they are."

"And your comment about not being in Rapid City going unchallenged would suggest they aren't."

He nodded. "What else?"

Nicole furrowed her chin, thinking.

"Other end of the spectrum," Jimmy said, "we don't get off in a few miles, just keep going east into the night."

"And leave all our stuff in the hotel?"

"Okay, we stop to pack first."

"And just leave Kira's fate up to the Gardiners?"

"Didn't say I liked the option, but we're brainstorming."

"Do we . . ."

"Do we what?"

"Do we even know that they are Gardiners? For all we know, she's been making up a story the entire time. Jimmy, I know you won't like it, but we have to at least consider the possibility that Kira isn't the innocent victim she seems."

She was right, he didn't like it. He searched his mind for a rebuttal, and found one quickly. "I think we're safe assuming the guys threatening physical harm and warning against going to the cops are the bad guys."

"Probably, but we need to be open-minded, given everything that's happened."

He had no rebuttal for that.

"And we need to at least ask the question of how much we owe Kira. She's clearly been duplicitous to some degree with us."

"Unless they're wrong and she didn't hide a drive in our stuff."

"In which case she threw us under the bus."

Jimmy sighed. "Let's go check your backpack, if they haven't beaten us to it. Then we can decide what to do next. Maybe it's easy and she did hide it and we can exchange it and ask her our questions once she's—"

"Jimmy?"

"Yeah?" he asked as he signaled for the exit ramp to Elk Vale Road.

"How . . . If they're the ones who ransacked our rooms, how is that they're on their way to Rapid City? Shouldn't they be here?"

Jimmy let his foot off the gas. "They told me on the first call they were six hours away. That would correspond with being in Denver."

"Then who hit our rooms?"

"They could have hit them right after we left this morning."

"Then why wait to call until dinner time?"

He coasted to a stop at the light, shaking his head.

"The alternative being," she said, "they have two teams, one with Kira and one here to search our hotel rooms, meaning they could be watching us right now meaning they know you were lying about not being in Rapid City."

Jimmy turned his eyes out his window, to their hotel several hundred yards away. Suddenly it didn't seem like a safe haven any longer.

CHAPTER TWENTY-SIX

Nicole looked dubiously at her brother. They were in the parking lot of a new, sprawling Exxon station on the hill overlooking the road that led down to their hotel. They had switched seats, her now behind the wheel. Her revelation that the Gardiners might very well be monitoring them had seemingly spooked him, but also put his brain into high gear. Maybe it was survival mode.

"We have to check that backpack, Nic."

"I know. I just don't know why we can't both go in."

"Because I don't want to put you in harm's way."

"You're scaring me, Jimmy."

"Good, then I have company." He nodded for her to start driving, and she did, back onto the frontage road, down the hill, and into the Cambria Suites parking lot. "Pull up under the carport. As soon as I'm out, lock the doors, then loop back around and park facing the other way. If anyone even approaches the vehicle, drive away."

"Where?"

"Start honking and try to find a cop."

"Is all this really necessary?"

"I don't know." He'd kept his eyes roving as they'd entered the parking lot, and now turned to her as she braked under the sweeping carport. "I love you, Nic."

That scared her more than anything. Jimmy had only used those words once or twice before—and the fact that he was telling her now suggested they were in real danger. She mumbled something back, but it didn't matter; he was already out the door.

She swallowed the lump in her throat, locked the doors, and drove to the corner of the lot and made a Y-turn before returning to the carport. Then she waited, her eyes constantly on the parking lot entrance, the Jeep's mirrors, and the door Jimmy had just entered. He had taken both of their keycards, to the new rooms provided by the hotel, where he would grab Nicole's backpack, stuff as many of their clothes into a duffel as possible, and come back down. She tried to be patient, tried not to count the minutes, tried not to think of a motorcycle gang materializing out of the haze and surrounding the Jeep.

Jimmy was gone less than ten minutes, and returned with her backpack slung over his shoulder and his duffel in tow. Instead of circling the Jeep, he motioned for her to unlock the doors, then climbed in the backseat. He tossed his duffel on the far seat and began rifling through the backpack.

"Where to?" Nicole asked.

"Fifth and Broadway, driver, and step on it."

"At least you've kept your sense of humor," she said with an eyebrow raise in the mirror.

"Hmm, was that funny? I didn't think so."

"Not really."

"Head back to the main road and go north."

"North?"

"I want to see if we have a tail." He had already scrutinized the bumpers and wheel wells of the Jeep, looking for any tracking device. Nicole had doubted they would have an antenna and blinking red light to easily identify them like the ones in the movies, but it had been worth checking.

"You grab more than you planned?" she asked as she turned out of the parking lot. A blue four-door had backed out of a parking spot in the hotel's back lot, and she watched it carefully.

"I got a couple changes of clothes for each of us, and unmentionables—sorry."

"It's okay."

"Also scooped up everything on your bathroom counter."

"This is so weird," Nicole said, allowing a little relief to flood her when the blue four-door turned the other way. She followed the road they had taken a few minutes ago, past the Exxon station, and to the stop sign at Elk Vale Road while Jimmy alternated between digging through her backpack pockets and looking all around.

Nicole waited for a southbound dump truck, then turned north. Almost immediately they were into the country, heading down into a valley bound by a low ridge a few miles away. They drove through pastureland, over a small creek, then past a soccer complex. She spotted another car a long way back, but was sure it had come from south on Elk Vale Road.

They passed one intersection, continuing for another mile through more open grass. The car behind them had turned off, and Nicole felt confident no one was tailing them.

"Turn left here," Jimmy said as they approached a second intersection. Nicole turned onto a gravel drive. "There's nothing here," he said, setting down the backpack.

"Nothing?"

"Where else could she possibly have put something? A flash drive could be pretty tiny."

"Stuff it in your pocket?"

"Only if she's a pickpocket."

"Check between the seat cushions. Maybe she hid it there while we were driving."

"Why would she do that?"

"I don't know. We need to figure out what to do, Jimmy."

He craned his neck every direction. "Take your next left, back toward town. We need to find a place to stay."

"Any suggestions?"

He didn't respond, and Nicole looked to see his face in his phone.

"I'm legit low on battery this time. Borrow yours?"

She lifted her purse from the console between the seats and swung it back to him.

"You don't mind?"

"You're the second today, so go for it." She turned south, back onto pavement, through pastures and then various industrial buildings. The sun was low over the dark ridges to the west, and the dashboard clock told her it was seven-twenty. For the next fifteen minutes, Jimmy gave her directions into and through Rapid City, back close to downtown, then south on Mount Rushmore Road, which doubled as Highway 16. He also kicked out ideas of what to do. Call back and plead for mercy? Call back and bluff that they had the drive? Call the cops? Call a private investigator? Hoof for home?

She got the feeling he was grasping at straws—and leading them right out of Rapid City. She finally asked, "Jimmy, do you know where we're going?"

"Yeah, top of the hill."

"What's at the top of the hill?"

"Plains Vista Lodge."

"We've passed a dozen other places to stay."

"Found a room with a view, two beds, and parking in the rear. And it's on the opposite side of town."

Highway 16 climbed out of town and made a gentle S curve at the top of the ridge. Looking back over her shoulder, Nicole emitted a soft, "Wow," as she saw the city in the valley below, and, beyond it, the sun-bathed prairie as far as her eye could see.

"Right up there," Jimmy said, stretching his arm beside her to point. She moved into the turn lane in the divided highway, then, when traffic allowed, turned into a driveway between a strand of ponderosa pines and a brown, one-story building that stretched along a ridgeline at a forty-five-degree angle from the highway. Rooms faced northeast, toward the valley, and the doors—along with the parking spots in front of them—were shielded from the highway by the building, the ponderosas, or the next ridge north. There were only two other cars in the lot, and, at Jimmy's advice, Nicole backed into a spot.

"You reserve a room?" she asked.

"Figured cash and no online trail would be better."

"You have the cash?"

"No, but you let me rifle through your purse."

She smirked at him in the mirror, and they got out. "I'll get a room," Jimmy said. She nodded and waited, taking deep breaths, looking over the pines toward an antenna tower on the next ridge. The sun had set, not behind the ridge but behind a bank of gray clouds pushing in. The wind was stronger than it had been all day, still warm, but the air was no longer unpleasant.

Jimmy returned in just a few minutes. "Room 8," he announced, pointing to the far end of the building. Then he held up his phone. "They called while I was in there."

"What'd you say?"

"I didn't answer." He sagged his shoulders. "Nic, I have no idea what to do."

"Actually," she said, tucking windblown hair behind her ear, "I think I might."

CHAPTER TWENTY-SEVEN

Jimmy listened as Nicole outlined her plan, sitting cross-legged on one of the two beds in Room 8 at the Plains Vista Lodge, while he paced back and forth on the threadbare carpet. The room was simple, clean enough if not comfortable, with space for two queen beds and to walk around them and not much more. But the view made up for it, looking down at the eastern two-thirds of Rapid City, the lights twinkling on what had become a blustery night.

The plan sounded more like a Jimmy plan than a Nicole plan, but she assuaged his concerns by saying she'd listened as he'd brainstormed on the way over and had taken snippets from various ideas of his and coalesced them into a single plan. "Coalesced" had been her word. The plan had cemented while he'd been checking into the lodge, which he argued had taken two minutes. But again, she had answers to his objections.

"Our backs are against the wall here, and I think it's the best we can come up with," she concluded, her head following him back and forth across the room. "Short of calling the cops or heading for home. And, Jimmy . . . the way these guys are going, who's to say they wouldn't follow us home?"

He stopped at the far end of the room. Then he sighed. "I think it's solid."

"I think it's the best we can come up with," she said again.

"But we need to work out some details."

143

"So let's get busy," she said. "Before they call again."

"I need some coffee."

"Of course you do."

"I think they had a machine in the lobby. I'm going to get a cup."

"I'll go," she said. "I need to stretch my legs."

He nodded and let her go, pacing while she was gone, thinking through holes—or potential holes in her plan. He stopped and tipped his head back, looking up at the ceiling. *God, help us out, please. And watch over Kira too, whatever she's into.*

He paced a little more, then realized Nicole had been gone too long. Maybe she struck up a conversation with the old woman minding the front desk, or maybe she'd stopped to pray too. Or maybe she'd been snatched by the Gardiners and was trussed up on the back of one of their hogs.

He pulled open the door and turned to see Nicole leaning against the wall.

"Sorry," she said, holding a Styrofoam cup of coffee. "But check this out."

He followed her eyes over the valley to the north, where constant muffled flashes lit a bank of thunderheads orange and pink. Every now and again, a jagged bolt seemed to split the sky, its light temporarily blinding.

"Don't you find this reassuring?" she asked.

"No."

She looked at him.

"Why would I?"

"Because it reminds me that God is still in charge no matter what happens."

He nodded. "The lightning reminds you of that?"

"Yes."

"I'd have picked something less destructive as means of reassurance, but okay. Can I have my coffee?"

Nicole rolled her eyes and handed him the cup, then followed him into the room. He bolted the door, then drew the blinds, not so much for privacy as to keep his sister from being distracted by the reassuring

144

lightning. She pulled out her laptop, which he had thought to throw in the duffel, and set it on the edge of the bed.

"You have a place in mind already?" he asked.

In reply, she began whistling "Hail to the Chief."

*   *   *

An hour—and another ignored phone call from the Gardiners—later, Jimmy and Nicole had a plan outlined. They had gone over it several times, tweaking and looking for flaws. There were none, other than for the fact that they still had no idea what drive the Gardiners wanted. But there was nothing they could do about that.

At twenty to ten, Jimmy set his phone on the corner of the bed. Nicole sat on the edge of the other. He looked at her. "Time this."

"Time it?"

"At thirty-five seconds, raise your hand."

"Why thirty-five seconds?"

"Because it takes forty to trace a call, and I want to hang up in time."

"How do you know it takes forty seconds?"

"That's what the German lady said on *The 355*."

"The what?"

"That movie about the lady secret agents."

"Are you for real right now?"

"I'd always thought it was thirty seconds, but they would have researched that, right?"

Nicole sighed.

"Ready?" he asked.

"Ready."

"Thirty-five seconds," he said, then tapped to call Gruff Voice.

He answered after one ring. "Where have you been?"

"You mean you don't know?" Jimmy asked.

"Do you have the drive?"

"I want to talk to Kira."

"The drive for the girl. That's the deal."

"Okay," Jimmy said with a sigh.

"Are you in Rapid City?"

"Yes."

"Where?"

Jimmy laughed. Nicole held up two fingers, then closed them against her thumb to make a zero.

"Take Exit 61 off I-90 on the east side of town," Gruff Voice said. "Go south and take your second right, Eglin Street. You'll wind past an oil storage facility and go four-tenths of a mile to a dirt driveway across from a recycling center. Cross the railroad tracks, and follow the dirt drive until you get—"

Nicole held up her hand, and Jimmy immediately tapped the end call button, cutting off Gruff Voice.

He sat back.

"Are you sure that was a good idea?" Nicole asked.

"No. And I hope that German lady knew what she was talking about."

"Now what?"

"Now we start over," he said. "Thirty-five seconds again."

"Whatever you say."

He tapped his phone screen several times to redial. Again, Gruff Voice answered on the first ring. "Bad battery?"

"We're picking the meeting location," Jimmy said.

"You're not in position to bargain."

"Guess it depends what's on that drive and how much it means to you," Jimmy said. "I'd hate for it to fall down a sewer drain or get mailed to KOTA-TV. As for the girl, we met her day before yesterday. She's not exactly an old friend."

Nicole flashed him the twenty-second signal again.

"Get to it," Gruff Voice said after a few seconds' pause.

"Meet us tomorrow at ten a.m.—"

"Tomorrow's too late."

"Tomorrow or not at all," Jimmy said.

Gruff Voice sighed again. "Where?"

Nicole held up three fingers, then a zero.

"I'll call you back," Jimmy said and ended the call again.

"He's going to be mad," Nicole said.

"I'm not exactly jumping for joy."

She raised an eyebrow.

"One more time," Jimmy said. She nodded, and he called again.

"I'm not tracing the call," Gruff Voice said after one ring.

"Tomorrow at ten a.m. at Mount Rushmore."

"Mount Rushmore?"

"Lots of people. A safe place."

"Where?"

"Avenue of Flags. Meet us under the South Dakota flag. Bring Kira, we'll bring the drive. If she's not there, we start screaming for the cops. If she's hurt, your drive is toast."

"We'll be there and she'll be there, unhurt."

"No cops by us, no tricks by you."

"Agreed."

Nicole flashed three-zero, and Jimmy ended the call. "You'll notice I didn't say no tricks by us," he said with a wink.

"You think this will work?" she asked.

He looked at his sister, at wide brown eyes. Then he squared his jaw, and in a dead-on Sean Connery said, "I give us one chance in three."

*   *   *

Nicole took a while to fall asleep, finally drifting away to the sound of steady rainfall. It had arrived shortly after their last call with the Gardiners, slapping the siding of the lodge as gusty wind whipped it across the mountains. After ten minutes, it settled into the pitter-patter that eventually helped her fall asleep. Then thunder woke her up.

She blinked a few times, allowing her eyes to grow accustomed to the darkness and to confirm what she thought she'd seen initially—Jimmy standing and looking out the window.

"You keeping watch?" she asked with a somewhat croaky voice.

"No." He looked over. "I find the rain relaxing."

"Sleep is supposed to be relaxing."

"Maybe, but I'm not tired." He tapped his head. "This, this is tired."

Nicole glanced at the clock. It was twenty to one. She wondered if Jimmy, like her, was reminded of the middle of the night two nights ago, of pie with Kira at the Hole-in-the-Wall Café. "You should get some sleep, Jimmy. You need to be sharp tomorrow morning."

"Yeah."

She laid her head back down.

"Nic?"

Slowly, she propped herself on her elbows again.

"Can I ask you something?"

She sat all the way up, stifling a yawn. "What?"

"You having second thoughts?"

"No," she said after a moment. "Not really."

"But a little?"

"I have the same doubts we've had since the beginning. But nothing more."

He nodded.

"Are you?"

"The same," he said.

Nicole nodded slowly. "Jimmy, I trust your gut. If you think we should abort, try something else, I'll follow your lead."

"Like you've said, this is the best we can come up with."

"Even so."

"I'll sleep on it," he said. "Eventually."

She nodded. "Night again, Jimmy."

"Night, Nic."

She laid back down, closed her eyes, and very slowly succumbed to sleep as the rain pattered on. Just before she dozed off, she was pretty sure she heard Jimmy crawl into his bed.

CHAPTER TWENTY-EIGHT

The route to Mount Rushmore was meandering, following Highway 16 out of Rapid City into the Black Hills, then Highway 16A into the canyon town of Keystone, then Highway 244 along the top of a ridge offering views of Custer State Park. Even had Jimmy not studied a map the night before and again that morning, he would have had no trouble following the numerous signs marking the way to one of America's most famous landmarks.

He and Nicole had been up early, finding the night's storms gone and a bright, sunny, almost cool morning in their wake. After breakfast at Colonial House on the outskirts of Rapid City, during which they had not only fueled their bodies for the day ahead but also gone over the details of their plan again, they had driven to a Walmart on the northeast side of town, where they had picked up a few items they would need for the day. The next stop had been an Enterprise Rent-a-Car not far from where they'd had lunch with Kira two days before. There they'd rented the most non-descript economy car they could, a silver Mitsubishi Mirage. In the parking lot, they had done one final assessment, reassured each other as best they could, and hugged.

Then Jimmy had gotten into the Mirage and set his course for Mount Rushmore. Nicole, meanwhile, had used her laptop and a nearby McDonald's Wi-Fi to type an e-mail briefly explaining everything that had happened over the last few days, along with an outline of their intended plan, and set it to send to the Custer County Sheriff's Department at noon if she hadn't deleted it. It was the best failsafe they could think of.

At quarter after nine, Jimmy turned into the Mount Rushmore National Memorial entrance drive. He paid for parking at the entrance station, then proceeded to the parking garage. He spent five minutes driving through it, looking for a spot as close to the exit as possible. He parked, checked the time, and got out. He fitted a brown Wyoming Cowboys baseball cap—also purchased at Walmart—over his hair, then donned a pair of sunglasses—new as well. He checked his reflection in the Mirage's window and determined his own mother wouldn't recognize him. Then again, his own mother hadn't seen him in three years.

He started walking, as he did inserting a Bluetooth earpiece into his ear. It was paired with his cell phone, and when he exited the garage stairwell and figured he had clear reception, he called Nicole.

"I'm here," he said when she answered.

"I'm just passing . . . an NFL Gift Shop and Christmas Village."

Jimmy squinted. "You're fifteen to twenty minutes out yet."

"I'll be right on time."

"I'll call you on the red phone when I'm in position," he said.

"All right. Keep your eyes peeled. They could be there already."

"Counting on it," he said, then ended the call. He crossed the street and passed under a square archway, then down a long path between ponderosa pines and giant boulders. Up ahead were more arches, and towering over them, the white granite faces of four American presidents. But Jimmy wasn't paying attention to the rugged scenery around him or the carvings in front of him. His eyes were on the hundreds of tourists milling around him, going into or coming out of the restrooms on his left or the bookstore on his right, or heading closer to the mountain. He looked for leather, surmising the Gardiners weren't the sort to go undercover—especially in a place where there was already plenty of leather. More than anything, he looked for Kira.

He passed under two more arches to a wide patio leading to either a gift shop or the Carvers Café. Ideally, he and Nicole would be taking their time, browsing for souvenirs, or sampling vanilla ice cream rumored to be Thomas Jefferson's own recipe. Instead, he kept his head down as much as he could, continuing into the Avenue of Flags. The granite tiles forming the path led between fourteen square columns, atop each of which were four flagpoles, containing the banners for each of the country's fifty states and six territories. They were in alphabetical order, and South Dakota's sky blue flag was on the next to the last column on the left. There was no one standing beneath it or anywhere near it, but Jimmy was still fifteen to twenty minutes early.

One last arch led to a wide patio, beyond which was an amphitheater sloping down the hillside. The faces of Presidents Washington, Jefferson, Roosevelt, and Lincoln stood regally against a blue sky. Around them, and especially beneath them where the slag spilled down the mountainside, trees grew out of the rock. The same trees cascaded down into the valley and around the amphitheater—and around the Presidential Trail, which wound down from the patio to the base of the mountain, then through the trees to the Sculptor's Studio, and back up a steep climb to the patio.

Without casting more than a passing glance at the mountain face, Jimmy turned down the Presidential Trail. A concrete path quickly disappeared into the trees, so that only an occasional glimpse of the amphitheater seats or the patio was visible through their boughs. When the trail turned, the concrete gave way to a wooden bridge along the side of the mountain, still deep in the trees. Jimmy followed it to a turnout, then climbed a couple dozen stairs on the turnout to get to an observation deck looking almost straight up at the carvings. For the first time fearing that he might not have cell service, Jimmy again retrieved his phone. He checked the time—quarter to ten—and called one of three prepaid phones he and Nicole had purchased at Walmart. She answered after two rings.

"Hey."

"I'm in position," he said.

"Work like we thought?"

"There are two turnouts, then a big boulder, then a deck a little ways after that. That'll work."

"Okay."

"Where are you?"

"About a mile out of Keystone."

"Stay with me until you park. I'm going to go scope out that lower deck."

*　　　*　　　*

Following her brother's earlier advice, Nicole circled the parking garage until she found a spot that would enable her to exit the garage quickly. "Jimmy, I'm here," she announced.

"I'm back. The lower deck is an absolute go."

"Past the second turnout on the planks, then past the big boulder?"

"Yes."

"All right, I'm getting out."

"Okay, put the red phone on speaker as loud as it goes, and put it in your pocket, then give me a 'Testing one-two-three.'"

Nicole wore a pair of blue jeans and a loose, blousy peach top. It hung down far enough to conceal the small front pocket of her jeans, into which the red phone just barely fit. She slid it in, then announced that she was walking through the parking garage. She stopped, removed it, and lifted it to her chin. "You hear that?"

"Loud and clear."

"Good."

"You have everything?"

"White and blue phones both in my back left pocket."

"Bear spray?"

"In my purse," she said. It had been purchased at Walmart too, not for fear of hungry carnivores, but as a precaution in case things went sideways.

"Okay. Any questions?"

"No."

"Okay. Turn down the volume on the red phone until you can't hear me anymore."

"You sure that's necessary?"

"Some kid starts crying or a chopper flies over or something, I don't want them hearing it from your pocket."

"Okay."

"And let me know when you pass the Borglum bust."

"Will do."

"'Fourscore and seven years ago, our fore . . .'"

Jimmy's voice faded away, and Nicole said a brief prayer as she climbed the stairs out of the parking garage, knowing that she was now on her own.

CHAPTER TWENTY-NINE

Twice, Nicole thought she spotted Kira's blond/brown hair ahead of her on the sidewalk, but the first person was walking with another women and two young children, and the other was by herself and too tall. The pine scent, the calls of birds and chirp of insects, the hubbub of hundreds of tourists were all lost on her even as her brain subconsciously observed them. Similarly, the grandeur of Gutzon Borglum's masterpiece was a mere backdrop for the drama about to unfold.

Nicole checked her watch as she passed beneath a stone arch supported by a pair of square columns. It was exactly ten o'clock. "I'm at Borglum," she said, glancing to her left at the giant bust of the man who had sculpted Rushmore. "Too crowded ahead to see if they're there." She took a deep breath, trying to calm her heartbeat, and resumed walking, dodging a large family all wearing the same shirts and an elderly couple shuffling along arm in arm. She reached the first column in the Avenue of Flags, the bright colors floating lazily in the breeze serving as a perfect frame for the faces on Mount Rushmore.

Keeping her head on a swivel, Nicole passed several more columns adorned with flags. When she reached the fourth, the crowd of people in front of her parted such that she could see the base of the last two columns on the left. Beneath a flapping blue flag, Kira stood facing her way. She wore jeans and the black T-shirt with the yellow and white Missouri Tiger on the front. Her hair was in a ponytail, but wisps hung loose in the breeze. As Nicole drew closer, she saw two men with Kira.

One stood on her right, Nicole's left, and wore a tight, black T-shirt with faded jeans. He wasn't big but muscular, and his eyes and expression were hidden by the brim of a black baseball cap with the same BHG emblem as she'd seen on vests previously. The other man stood behind Kira's left shoulder. He was tall and thick, and wore a white T-shirt and a black vest, also with jeans. His head was bald, reflecting the sun, which also accentuated a full, white beard. Neither of them paid attention to Nicole as she drew within a few dozen paces, or noticed that a thin-lipped, almost sad smile spread over Kira's face. She looked tired, but none the worse for wear.

Nicole took a deep breath, sent a one-word prayer skyward, and marched up to the trio. "Kira, are you all right?"

"I'm fine," she answered softly.

"Which of you all is in charge?" Nicole asked before either man could speak. They had both reacted to her, the one with the ball cap taking a step to his right, hands folded in front of him, looking like a bouncer. The bald one had edged to his left and forward, standing beside Kira and in Nicole's path.

He dipped his chin down and back up. "I am. Lance Gardiner." His voice was gruff, and she was pretty sure she was talking to the man who'd called Jimmy the night before—and also the leader of the Gardiner clan.

"Nicole," she answered, relieved that her voice didn't crack.

"Do you have the drive?"

"Is she unhurt?"

"You just asked her."

"Now I'm asking you. Did you hurt her?"

"No."

Nicole nodded.

"The drive?"

"My brother has it."

"Where is he?"

She held up her left palm, then slowly reached it to her back pocket and withdrew the white phone. She extended it to Lance. "Take this," she said, and he squinted at the phone but took it from her hand. "Follow the trail from the patio down to your left. At the bottom of the hill, the trail becomes a wood bridge leading through the woods. Go past the turnouts and around a huge boulder and the trail will open to a deck. Jimmy will meet you there with the drive. Do what you need to authenticate it, then call the number programmed into that phone." She reached into her pocket in a similar fashion and withdrew a blue phone. "It's to this one, which he'll have," she said, tipping her head toward the guy with the ball cap. She then extended it to him. "You tell him all is clear, and Kira and I walk away. You have the drive and walk away, and that's it."

Lance pursed his lips for a moment. Then he nodded. "Have it your way. But if this is some trick . . ."

"We're tourists, not spies," Nicole said. "We just want to all walk away from this."

"Okay." He turned, picked up a shoulder bag that Nicole hadn't seen previously from beside the column, and started walking. Nicole watched him for a moment, then looked at Kira, hoping to silently convey confidence that she didn't feel.

*　　　　　*　　　　　*

Binoculars would have been a good purchase, Jimmy realized as he heard the end of Nicole's conversation with Lance Gardiner. He wasn't even sure they sold binoculars anymore, or if there was a new, high-tech replacement device for them. At any rate, "could have" and "should have" were out the window. So he waited, watching through the trees for Lance, hoping he'd recognize him. Kira had made some comment at Wall Drug about him after spotting a biker with a bald head and white beard, so he was going off that.

It had taken him about five minutes to walk to this point, and he figured Lance would push it. So he kept his eyes peeled, while also listening to the phone in Nicole's pocket on his Bluetooth. Nobody spoke—not Nicole, not Kira, not the other guy Lance had brought. That wasn't a surprise.

Jimmy saw movement in the trees below, but it was a young couple with a stroller. The next time it was a family all dressed alike. Then a ray of sunlight that penetrated the tree cover glinted off a bald head. A second later, Jimmy saw him more clearly—big, tall, bald, white beard, a black leather vest, and he would bet his savings account a gruff voice. Jimmy watched him in and out of the trees until he disappeared behind a huge boulder. Jimmy moved a few steps to his left, around a woman taking a picture up at the presidents. At the very end of the spur walkway, he had a vantage point to the deck where Nicole had instructed Lance to stop. Jimmy saw him arrive and pause.

Now for the hard part. He had no idea how long it would theoretically take Lance to authenticate the drive. It might be as simple as seeing it. He might have to plug it into a laptop or tablet, and he did have a case of some sort in his right hand. He might have to verify multiple files or check lines of data. It could take seconds or minutes. That length of time, which Lance and his associate would know, had to be balanced with a guess as to how long Lance would wait for Jimmy to arrive before getting suspicious or impatient. Nicole had said Jimmy would meet him there, not that Jimmy was waiting there, and he hoped Lance picked up and homed in on that distinction. And Lance's associate didn't know how long it would take Lance to get to the meeting location, although if they had scouted, they'd likely have a close guess. All that meant Jimmy could be way earlier than necessary or way too much later, so he'd already committed to two minutes exactly once Lance reached the spot.

Jimmy ended the call from his phone to the red phone, then used his phone's clock to tick off one hundred ten seconds, checking Lance's position and his own surroundings every fifteen seconds. Lance paced back and forth without seeming terribly impatient. No one else on Jimmy's radar seemed relevant.

At one minute fifty seconds, Jimmy reached into his pocket and withdrew the fourth prepaid phone he and Nicole had purchased that morning, the black phone. With one last look at Lance, he tapped the single number programmed into it, put it to his ear, and waited.

CHAPTER THIRTY

"Yeah?" a terse but clear voice answered.

Jimmy squinted behind his sunglasses, focusing on a crooked tree limb twenty feet away. "I have the drive," he said in a gruff voice, one meant to imitate Lance. He was fortunate that he'd had several conversations with the man the night before, giving him more of a sample to emulate. He and Nicole had both suspected the caller might be the one to show up with Kira, but had arranged the red phone in her pocket in case, giving Jimmy at least a few snippets on which to base his impersonation. That would have been cutting it close, even with his ability to mimic. But he felt confident with the amount of time he'd listened to Lance that his imitation was solid, and hoped that over a phone and with just a few words spoken, Lance's associate would think so too.

"It's good?" the man asked.

"Yeah. You can let them go."

He took a breath, waiting. The blind spot in their plan—beside not knowing how Lance would have to authenticate the drive and not knowing the timing—was uncertainty as to whether or not Lance and his associate would have some specific, agreed upon jargon Jimmy wouldn't know to use. And the longer he didn't hear a response from the associate, the more he started to worry.

"Okay."

Jimmy pushed his luck. "I'm coming to you."

"I'll wait here."

"Good," Jimmy said, then ended the call. He took a deep breath and prayed it had worked.

*   *   *

The guy with the ball cap lowered the blue phone. He looked at Kira. "You can go."

Her eyes were wide, likely in shock, and Nicole extended her hand to Kira's to encourage her. As if rooted in concrete, she slid her foot and took a step.

"Hey. You want your phone back?"

"Keep it," Nicole said. She grabbed Kira's wrist and turned back toward the entrance, at first pulling Kira until she caught up.

"What is goin—"

"Keep walking," Nicole hissed. She tried to walk normally and willed herself not to look back, even though she could almost feel the man's eyes boring into her. She expected to hear him yell any second, realizing he'd been had. But every column of flags marked another twenty or twenty-five feet of separation, and put more and more tourists between them. Assuming he wasn't following them.

"What happened?" Kira asked again. "How did you do that?" she added, looking behind her.

"Let's just get out of here first," Nicole said, scanning left and right as the sidewalk widened and they now incurred cross traffic from the gift shop and café. She doubted Lance and the guy with the ball cap had come alone, meaning he wouldn't have to chase them himself. If something tipped him off, he could radio his pals stationed elsewhere around the park to intervene. For that matter, it was about time for Travis to suddenly appear. Nicole wasn't going to relax until they were on the road, if even then.

*   *   *

Jimmy waited. There was nothing to be gained by leaving now, as he was already six to seven minutes behind Nicole and Kira, unless he ran which would draw attention to himself. Eventually, Lance and his associates would realize they'd been duped, and at that point, Jimmy hoped to look like just another tourist from Wyoming. For now, he pretended to look at his phone while watching Lance. Judging by the way he paced back and forth, he was getting impatient.

"Excuse me, would you mind taking our picture?"

Jimmy turned to look at a young woman in a Wall Drug shirt extending an actual camera to him. He couldn't very well refuse, so quickly took a few shots of the woman and her male companion. He passed back the camera, received her thanks, and turned to look at Lance again.

He was gone.

Jimmy waited to see if Lance walked through his vision on the trail below. A minute passed. Jimmy counted thirty, painstaking more seconds. When Lance didn't cross in front of him, Jimmy assumed he'd gone the other way. So he walked back to the main trail and returned the way he had come, looking over his shoulder as he turned the corner back onto the concrete, not seeing Lance behind him as he did.

His phone rang.

He stopped and frowned. It wasn't the iconic Marimba ringtone, but a more generic chirp. Meaning it wasn't his phone, but . . . the black phone. He stopped and fished it out of his pocket. "Nic?"

He was greeted with silence, and quickly ended the call, at the same time looking up. Not fifty feet in front of him on the trail was a man in a tight black T-shirt and a black baseball cap. He had a phone to his ear, and his eyes homed in on Jimmy as he started to run toward him.

*　　　　　　*　　　　　　*

Nicole and Kira walked through the outermost archway and crossed the street to the plaza between Mount Rushmore's two parking garages. Nicole hadn't noticed on her arrival, but the entire park and complex was situated on a ridge, and before her the panorama of the southeastern Black Hills stretched out against a blue canvas.

"Where's Jimmy?" Kira asked.

"On the trail."

"How did you do that? How'd you make them let me go?"

"I'll tell you when we get to the car," Nicole said, turning toward her left as she started down the stairs. She looked down to get her footing, then lifted her head and saw Johnny coming from the top level of the parking garage. She stopped suddenly, causing Kira to bump into her shoulder.

"What is—"

Kira never finished her question. Johnny had spotted them and started running their way. He was between them and the stairs down to the proper level of the parking garage. So Nicole did the only thing possible. She nudged Kira to the right, and both women took off running.

CHAPTER THIRTY-ONE

Jimmy didn't run, but fast-walked back the way he had come, into the trees. He glanced back once and saw that the man with the ball cap was following him at a similar pace. He was close enough that he would be able to see if Jimmy took the first turnout, leading to a hollowed out boulder that might otherwise serve as a good hiding spot. So Jimmy kept moving, hoping to lose him in the crowd of people ahead on the path. But they had thinned. He slipped past one family with two little kids and then accelerated to a jog, his shoes thudding on the wood.

He looked back again, didn't spot Ball Cap immediately, and tossed his brown Wyoming cap as far into the trees as he could—accidentally knocking off his Bluetooth in the process. He let it fall. He should have planned for this contingency and worn two shirts so he could further change his appearance. But he was relegated to trying to outrun the man, who another glance back confirmed was still in pursuit. Jimmy went up a rise, past the stairs leading to his original vantage point, and then down several more flights that turned at left and right angles as they descended the mountain slope.

At the base, Jimmy stopped and turned back. He could see Ball Cap halfway down the stairs, so there was no time for Jimmy to catch his breath, even though he needed to. He looked over the railing and thought about going off the path, but the terrain was too rugged, and he wasn't going to get far. So he turned to keep running, hoping that sooner or later he'd find a crowd to blend into or a park ranger to summon for help.

Instead, as he rounded the next corner, he saw Lance at the top of a short rise of stairs, coming his way. Jimmy looked back. Ball Cap was no more than a dozen yards behind him and closing. Ahead, Lance was even closer. And the Presidential Trail was void of any other pedestrians.

Jimmy was trapped.

*   *   *

Kira wore the same tennis shoes she had when they'd picked her up, to no surprise, and made good time as she followed the contours of the path as it wove through tall grass and small trees. Nicole followed close behind, glancing over her shoulder as she turned. Johnny had followed them onto the main plaza, and now was halfway between the path Nicole and Kira had taken and another that circled around from the other side. He hesitated for a moment before continuing after them.

The path dropped down a flight of ten stairs, then met with the one from the other side at a giant boulder. Shortly thereafter, it split again, running right beside several partially exposed boulders or left into a copse of pines. It also led toward their parking garage, so Nicole nodded at Kira who had paused and looked back, and they ran side-by-side to the left. They had to be drawing attention, but Nicole was too focused on getting away to notice.

They ran pell-mell into the parking garage, nearly running over a man in cowboy attire, right on down to the Sam Elliott mustache. Nicole muttered an apology, took a second to get her bearings, then dashed to her left, Kira now a half step behind. She tried fishing for a key in her purse as she ran, but it wasn't possible, so she turned down a lane behind a pickup with a cab and stopped. Breathing heavily, she dug into her purse for the spare key for the rented Mirage, passing over the bear spray as she did. Her fingers closed over the small cannister as she turned her head to the side to look through the window of the cab. Kira brushed in a little closer to make sure she was hidden as Johnny appeared, backlit by the sun. He looked around and turned right, walking slowly, head roving from side to side.

"Any idea how many of them are here?" Nicole whispered.

Kira shook her head.

Nicole looked over her other shoulder. Johnny disappeared behind several different vehicles. Nicole released her grip on the bear spray and lifted her fingers to point at the Mirage, just across the aisle and a few slots down. Kira nodded, and, with one more look over her shoulder, Nicole set out walking at a normal pace. Kira crossed behind her at the rear bumper, and Nicole chanced another look back. No sign of Johnny.

The click of slamming doors echoed through the garage, followed right after by the start of an engine. The noise covered for Nicole and Kira to open their doors, get in, and close the doors as quietly as possible. Nicole flicked the button to lock them, then started the car.

"What about Jimmy?" Kira asked as Nicole backed out of the spot.

Head still on a swivel, she started forward, seeing no signs of Johnny. "He's going to take the Jeep," she said. It had been his idea for her and Kira to take the Mirage and leave him with the Jeep, just in case the Gardiners were onto them. It seemed prudent now.

Nicole turned right, to the exit, and then hung a quick left behind an RV. They drove through a short tunnel underneath the plaza where they had spotted Johnny, then back into blinding sunlight. Nicole winced, wondering where her sunglasses were. She'd had them . . .

"Where is Jimmy? What's he doing?"

"That was him, calling the guy with the cap, imitating Lance."

"How . . ."

"He's got a gift," Nicole said.

"And we're just leaving him behind?"

"That's the plan," Nicole said as she followed the RV on the single lane that wound around the other parking garage toward the main road. "He wanted to make sure we were safe, top priority."

"What a guy."

"Yeah." The RV slowed to let another vehicle out of the garage, and Nicole reached back to the console where she'd set her purse. She lifted it and swung it over to Kira. "My phone is in there," she said. "See if you can get ahold of *that guy* and warn him that Lance and his buddy have reinforcements."

*   *   *

As Lance and Ball Cap drew closer, Jimmy considered his options. He could scream like Shawn and Gus running from that sorority house, but this was the twenty-first century, and people didn't come to the aid of their fellow man. He could jump the rail after all, and probably sprain his ankle before he made it over the first boulder. He could do a running jump punch at Lance's head, but would probably miss and get picked up by the scruff of his neck. Or he could remain calm and hope that the leader of the Gardiners had either a level head and/or a sense of decorum. Lance and Ball Cap likely didn't want to start a fight at a national monument.

So he stopped and waited beside a bench under a tall pine with no lower branches that seemed to stand as a sentinel over the trail. Lance and Ball Cap both closed in, staying about six feet away, as the phone in Jimmy's pocket chirped again. Ball Cap held up his phone, the blue phone, the one Nicole had provided him, and looked at Lance. "It's him," he said simply.

"Jimmy?" Lance said.

He nodded.

"I'm Lance Gardiner. This is my nephew Cade." He held out a hand to gesture at Ball Cap/Cade, and left it extended. "We're not the bad guys."

Jimmy looked at Lance, at his weathered face, muscled arms, black vest with the BHG patch over the heart. He processed his gruff-sounding but not harsh words. Then he frowned. "It would be a lot easier to believe that if you hadn't kidnapped Kira and called us to trade her life for a flash drive."

"I can explain that all," Lance said. "But it is imperative that we recover that drive. Where is it?"

"I told you," Jimmy said, taking off his sunglasses, "we never had it. Kira never said anything about a flash drive and she never gave it to us. We checked the one bag we had with us yesterday afternoon, we checked the Jeep, and you checked everywhere else. We don't have it."

If Lance's expression was any indication, he believed Jimmy. Or, at least, didn't completely disbelieve him.

"Then why are you here?" Cade asked.

"Because we weren't going to let you hurt Kira if we could help it. We figured we could bluff you into an exchange that would at least give her time to get away."

Lance took a step closer, his face hard. "If you're telling the truth, and if you don't have the drive and we don't have Kira, then we have a very big problem."

CHAPTER THIRTY-TWO

"He's not answering," Kira said, lowering the phone for the second time. Nicole, meanwhile, had turned onto Highway 244 and made it around a corner so that, as she looked in the rearview mirror, there was nothing to indicate there was a national monument a few hundred yards away. Nor was there any sign they were being followed.

"Let's not panic yet," Nicole said, as much for herself as for Kira. "He could be on the move, or may have turned his phone off to avoid drawing attention."

"So where are we going?"

"We have a rendezvous point," Nicole said.

Kira looked at her skeptically.

"Jimmy's idea," Nicole said in answer.

"And then what?"

"We didn't know," Nicole said. "It depended on if we made a clean getaway or not, on whether or not . . . you were okay," she finished with a tilt of her head.

Kira nodded.

"Are you okay?"

"In a manner of speaking."

"How did they find you, anyhow?"

"I don't know. I got off the bus in Denver, found a hotel, and the next morning when I went down to go get breakfast, they were waiting in the parking lot. Cade—the one with the ball cap—pulled a gun and told me to get into the back of this pickup. They drove me to some house in the country where we sat all day."

"While they ransacked our room."

"What?"

As they wound into and through Keystone, Nicole recapped for Kira their experience of the day before, from returning from the Badlands to find their hotel tossed to the call from Lance at dinner to Travis wandering over and sitting down at their table. Kira said nothing throughout, but lifted up the phone when Nicole was done. "I'm going to try Jimmy again," she said.

Nicole could hear the phone purring in her hand, then heard Jimmy's voice. But her rising heart quickly sank when Kira lowered the phone and said, "Voice mail."

"Jimmy," Nicole muttered, "what is going on?"

*   *   *

Jimmy's phone—his actual phone, not one of the "burners" they'd bought and activated that morning—was vibrating in his pocket. But he had a feeling if he suddenly reached for a pocket, he'd be kissing lumber in half a second. So he ignored it and focused on Lance. "Why do you say that?"

"What did Kira tell you about who she was?"

"A girl running away from her crazy ex and family. Her words not mine," Jimmy said with a half smile in the hopes of diffusing the situation. Two women in yoga pants and bright workout quarter-zips were approaching from his left, and he thought about trying to send an SOS with his eyes, but what could they do? Besides, they were involved in their own conversation, and passed the trio without so much as a look.

"She was dating my nephew, Cade's cousin Braden," Lance said when they were gone. "She tell you why she left?"

"Said you were acting suspicious, seemed to be hiding something, and threatened her."

"That all?"

"In a nutshell. She said you were big into bikes and guns and she was afraid you were planning some attack on a federal building or something."

Cade emitted what might have been considered a chuckle.

"Nothing of the sort," Lance said.

"Look, I don't care if you guys wanna ride Harleys and shoot AR-15s into the prairie. To each his own. And I'm willing to let felonies be bygones and we all go our separate ways."

"Afraid we can't do that," Lance said. "Not without the drive."

"What's on it?"

"That's private."

"Well, we don't have it. If we find it, we'll mail it to you, how's that?" Jimmy took a step, and Cade held out a hand. Jimmy looked at Lance. "You going to kidnap me too?"

"No. You're free to leave."

"Good," he said, taking another step.

"But I asked who you thought Kira was," Lance said. "I didn't tell you who she is. And since I presume she's alone with your sister right now, you might want to know."

At that moment, Cade lifted a phone from his pocket and put it to his ear. "Yeah? . . . Okay. . . . Yes." He lowered it, then shook his head at Lance.

Jimmy looked back and forth between them.

Lance nodded, and Cade said, "That was one of our guys, confirming your sister and Kira got away."

"You tried to stop them?" Jimmy asked.

"We did," Lance said. "Kira is not who you think, and she's dangerous."

"Who is she?"

Lance took a step forward, close enough that Jimmy could hear him breathe, almost like the purr of a jungle cat, just before it strikes. The veins in his biceps looked ready to pop, and Jimmy could just envision Lance grinding him to powder. Even so, he stood his ground.

Lance's eyes never wavered, boring into Jimmy, as he said, "We think she is a foreign intelligence operative."

Jimmy frowned.

"A spy."

Jimmy swallowed. "A sp—You think . . ."

Lance nodded. "Because of that, we believe your sister may be in danger. So it is imperative that we find them as soon as possible." He leaned even closer. "Now, do you want to help or not?"

*　　　　　*　　　　　*

The two women were silent as they headed north out of Keystone and back onto Highway 16 to Rapid City. Nicole's thoughts were on Jimmy. Had he been compromised? Was he trying to keep a low profile? Was he distracted and didn't hear/feel his phone? If this were a Saturday morning back in Eau Claire, sure, but Jimmy should know to make contact unless something was wrong. Then again, that's why they had the rendezvous point.

Nicole also didn't know what to make of Kira, her story, the drive Lance claimed she had given them—that he claimed *she* claimed she had given them. Nicole was somewhat shocked that the non-exchange exchange had worked, at least as far as getting her and Kira away clean. What would the Gardiners do now? In theory, they didn't know what Jimmy looked like or have a way to identify him in the crowd of people at Mount Rushmore. But they might have a photo, would certainly know the Jeep. And to Kira's earlier question, even if they all arrived at the rendezvous point clean, what then? Nicole and Jimmy had been so concerned with the first part of their plan that they'd never considered what to do if it worked.

She turned to look at Kira, wanting to grill her, wanting to ask a hundred questions and finally get some answers. And yet, as she saw Kira staring out the window, biting her lower lip, she got the feeling she needed to tread carefully.

"Kira."

She turned her head but said nothing.

"Did they . . . hurt you?"

Kira slowly shook her head. "No. They were firm with me, getting me in and out of the truck and stuff, but they didn't hurt me. But I was scared they might. Braden was yelling and screaming, and I thought he was going to take a swing at me, but it was Lance who really scared me. He kept asking about a flash drive. I told them I didn't have anything, that I didn't know what they were talking about." She looked back out her window. "I held out as long as I could, until I was convinced they *would* hurt me. That's when I told them I gave it to you. I . . . I didn't know what else to do. I thought it might buy me some time to figure a way out. I never thought they'd come after you the way they did." She looked back. "I'm so sorry I got you into this mess, Nicole."

Nicole swallowed and nodded. She took a breath. "Do you know that they're talking about? Do you have the drive?"

"I don't," Kira said. She gulped. "But there is something I haven't told you."

CHAPTER THIRTY-THREE

Jimmy didn't know whether to laugh or freak out. A huff escaped his lips and he turned to the side, running his fingers through his hair. Kira, a spy. The sweet, cute girl who had taken selfies in the Wall Drug back yard and fallen over while giggling by the Hole-in-the-Wall Inn's pool was a "foreign intelligence operative"? And her act of espionage was to date a biker in South Dakota? He pivoted back to Lance, whose expression hadn't changed.

"Why would you think she's a spy? Spying on what? Are you guys really part of the Serbian mafia or something?"

"It's complicated and delicate," Lance said. "Come with us, and we'll lay it out for you."

Instead of a huff, Jimmy emitted a full laugh. "Come with you? Do I look crazy?"

"There are too many ears around here. There's a bar in town, in Keystone, where we can talk a little more freely. Come with us, and if you don't want to help us find Kira and your sister, one of my men will drive you back here."

"Last night you threatened to hurt Kira if I didn't bring you a mysterious drive, and now I'm supposed to trust you?"

"If you want answers, yes. But you are free to go and look for them on your own."

Jimmy took a breath. If Nicole and Kira had gotten away clean, they would be headed to the rendezvous point. Jimmy could be there in half an hour. If he ran to the Jeep and sped, he might almost catch them before they got there, before Kira would have a chance to . . . hurt his sister? That made no sense. Kira wasn't a threat. There was nothing to worry about.

And yet, something in Lance's words and the calm demeanor with which he delivered them suggested to Jimmy there was more to this biker gang's top dog than he originally thought. Did that mean there was more to his story too, and to his allegations about Kira?

Jimmy slowly nodded. "Okay. But you should know, we have a failsafe. If you try something . . ."

Lance held up both hands. "No tricks."

"Unlike you," Cade said.

Jimmy and Lance both shot him a glare.

"We should get a move on," Lance said.

Jimmy nodded again. Lance signaled for Cade to lead, and Jimmy fell in between them. They walked in silence back to the patio overlooking the amphitheater, then through the Avenue of Flags. Jimmy tried to make sense of this all—Kira being on the run, the mysterious flash drive, the Gardiners, Travis. None of it added up. Nor could he figure out what Lance could say or do to convince him that Kira was a spy and that the Gardiners were trustworthy. Yet, he couldn't let it go without hearing them out.

As they passed under the arch and crossed the entrance drive, Jimmy felt his phone vibrate again. It had to be Nicole, but he doubted Lance would let him take the call. Or that if he did, some Gardiner hidden out of sight wouldn't ping Nicole's phone during the process and find out where she was. Besides, if he did talk to her, he didn't know what to say or ask.

Cade led the way to a bank of Harley-Davidson motorcycles lined up on the top section of the parking garage, their chrome flashing in the morning sunshine. Two other men, similarly attired as Lance and Cade, were waiting. One had darker skin and wavy black hair. The other was white and looked like he could be Cade's older brother.

Lance made quick introductions to Johnny and Casper, then nodded at the nearest bike. "You can ride with me." He lifted a helmet off the handlebar.

"Don't you need that?"

"Hopefully not," Lance said with a wink. Jimmy strapped the helmet on, then climbed on the backseat of the motorcycle.

Lance sat down in front of him, then looked over his shoulder. "You ever ride before?"

Jimmy shook his head.

"Wrap your arms around my midsection, don't be weirded out, and hang on."

Before Jimmy could reply, his eardrums nearly exploded as all four riders started their Harleys.

*   *   *

"The Gardiners weren't chasing me because of my relationship with Braden or because I *might* have overheard something," Kira said as they wound through the trees and ravines of the Black Hills. "Before I left, I took a flash drive from a safe in Lance's office."

"How?" Nicole asked.

"Braden told me where it was."

"He told you?"

"He got really drunk one night, after a party for his buddy. I was there when he came home, spent the night making sure he didn't drown himself or break something falling over the steps. We talked, my curiosity won out, and I pried a little and he divulged everything. Next morning when he sobered up, I was terrified he'd remember what I'd done, but he didn't remember anything after the first five or six beers."

"Did he tell you Lance's combination too? Or are you also a safecracker?"

"Braden knew it. He handled a lot of the family's finances and needed access to stuff stored there."

Nicole frowned. Something about Kira's statement didn't quite make sense. But that had been the case since they'd met her, and Nicole still couldn't put her finger on what was wrong.

"Why did you take it, Kira? Why not just go?"

"Because . . ." She winced sheepishly. "I was paid to take it."

"Paid? You were paid to take it?"

"In a manner of speaking."

"By who?"

"A major national news company. I'm not just a girl from Missouri, Nicole. I'm a reporter, and I've spent the last three and a half months embedded with the Gardiners." She held up her forefinger and thumb a half inch apart. "I was *this* close to breaking a huge story when I realized they were onto me and had to run, quite possibly for my life."

*   *   *

There wasn't much to Keystone. A pair of sweeping turns formed an S on the southern end of town as Highway 16A passed the usual tourist-town attractions—roadside motels, kitschy souvenir shops, a campground, mini golf, a wax museum. Then the highway straightened out to form a traditional main street, lined on both sides by more gift shops and restaurants.

Holding Lance's midsection—which was firmer than it looked—Jimmy pondered his life choices as the four hogs roared through town. Just before they reached a bridge over a small creek and then the main intersection in Keystone, the bikes turned right, causing Jimmy to dig his clenched hands into Lance's stomach as they banked. Riding "pillion" on a Harley was completely different than riding your own dirt bike through the Wisconsin north woods.

Single file, the four bikes rumbled down something between a street and a parking lot, the creek bed on the left and a Ramada on the right. It gave way to a two-story building that resembled an old mine, especially being built at the base of a hill that towered over it. The building contained a mirror maze, an antique shop, and a saloon. No surprise, the bikes swung into a side lot beside the saloon. A few more Harleys were already parked there.

The five riders dismounted, and Lance made eye contact with Jimmy as he removed the helmet and handed it back. "I meant what I said before. Any time you want to leave, you let me know."

"Okay."

"We're a bunch of bikers who wear leather, but we don't eat puppies or anything."

Jimmy nodded and followed Lance inside Dave's Saloon, a cross between an old west tavern and a biker bar, or so Jimmy guessed, having never been in either. The music wasn't too loud, and at a little before eleven, the bar was mostly empty. Even so, Lance led the group into a back room where five other men and one woman were seated at or standing around a large table. Glasses of liquid too dark to be beer and mugs of coffee sat on the table.

"Everybody, this is Jimmy. Jimmy, I'd make introductions but I'm sure you don't care. You want anything to drink, you hungry?"

Jimmy frowned, still baffled that the guy who'd bartered with Kira's wellbeing—if not her life—the night before was now playing waiter. But he was thirsty. "I could use a water," he said.

"Casper, would you?"

"Yeah," he said and retreated to the bar.

"Have a seat," Lance said, gesturing at an open spot at the end of the table. A window at the back of the room allowed sunlight to bounce off the table, and Jimmy shifted in his seat so it wasn't in his eye. Lance pulled out the chair adjacent to him and sat down, facing Jimmy. He leaned forward, forearms resting on his knees.

"I am going to explain everything to you," he said. "Who Kira is, why we did what we did, and why it is so important that we get our hands on that drive. But before I do, I have a favor to ask you."

"What's that?" Jimmy asked.

"That, other than your sister, you never tell anyone what I am about to tell you."

CHAPTER THIRTY-FOUR

Rally Point Bravo, as Jimmy had absurdly christened it, was a Travelodge on Highway 16, just down the hill from Plains Vista Lodge on the edge of Rapid City. It overlooked a Culver's, which was a slice of childhood and home for Nicole, and even made her mouth water despite the circumstances. It was, after all, late morning going on lunchtime. But she had more important things to worry about than hunger. Jimmy had not answered Kira's calls, had not texted or called himself, and had not somehow beaten them to "RPB."

Then there was Kira's bombshell.

Nicole hadn't asked any follow-up questions for the rest of the drive, trying to process what Kira had already said, including what that meant about everything else she and Jimmy thought they knew about her. They had checked into their room, small and simple, and Nicole had used the bathroom and emerged to find Kira sitting against the headboard of the single bed. Before Nicole could ask the questions that had been tumbling through her brain—What had Kira been investigating? Why? To what end? What did the flash drive have to do with it?—Kira leaned forward.

"We should turn off our phones."

"Why?"

"So they can't track us somehow."

"You think they can track our phones?"

"The way they've found us every step of the way . . . maybe. Besides, you and Jimmy have a rendezvous point set up for just such an emergency, right?"

Nicole thought for a moment, then agreed. She canceled the e-mail to the Custer County Sheriff's Department, seeing as how the scenario had changed and she could always call them, then powered off her phone. She placed it on the desk next to her purse, then walked to the end of the bed. "Where's the drive now? You don't have it on you, clearly, and you didn't give it to us. So where is it?"

"Hidden."

"Where?"

"I'd rather not divulge that, yet."

"Why? You don't trust me?"

"It's not that," Kira said. "It's that I don't . . . I don't trust your ability to withhold interrogation, despite your best intents, if it comes to that."

"Plausible deniability?"

She nodded.

"Something doesn't add up here, Kira," Nicole said, pacing to the window and turning around. "Why wouldn't you take the drive to your editor or upload it to the cloud or somewhere safe?"

"I would have, eventually. But when I tried to open it, I found it was encrypted. I couldn't open it, couldn't copy it. I knew I would need somebody with some major hacking skills, so I had to buy time. When I realized they were chasing me, I determined the only thing I couldn't do was be captured with the drive. So I ditched it, figuring I could always come back once the heat died down."

"What's on this drive anyhow?"

"Supposedly, according to my employer, evidence of a wide host of illegal activities—drug trafficking, prostitution, organized crime in Pierre, if you'll believe it, and a host of anti-government undertakings."

"They keep all that on a flash drive?"

Kira shrugged.

Nicole exhaled. "So what do we do?"

"It's safe right now. So we wait. If Jimmy comes back, we get out of here."

"And go where? You make it sound like . . . like *Butch and Sundance*," she said with a sigh.

"I don't know. Head for home."

"Home," Nicole said. "Our home or your home?"

"Your home. It's completely the other direction, and somewhere along the line—Sioux Falls, Minneapolis, Eau Claire—I'll get another bus to somewhere else."

"And you spend the rest of your life on the run?"

"Not the rest of my life. If I can get away—clean, I mean—I can disappear. In a few weeks, I come back for the drive, get it decrypted, write my story that exposes the Gardiners as the crazy, criminal, far-right militia group they are, and . . . it'll all be over."

Nicole nodded. "And what if Jimmy doesn't come back?"

"Then we go get the drive and make an exchange."

"I don't think they'll fall for that again."

"This time it won't be a fake exchange."

"You'd give up the drive?"

"To save Jimmy's life, yes."

Nicole exhaled. "Why not go to the police?"

"Selfishly, because I don't want this story getting scooped. But it's also for Jimmy's sake. If we call the cops, and the Gardiners get word of it, they'll disappear—with Jimmy. And all we could do is dispatch them to Mount Rushmore, where the Gardiners likely have someone stationed, if they're smart. The cops show up, they won't find anything, and our chance of getting them to trust us for an exchange is out. Either way, wherever Jimmy is right now, our best bet is to handle this ourselves."

"So what do you suggest we do?"

"For now . . . wait. Give Jimmy a little more time."

Nicole didn't know why, but she decided to trust Kira's advice.

*   *   *

Lance tapped the shield-shaped patch on his vest. The patch was black, rimmed in very thin lines of red and gold. The interlocking B and H were red and the G gold, to match the lines. "This stands for Black Hills

GOLD," Lance said. "Guardians Of Liberty's Dream—G-O-L-D. We're a chapter of America GOLD, which has over five thousand members across the country." He shook his head a few times. "You ever heard of either?"

Jimmy slowly shook his head, then acknowledged Casper with a short nod as he set a glass of water in front of him.

"We've made a few headlines over the years," Lance said. "We're generally portrayed by the media as 'far right-wing' or 'alt-right' or even 'fascists.' But they don't really know us, which is somewhat intentional. Our stated goal is to protect and preserve the Constitution and the freedom it entails, but most people hear that and think we're a militia doing maneuvers on weekends and just waiting for World War III to start so we can get our guns off."

Jimmy took a sip of water.

"In truth, we 'fight' through educational and legislative methods, and always via legal methods."

Jimmy wanted to say, "Except when you kidnap young women," but swallowed another sip of water and kept his mouth shut.

"Even so, all it takes is one person who gets the wrong idea—makes some assumptions or stereotypes—to paint us as domestic terrorists."

"What about Kira?" Jimmy asked.

"I'm getting there," Lance said with a nod. "I mentioned our goal is to use legislation and education to try to win people over to Constitutional ideas. But we also recognize that the course of history is against us, is against freedom. We know that government is inclined by its very nature to seize that freedom, to breed corruption. And that is why we have taken measures in case our government turns against us or fails to protect us from outside intrusion. For decades, our members have been collecting weapons, collecting financial resources, collecting names of friendly persons and entities in our country and among our allies so that, God forbid, should that day come, we will not go down without a fight."

Lance shifted in his chair. A couple of the ice cubes in Jimmy's glass melted enough that they shifted position, tinking against the edge of the glass. He swallowed, trying to process all that Lance was telling him.

"We have no intention, now or ever, of attacking or overthrowing our government," Lance said. "Our preparations are purely defensive, and to be considered a last-ditch recourse if worst comes to worst. And every weapon we have stockpiled, every dollar we have squared away, has been legally obtained. Legal, according to the Constitution. We are aboveboard, as a chapter and as a national movement."

Jimmy opened his mouth to comment on Kira's kidnapping, but said nothing.

Lance waited a beat, then continued. "However, if the wrong people caught wind of any of that, it would be easy to paint us in a bad light—or a light that a lot of people would see as a bad light. All those labels—'alt right,' 'domestic terrorist,' 'literally Hitler'—would get thrown around. And a lot of people see people who look like us, see a gun on our hip, maybe, and feel threatened. Not only would our efforts to inform and persuade people be hindered, but we might also face serious pressure from various governments. So we keep the circle of people who know about our worst-case scenario preparations tight."

Jimmy nodded, waiting for the connection to Kira, trying to decide if Lance and his pals were true patriots or insurrectionists.

"It goes without saying, if our caches of weapons and resources, or names of allies, were released, they would likely face confiscation and persecution. So the list is kept closely guarded on two heavily encrypted, independent flash drives, each of which has the decryption key for the other. Black Hills GOLD has been tasked with maintaining one of these two drives for the entire organization. As the leader of Black Hills GOLD, I keep the drive in a safe that only a few people have access to." His brow furrowed as he looked squarely at Jimmy. "Kira stole that drive. It is essential to the security of our organization, and to others like it who would similarly be falsely vilified if that information came out, that we recover it before she is able to decrypt the data on it or pass the drive to someone else." He leaned back. "That's why we went to such drastic efforts to get it back, and that is why we insisted that the police not be involved—not because we're on the wrong side of the law, but because we are doing everything in our power to keep this contained."

Jimmy took a deep breath and leaned back. His mouth was suddenly dry, and he reached for his glass of water, slick from condensation on the outside. He took a drink, felt the drops of condensation on his lap. He set the glass back down and squared up Lance. He shook his head. "That still doesn't justify kidnapping Kira, holding her against her will, threatening to hurt her. And it doesn't align with you claiming to be legal and aboveboard."

"It does if you know who Kira really is."

"A spy," Jimmy said.

"Yes."

"If she was a spy, how'd she infiltrate your group and start dating your nephew?"

"Because she was very good. We vetted her carefully, and her story held up—she appeared to be a young woman from Missouri looking for a change of pace. But we started to get suspicious a few weeks back, and then really suspicious when I caught her sneaking around my office, allegedly looking for Braden. We reached out to several contacts and resources from our list of allies I mentioned a minute ago, and confirmed her real name is Kira Angeloff, a native of Nizhny Novgorod, Russia. Unfortunately, she was a half-step ahead of us and was gone before we identified her."

Jimmy ran his hand through his hair, feeling flushed and almost short of breath as he digested everything Lance was saying.

The leader of Black Hills GOLD continued. "We were unable to confirm, but we believe she is a member of the Russian SVR, their foreign intelligence agency. Given that turn of events, our drastic measures were not, in our opinion, excessive. And for what it's worth, we didn't touch a hair of her head."

Jimmy exhaled and leaned forward. "So you're telling me this woman, who is alone with my sister, is not a sweet kid from the Show-Me State but an intelligence agent from our greatest enemy on the planet?"

"I'd argue China is our greatest enemy," Lance said with a hint of a grin, "but that's correct."

"And how do I know that any of this is the truth?" Jimmy asked. "How do I know this isn't some concocted story to get me to lead you right to her?"

Lance leaned back. He stroked his beard, tipping his head back. Then he looked at Jimmy again. "I know we've given you a lot to chew on, Jimmy. So I'll give you a few minutes to think, to digest it all. In fact, go for a walk. We'll stay here. That should be a show of good faith, because if we wanted, we could keep you from leaving this room right now. But we're not going to. And we've told you things we'd really rather not get out, as another show of good faith."

Jimmy nodded.

"And consider this. If I'm lying to you, if you lead us to Kira and your sister, all we want is the drive. Kira's accusations won't hold much water without evidence, especially if we can expose her as a Russian agent. That was the original deal, remember, the drive for Kira. I guess you have to take my word that we would have honored that agreement. On the other hand, if I'm telling the truth, your sister could be in danger, and if you go back to them without us, you both could be. Not to mention the harm that would come to us if her info gets leaked."

Jimmy swallowed.

Lance sat back and said. "Go ahead, get up, stretch your legs, think it over. We'll be right here."

Jimmy stood.

"But," Lance said as he turned to walk out, "for all our sakes, I urge you to think quickly. The clock is ticking."

CHAPTER THIRTY-FIVE

Nicole watched the clock tick to 11:26. It had been thirty minutes since they'd arrived at the Travelodge, meaning roughly an hour since they'd left the parking structure at Mount Rushmore. She and Kira had switched places. Nicole was now seated cross-legged on the bed and Kira was pacing back and forth. She seemed preoccupied, not giving more than one-word answers or quick brush-offs to Nicole's questions. Was "falling" for Braden part of your cover? Yes. Were the Gardiners onto you before you left? No. Is the flash drive that incriminating? Yes. Through it all, something still seemed off about her story, but Nicole couldn't figure it out. But it beat trying to wonder what had happened to Jimmy.

"It's eleven-thirty," Kira noted. "I think we should leave."

"Leave?"

"If something wasn't wrong, Jimmy would be here by now."

Nicole tried to argue with her, but couldn't. She was right. Maybe he'd had Jeep trouble again, but then he would have called or texted by the time they shut down their phones—unless he'd lost reception, which hadn't been an issue so far. But, other than for that, unless something had gone wrong, there was no reason for him not to have made contact or arrived at their pre-arranged rally point. Even so, Nicole wasn't sure they should leave.

"Why not just wait?"

"We have to assume the Gardiners have him. Somehow. Which means one of two things. Either they'll want to make a trade, in which case the sooner we get the drive, the better. Or two, they'll get him to divulge our location. They could show up any minute and then we'd have no leverage point."

"You'd still have the location of the drive."

"But no way to exchange it. We'd be at their mercy."

"I don't know . . ."

"I was willing to wait a little while, but now . . . I hate to say it, Nicole, but something has gone wrong."

She swallowed, unable to deny that any longer.

"If there is an innocent explanation, and he does show up after we leave, we can leave a note for him."

Nicole did the math—how long it took to walk from the bottom of the Presidential Trail to the parking garage, to get out of the garage, to drive from there to here, even if he had to deal with traffic congestion and red lights and a stop to get gas . . . There was no way he wouldn't be back by now.

She looked at Kira, her face grim but yet soft. Slowly, Nicole nodded. "Let's give him another fifteen minutes—more like thirteen. Quarter 'til."

Kira nodded.

While she waited, Nicole wrote Jimmy a note on the hotel stationery. Her attempts at spycraft were ridiculous, but she didn't know what else to do.

At 11:45, Jimmy had still not arrived, and there was no sign of him in the parking lot. Her heart pounding at the possibilities, and pushing back against the idea of leaving without her brother, Nicole stopped pacing as Kira emerged from the bathroom.

"You ready?" Kira asked.

"Yeah. Where are we going?"

Kira raised her eyebrows. "How's your supply of fudge and taffy?"

*　　　　　*　　　　　*

Jimmy stared at the steep rock outcropping across the creek bed and street, marveling that pine trees could grow from its slopes. He should have been concentrating on Lance's revelation—alleged revelation—a few minutes ago. Instead, he found his brain distracted by everything else—rocks and trees, a mom struggling to get a baby into a carrier and a toddler into a stroller down the way, what Mount Rushmore had looked like before the carving, if the local authorities were called "Keystone Kops." Not to mention where Nicole was and if she was safe.

He'd tried calling her after stepping outside, but her phone just rang and rang and rang. He thought about calling Kira, but didn't know if he trusted her. That was scary. He'd been defending Kira to his sister since the beginning, and not just because she was cute. He genuinely believed her—believed her story. And yet, something about Lance's words and the way he'd said them was convincing. But did that mean Lance was telling the truth or was a very good liar?

Jimmy paced west for a hundred feet, allowing his mind to wander to the what ifs. What if Lance was right, that Kira was a Russian spy, alone with his sister? She'd have no reason to harm Nicole, would she? She'd want to get the drive back, from wherever it was, and would likely maintain her cover, right? Now that she and Nicole were in the clear, she wouldn't suddenly whip out a bad accent, start praising Putin, and put a Makarov to Nicole's head and demand her help. Would she? And what if Jimmy led Lance and the other members of Black Hills GOLD to them. Then she *might* do something drastic, might feel cornered, might hurt Nicole.

On the other hand, what if Jimmy did nothing and Lance was telling the truth? Jimmy had no interest in wading into BHG's politics, determining how right they were on the spectrum and how far right was too right. Nor did he know what a Russian agent would do with the drive. Expose BHG's true purposes to the American people, painting them as domestic terrorists and letting the narrative take its course? Send operatives to confiscate their weapons and money? Would it endanger allies of freedom around the world? And what would Kira and Nicole do in the meantime? Go get the drive ASAP? Hole up and wait for him? Could he ditch Lance and get back to Eau Claire with Nicole and Kira and sort things out then, or with some or other police department? Did he dare take that chance?

One hundred feet became two hundred, and he stopped in front of the Ramada's carport and turned around. Then there was the possibility Lance had concocted some story to cover BHG's real identity and purpose, and Kira's fears about them were true. Maybe she had taken a drive, maybe she hadn't.

He stopped.

Black Hills GOLD had Kira in their hands. They hadn't hurt her. That validated their claims that they were ultimately after a flash drive, and invalidated hers. She'd told Jimmy and Nicole she didn't have anything on the Gardiners, and had definitely not revealed the existence of a flash drive. One-zero, Lance.

Then there was the fact that Jimmy was a free man, albeit one without wheels. But Lance had let him go after revealing his secrets. Jimmy could be on the phone with the FBI right now. The show of good faith was just that. Two-zero, Lance.

Then there was the fact that Nicole, never one to rush to judgment, had been suspicious of Kira all along. Was she jealous of Jimmy's time? Coping with her own romantic issues? Or picking up on something? Two-and-a-half-zero, Lance?

Jimmy was almost back to the entrance to Dave's Saloon, and he needed to figure out something quick. He recalled Lance's story. He thought of Kira. A battle waged between his head and his heart. He considered the stakes, potential consequences of his decision.

He stopped outside the entrance. He pulled out his phone and tried Nicole again. No answer. He tried Kira. No answer. He took a deep breath. He prayed. He willed himself to think. He asked himself what Nathan Ford would do.

Something crazy, he realized, which was exactly the plan that was forming in his brain.

CHAPTER THIRTY-SIX

Lance didn't move when Jimmy returned to the back room of Dave's Saloon. He swiveled slightly in his seat to face Jimmy, and the chatter among the other members of Black Hills GOLD died out instantly. "Well?" Lance asked.

"I may not be in position to make a deal," Jimmy said through a dry mouth, "but I'll make one anyhow."

Lanced looked at him.

"I think it's pretty clear that Kira took something from you. You wouldn't have chased en masse across the state after her for info that was just in her head, and you certainly wouldn't have ransacked our room or tried to contact us if so."

Lance nodded.

"So here's the deal. Nicole and I established a rendezvous point, where we would meet up afterward if things went sideways. I'll take you there, but only you. The rest of your guys wait here. When we get there, you wait outside and I'll go in. I'll talk to Kira, because I figure there are three possibilities." Jimmy could barely swallow, and wished his water was in reach. He cleared his throat. "One, Kira is in fact an undercover Russian agent and took the flash drive with the intel on it you mentioned. Two, she's an undercover fed or cop and has a drive with some other info on it. Three, she's just a sweet girl from Missouri who stumbled into something way over her head."

Jimmy managed to swallow again, aware that a dozen sets of eyes were on him. Nobody had moved but to take a drink or take a drag on a cigarette, and yet he felt as if they were all closing in on him. "If it's the final option," he continued, "I'll convince her to tell me where the drive is, and I and I alone will take you there. I'll give you the drive, and you don't even need to give me a ride back. Our business will be concluded, right?"

Lance gave a slight nod. Jimmy would have preferred a contract signed in blood, or at least a verbal "Yeah," but he'd take what he could get.

"If it's option two, that's she's a fed, she won't be willing to hand over the drive. We'll call the cops right then and there and lock ourselves inside until they get there."

Lance said nothing.

"If it's the first option, then not only will she not go for the deal, but when I tell her you're outside, she'll probably turn on me. Which is why I'll have you on speed dial to come in and save me. And then you'll know that we don't have the drive and can . . ." He nearly gagged as he swallowed dryness this time. "You can do what you need to in order to find it."

Lance leaned back in his chair, stroking his chin. "That's weighted pretty heavily in your favor. If we're right and Kira is who we say she is— and she is—we still don't have the drive."

"No, but if that's the case, I can't get you the drive, and Nicole and I are of no use to you as leverage because clearly a Russian operative from Nancy Nowitzki or wherever it was isn't going to give up national secrets for a couple of kids from Wisconsin."

Lance looked at him for an uncomfortable length of time. Then he turned to Cade on his left. Lance leaned forward. "I'll take your deal."

"You will?"

"We've got our backs against the wall. And I believe you don't know where the drive is, or you'd have brought it to the exchange."

Jimmy huffed out a laugh.

"Something funny?"

"Just that you feel like it's *your* backs against the wall."

189

Lance stood. "How far is this rendezvous point?"

"I'd rather not say."

Lance reached under his shirt and pulled a pistol from a holster inside his waistband. Jimmy couldn't help but flinch, but Lance set the gun on the table, nodding at Cade. "A show of good faith," the BHG leader said.

"Thank you."

"How are you going to give me directions while we're on a Harley?"

"In increments. I'll tell you which way to go out of the parking lot, then which way at the next stop, and so on."

Lance nodded. He looked at Cade, then to all the guys. "We'll honor the deal." He turned to Jimmy. "Less than half an hour?"

Jimmy nodded.

"I'll call you when I get there," Lance said to Cade, then turned his head back to Jimmy again. "That'll give you more than enough time to have your conversation, and for your sister and Kira to get out of there after we leave, *if* she's the innocent girl you say."

Jimmy swallowed. "Fair enough."

"All right. Then let's get rolling."

*　　　　　*　　　　　*

Nicole tapped her fingers on the steering wheel in frustration. She and Kira had both been hungry and had concluded there was no point continuing on empty stomachs for the short amount of time it would take to pop off the highway and grab a bite. That had been fifteen minutes ago, and they were still several cars back at a Panera Bread down the street from the SCHEELS they'd visited two days before.

Beside her, Kira was not fidgety but calm, almost detached, her eyes staring vacantly out the window. Nicole would have loved to know what she was thinking, but could barely figure out what she was thinking herself. Kira was a reporter writing an exposé on the Gardiners and had made off with a flash drive containing their illicit secrets, which she had hidden, all the while playing the happy-go-lucky hitchhiker. Just how upset Nicole was with her was to be determined, largely by how this all played out. For now, civility seemed the prudent course, at least until she could confer with Jimmy.

The car at the window took a paper bag from the server but didn't move, and Nicole let out something between a sigh and a growl. Kira turned her head, but only as if to see what the fuss was about. She said nothing.

"I'm going to check my phone," Nicole said.

Kira turned her head back again.

"We're on the move now—sort of—so if they do track it, it won't do much."

Kira seemed to think for a second, then nodded.

Nicole powered on her phone as the line finally moved. Her eyes widened when she saw an orange circle above her phone app, a white "3" inscribed in it. She quickly tapped the button and saw that she had missed three calls from Jimmy. "He called," she said.

Kira merely pointed at the line, which had moved again. Nicole accelerated, juggling her phone for her purse and digging out a credit card. She handed it to the server, then tapped to call Jimmy. The server stuck the card and receipt back out the window, and Nicole took them absentmindedly as Jimmy's phone purred. "Come on," she muttered. It clicked, and his voice mail message came on.

Nicole growled, turned off her phone again, and stuffed it in her purse quickly as the bag with their food arrived. She thanked the server, passed the bag to Kira, and accelerated out of the drive-thru lane.

"That's good, right," Kira said before opening the bag.

"He could have called under duress."

"Three times?"

"I don't know why he didn't leave a message," Nicole said, turning onto the street. When she straightened out the wheel, Kira handed her a paper sleeve with her panini in it.

"Try not to worry about it. We'll eat, give him some time to see you called, maybe get to the hotel, and call back."

Nicole sighed. "Yeah."

"We'll be there in forty-five minutes, have the drive in our possession within an hour. Then we get to dictate to the Gardiners, and *if* Jimmy is in trouble, we'll get him out."

Nicole nodded without conviction.

"And if he's not in trouble," Kira said with a beaming smile, "we can all meet up for more coffee at Wall Drug."

CHAPTER THIRTY-SEVEN

Several times on the twenty-minute ride from Keystone to Rapid City, Jimmy wondered how his "see an American icon" vacation with his sister had turned into him having his arms around a barrel of a man as they swept around corners at sixty miles per hour. That led to him questioning if he had lost his mind. Strolling into a bar full of bikers and giving their leader an ultimatum? Even considering that Kira, the girl with whom he'd had a late-night pie date and who had shared her heart over coffee by carvings of Butch and Sundance, was a Russian spy? Picking up a hitchhiker, cute or not, to begin with?

When he wasn't pondering life choices, giving Lance directions, and praying to stay alive for the remainder of the ride, he prayed for Nicole and Kira's safety and that he would have wisdom. His plan depended on either Kira or Lance being exactly who they said they were. If she was in fact the girl from CoMo who had left the heartbreak of home for the open spaces and opportunity of South Dakota, only to be entangled in a crazy family's mischief, Jimmy was sure he could get her to reveal the location of the drive and part with it. And if Lance was in fact the head of a pro-Constitution movement intent on upholding American values and Kira had stolen their most sacred intel, she would likely reveal her true nature when Jimmy showed up and announced Lance was outside. But what if it was somewhere in the middle? What if Kira wasn't the All-American girl next door, but also wasn't a Commie spy? What if Lance wasn't a Son of Anarchy but also wasn't a Son of the Revolution? Then what, James David Turner?

Highway 16 rode the top of a ridge that extended out of the Black Hills and split the majority of Rapid City from the western third. Just outside the city limits, the highway made a shallow S curve as it began to descend into town. The views were spectacular, but not from the back of a hog.

The road straightened and passed under a bridge, and Lance slowed as they approached a yellow light. When they stopped, Jimmy leaned forward and shouted into Lance's ear, "Next left. Travelodge."

Lance nodded.

Jimmy questioned his plan yet again. Lance had left his gun behind, but he could easily have another on his ankle or on his other hip, or a knife in a sheath. For that matter, he could beat Jimmy into powder with his bare hands. And yet, something in Lance's demeanor told Jimmy he wouldn't—despite his threats on the phone the night before.

Lance accelerated when the light turned green, and a pair of quick left turns had them in the parking lot of the Travelodge. As Lance coasted into an open parking spot, Jimmy looked around. He didn't spot the rented Mirage, but the hotel was made up of several buildings on multiple levels on both sides of the narrow side street. Besides, Nicole likely had had the good sense to park it out of sight.

Lance killed the engine, and Jimmy took off the helmet. The silence was deafening. He managed to dismount without looking like a rank amateur. "I'll go get the key," he said, "then walk to the room. Give me ten minutes."

Lance nodded. "I'm letting Cade know where we are."

Jimmy nodded and turned toward the lobby. It featured a seating area around a TV and a breakfast bar with a side dining room. A black woman with long, thin dreadlocks greeted him with a smile.

"I'm checking in under the name David Turner," he said. "I think my wife might have beaten me here."

The woman didn't bat an eye at the oddity of husband and wife checking in separately. That little quirk, along with making the reservation under his middle name, he hoped would be one more layer of insulation if anyone came looking. And it wasn't on the level of an Abraham-Sarah deception, and thus a heavenly reprimand, he didn't think.

The woman asked for ID, and Jimmy gave her his driver's license and explained that he went by his middle name. She bought it. She provided him a key, gave him his room number and directions to it, and announced when breakfast was served. He smiled through it and left the lobby within five minutes of getting off the Harley. He pictured the other members of Black Hills GOLD in a roaring, snorting convoy of steel and chrome, and quickened his step.

"Across the street," he said to Lance, pointing to an outbuilding right next door to a Culver's.

Lance, now standing beside his bike with his arms folded over his chest, nodded. Jimmy crossed the side street and walked briskly to the fourth door of the building on his left. It was two-story, brick, with the balconies of second-story rooms—accessible from the rear—over the ground-floor doors. Jimmy drew his key, then rapped seven times in rhythm on the door—the "all-clear" code he and Nicole had established.

He swiped the key and swung the door inward to find an empty room. No lights, not even in the bathroom.

Jimmy ran his hand through his hair, replaying his conversation with the dreadlocked woman at the front desk. *He* had been the one to say he thought his "wife" had checked in already, and she hadn't confirmed or denied it. So had Nicole and Kira gotten there and left for some reason, or never made it?

He started to reach for his phone to see if they had called or texted back when he spotted a slip of paper on the edge of the bed. He walked over and lifted it to find Nicole's handwriting.

Kira and I are okay.
Left to find Daddy Gene
If you're clean, text me the song you sang leaving Rochester
Else, text me the song you sang crossing the Missouri
Don't know if this is an Opportunity to Cry.
       Love, Nic

He stared at it for several minutes, mulling the odd syntax and trying to decipher Nicole's references correctly. If he was, it was good news until the end, which was . . .

Jimmy stopped, turning the note slightly. His eyes widened as he turned it back.

Then a wave of dread washed over him.

CHAPTER THIRTY-EIGHT

Jimmy stared at his phone, at the missed calls from Nicole, at the clock. He glanced to the note, rereading it. He closed his eyes and thought through song lyrics. He twice started a text and deleted it. Twelve minutes had passed since he'd told Lance, "Give me ten minutes." The rest of the gang would be there within ten minutes, and Jimmy didn't know if they were the cavalry or a lynching posse.

Despite Nicole's directions to text, he finally gave in and called. He waited through several interminable rings before her voice mail greeting started. He lowered the phone. He thought about calling Kira. Then he reread the note again, pondered the song lyrics again, and chose not to. He looked at the clock. Fourteen minutes.

With a deep breath, he pushed through the door and out into the parking lot. Lance was across the street, still leaning on his Harley. Jimmy alternated between a fast walk and a jog, dodging a car on the side street. "They're not there," he said to Lance, then thrust the note at him.

Lance scanned it and looked up at Jimmy.

"Look at the first letter of each line, except for the 'Love, Nic,'" Jimmy said.

"K-L-I-E-D," Lance said.

"Read the first word," Jimmy said, pointing to Kira's name, "then the first letter of the other lines."

"Kira lied." He looked up. "What's the rest mean?"

"There's an Alan Jackson song called 'Drive (for Daddy Gene)' with 'Daddy Gene' in parentheses."

"She's telling you they left to get the drive?"

Jimmy nodded.

"What about 'Opportunity to Cry'? That the Willie Nelson and Merle Haggard duet?"

Jimmy nodded again, ignoring the fact that Lance was apparently an outlaw country kindred spirit. "The song talks about not knowing wrong from right, not knowing if he would kiss or kill someone. I think she's torn on who Kira is."

"And she doesn't know what I've told you."

"But she knows that Kira lied about something. She didn't say that she was in danger, but she clearly questions Kira more than she did before. So why is she going with her?"

Lance handed back the note and crossed his arms. "Your call, Jimbo."

"I want to find my sister."

"You have any idea where the drive would be?"

"No. I mean . . . there's no way she had it on her when you grabbed her, is there?"

Lance shook his head.

"You searched our stuff, and we searched the one bag we had with us. And I looked in the Jeep where she was sitting, and she was never alone with it."

"She wouldn't likely put it in the Jeep," Lance said. "She'd stash it somewhere she could come back to."

"A place we ate, a place we stayed?"

"Maybe, but you go back to a restaurant or hotel, no guarantee you get to the same table or room."

"A bathroom at a restaurant, maybe?"

"Maybe."

Jimmy covered his mouth with his hand. He suddenly lowered it. "Wall Drug. We spent quite a bit of time there, and there are a ton of places to hide something."

"Was she ever alone there?"

Jimmy closed his eyes, replaying their afternoon. "We were together when we went in, walked around, had coffee and donuts . . . then she and Nicole shopped while I went off on my own and . . . Kira came and joined me. So she was alone for a while. Lot of places to hide something."

"That's got to be it," Lance said. He whipped out his phone, tapped it twice, and put it to his ear. "Casper. Divert everybody to Wall Drug, and haul. . . . I'll meet you there. . . . Out." He looked to Jimmy. "You coming?"

"Yeah."

Lance tossed him the helmet. "Mount up."

*   *   *

The silver grain bins were straight ahead as Nicole and Kira crossed the interstate on 4th Avenue, the "other" Wall Drug exit. The drive from Rapid City had both dragged and flown by. They'd said little, at first eating, and then in their own worlds. Nicole was worried about Jimmy, wondering why he'd called several times but not answered her call. Maybe he too was keeping his phone off so he couldn't be tracked.

"Where did you hide it?" Nicole asked.

Kira turned. "What?"

"Where in Wall Drug did you put the drive?"

She stopped absentmindedly twirling her hair. "In a Christmas tree."

Nicole raised an eyebrow.

"Figured they wouldn't take it down between now and then."

"I guess that makes sense."

They drove past the airport, then a small church, and through a neighborhood. Across three sets of railroad tracks and next to the grain bins, Nicole hung a right. Wall Drug was a block south.

"What do we do when we have it?"

Kira turned her head from looking out the window again. "Call Jimmy."

"And if he still doesn't answer, or hasn't texted me like I told him in the note?"

"Let's just get the drive first."

Nicole swung into a parking spot across the street from Wall Drug, in front of a building that resembled a fairy-tale castle. Gothic text identified it as "Gold Diggers." Nicole and Kira got out and stood on opposite sides of the Mirage, waiting for southbound traffic to pass. Nicole looked at the green and yellow signage on the brown façade across the street. It all seemed familiar, but the way re-reading a book five years later did. They couldn't have been here just three days ago, could they?

"Do you have a plan for retrieving it?" Nicole asked as they stepped over the curb.

"What do you mean?"

"I mean, you can't just start digging through their Christmas tree."

"How do you feel about distracting the nearest employee?"

"How?"

Kira shrugged. "Ask a question about something for sale, ask for directions, flirt."

Nicole stopped just outside the door.

"It won't take long," Kira said, pulling open the door. Nicole entered the pharmacy and waited for Kira to join her. Together, they walked through aisles of lotions and shampoos and other personal items, then turned and passed through the T-shirt shop. The next room over housed an unending assortment of souvenirs, and as they entered, Kira lightly touched Nicole's arm. "Over there."

Nicole turned and followed Kira's gaze to a thin faux Christmas tree decked with wooden ornaments. It was next to a tall, rotating display rack holding personalized nameplates and another, shorter display rack with engraved pocketknives. Nicole swung her head around, trying to pretend she was determining where to start browsing while actually looking for employees.

"Only security camera I see is in the corner up there," Kira said, signaling with her eyes. "I can avoid that."

"I don't see any employees."

"Browse the nameplates, and keep your eyes out."

"Right."

Nicole now followed Kira, who pretended to look at ornaments depicting the Badlands or Mount Rushmore. Nicole stood several feet away, spinning the display rack of nameplates while casually looking around for Wall Drug employees. She spotted a man in a Wall Drug polo shirt starting to come their way, but then he turned down a different aisle.

"Got it," Kira said, and Nicole let go of the display rack. She turned her head as Nicole briefly held up a two-inch long USB flash drive with a camouflage shell. Just that quick, it was in her pocket. Eyes wide, she looked at Nicole. "Let's go."

CHAPTER THIRTY-NINE

Jimmy and his buddies had gotten their BMX on a few times, taking their dirt bikes onto some semi-rough trails in the woods north of Eau Claire. The "danger" had given him a rush of adrenaline. Blasting down the interstate at close to ninety miles per hour on the back of Lance's Harley-Davidson was pure terror. He distracted himself by praying for Nicole and for wisdom and keeping an eye out for a silver Mirage ahead of them. Depending on how long Nicole and Kira had stayed at the Travelodge, they could have quite a head start.

Jimmy sighed with relief when Lance let off the throttle and took the first Wall exit. They crossed the interstate, then turned and drove past the Wall school, Wall Auto Helpers, and the Hole-in-the-Wall Inn. As Lance turned north onto Main Street, Jimmy looked over his shoulder and saw six more Harleys coming down South Boulevard. No surprise, they followed him and Lance through town to Wall Drug, where Lance parked just beyond the main "Wall Drug Store" sign. As Jimmy removed his helmet and breathed a sigh of relief, he recognized several of the riders also dismounting.

"Fan out," Lance said to the group. "Marlin, wait here for the others. Nobody *touch* his sister."

Several riders, Cade being one of them, headed for the "main" entrance to the mall. Lance turned left, pointing farther left to two other men while he headed for the nearest door. Jimmy, used to looking at his back, followed him. As Lance reached for the door, Jimmy felt a surge of anxiety rush through him, hoping that they would find Nicole and Kira inside . . . and hoping that they wouldn't.

*   *   *

Kira headed for the nearest exit, and Nicole fell in a pace behind. She couldn't help but think they looked suspicious, and could just imagine getting stopped by a worker who thought they'd shoplifted. She was also eager to check her phone again to see if Jimmy had texted. Hopefully he'd sent her "On the Road Again" and she and Kira could arrange to meet with him, get stories straight once and for all, and part ways. At this point, Nicole didn't care much who Kira was or what was on the camo flash drive or why she'd taken it from whoever the Gardiners really were. She just wanted to put South Dakota behind her.

Kira stopped suddenly.

"Wha—"

Kira darted left, and Nicole's eyes briefly followed her, then looked straight ahead where a barrel-chested man with a white beard and a black vest had entered the room. He mostly obscured Nicole's view of Jimmy, who didn't look any the worse for wear or under duress.

Nicole heard a crash and turned toward Kira. Before she got her head around, Kira pulled her arm. Nicole stumbled, and Kira looped her arm around her waist to catch her. Then Nicole felt a prick in her neck. Out the corner of her eye, she saw Kira's other arm and hand holding the broken shard of a coffee mug to her jugular vein.

"Stay back!" Kira said, even as someone in the store screamed and Jimmy shouted.

*   *   *

"Nic!"

Lance's outstretched hand caught Jimmy in the chest and kept him from rushing forward.

"You don't need to do this," Lance said, now looking at Kira. His voice was calm, but firm.

203

"Stay back," Kira said again.

Lance held up his open hand. "I'm not moving. Let the girl go."

"As soon as we're clear," Kira said. Holding the broken mug to Nicole's neck with her right hand, she grabbed her arm with her left. She whispered something in her ear, then took a step back. Jimmy wanted to follow, but Lance's other hand was still on his chest, keeping him in place.

Several people—customers and one employee—had gathered. One of them mentioned something about 9-1-1. Jimmy doubted it would do any good, because there couldn't be more than a few cops in Wall. Maybe state patrol, but most likely help from Rapid City. Jimmy's best hope was now a motorcycle gang.

"We're leaving," Kira said, having walked Nicole back several steps. "Anyone tries to follow us, she gets it."

"You hurt her, you lose your leverage," Lance said.

"Stay. Back."

"I'm still standing right here."

Jimmy saw movement to his right, in the hallway leading to the main mall. Two men in black were edging toward Nicole and Kira. Jimmy flicked his eyes to them, gauging how far they were from Kira. That was a mistake, because she caught his glance and whipped her head around. She spotted the men and spun Nicole around, at the same time pushing the mug into her skin and causing her to scream.

CHAPTER FORTY

"Stay calm," Kira hissed. The temporary pressure in Nicole's neck ceased, but Kira's iron grip on her arm didn't. Her feminine appearance belied her strength, but there was a lot about her that wasn't what it seemed to be.

Nicole chanced a look left and saw two more Gardiners coming out from the hallway with the stagecoach overhead. Kira continued to inch backward, and Nicole tried to make her legs cooperate so she wasn't dead weight. But she felt paralyzed, at the same time hoping one of the Gardiners had a gun but also terrified of them trying to take a shot without hitting her.

Kira bumped into a shelf, causing several items to fall to the floor. "Stay where you are," she shouted, pivoting her head from Lance and Jimmy to the other two, then the other direction entirely, and back. "Nic," she said quietly, "I won't hurt you if you don't struggle."

"You are hurting me."

Kira's right hand and arm moved, looping under Nicole's arm so that the mug shard was no longer at the side of her neck. Instead, Kira held it inches from her throat. "Okay, back up, one step at a time. Stay back!"

Nicole shuffled backward—left, right, left, right. They weren't in sync, and her feet kept bumping into Kira's. But they managed to make it around the corner and down another aisle. Lance and Jimmy inched along after them, and there were now four Gardiners—two right and two left—

along with half a dozen others moving along with them. Nicole kept expecting one of them to make a move, but they were very cautious.

"You're doing good," Kira said in Nicole's ear, with a calm voice, what Nicole would almost deem friendly. Amazing, how in the midst of this chaos and her terror, her brain was still trying to process who Kira was. Clearly not a runaway from Missouri trying to find herself, and likely not a reporter for a major national news company either.

They backed around a corner, with Kira continuing to guide Nicole by the arm and with reassuring commands while circumspectly barking at anyone who got too close. A loud bang startled Nicole, but not half as much as Kira's sudden move immediately after. She looped her right arm across Nicole's chest and under her left arm, grazing her arm with the shard as she did, then pulled Nicole backward with a gasping scream.

They were in a bathroom, in the middle of the building, and thus without an external wall with a window. It was also the men's room, Nicole noticed by the presence of urinals.

"Come on," Kira said, having released her grip around Nicole, but still holding her arm. She pulled her through the bathroom to the far side, where there was another door.

"Kira, wh—"

"Open it," Kira said, looking back over her shoulder. Nicole reached out a shaking hand for the door, and as soon as she opened it to reveal a vacant hallway, Kira pushed her through it with a firm but not mean, "Move."

Nicole stepped into the hallway, across which was employee access to the kitchen. Left, the hall ran back into one of the stores. Right, the hall opened to the souvenir shop again, or to a green door leading to the dining room with the Butch and Sundance carvings, or to an extension of the hallway leading to the back yard. Before Nicole could complete getting her bearings, Kira looped her arm around her again, putting the shard back to her neck. At the same time, she clenched Nicole's left arm and spun her around to face a heavyset man in a security guard's uniform.

* * *

Nicole disappeared into the men's room as if yanked in a harness. Jimmy turned his eyes to Lance, who had both hands outstretched, directing fellow members of Black Hills GOLD—who were multiplying—left and right. "Anybody know if there's a back way out of the bathroom?" Lance asked.

"Y-yes, s-sir," a young woman, maybe a teenager, answered. She was dressed in a Wall Drug shirt, and had a slight accent. "There's a h-h-hallway be-behind them."

"Cade, keep her flanked right," Lance said, pointing. The crowd had grown to over a dozen, including a couple employees, but Lance had taken charge. He was the general, directing his troops into battle. That analogy, as it ran through Jimmy's head, horrified him. Battles had casualties, often civilians.

"Johnny, make sure she doesn't come back through that way," Lance said. He turned to the teenage girl. "What's beyond the hall?"

Her eyes were wide.

"It's okay," he said, taking down his intensity a notch. "Where does the hallway behind the bathrooms lead?"

"The k-kitchen and the d-d-dining r-room and th-th-the . . . the back yard."

Lance whipped his head around. "Braden, Frank, get around to the street to the north and get to the alley."

Jimmy watched them depart, then turned after Lance, who was charging for the men's room.

*   *   *

"Ma'am, stop right there," the guard said, reaching for his gun.

He never got it drawn.

With lightning quick speed that convinced Nicole Kira could have only been a former soldier or secret agent or ninja, she released her grip on Nicole's arm and slid her right arm and hand holding the coffee mug shard from around her neck. In the same fluid motion, she also shoved Nicole in the back, sending her directly into the guard.

Instinctively, he reacted to catch Nicole as she stumbled, which provided Kira an opportunity to lunge forward and reach, not for his gun, but for his gun hand and arm. She grabbed him, spun him despite his being nearly twice her size, and planted a tennis shoe in the back of his left knee. He buckled as Nicole staggered out of the way and watched Kira, her foot still in the crook of the guard's knee, release his arm with her right hand, at the same time twisting it back with her left. She used her free right hand to unholster and draw his gun. Then she lifted her foot to the middle of his back and kicked him to the floor.

Nicole felt as if she was frozen in place, but it had all occurred in a matter of seconds. Seeing the gun in Kira's hand kept her from making any move to run, or to reach for her purse that she wore like a satchel, over her head and on her right side—a purse that contained a canister of bear spray. Kira spun several directions with the gun, causing a trio of women who had just come in from the back yard to scream and duck back out. Then, as if reading Nicole's thoughts, Kira turned her eyes and drilled Nicole with them.

Still before Nicole could move, Kira grabbed her hand and dragged her over in front of her, then looped her left arm under Nicole's left arm, far enough that she could grasp Nicole's right shoulder and use her as a shield. She swung the gun back past the restrooms just as Lance emerged from the men's room and two other men in black vests came from the souvenir shop.

Then Jimmy popped out of the women's room, right into Kira's line of sight. She pointed the gun right at him, and Nicole couldn't stop the scream that exploded from her lips.

CHAPTER FORTY-ONE

At the last second, Jimmy peeled off and, instead of following Lance into the men's room, took the door next to it into the women's room. Maybe he'd watched one too many spy movies and episodes of *Leverage* and *White Collar*, but wouldn't it be terribly clever of Kira to loop back, thinking everyone had either followed her or tried to cut her off on the other side?

There was a woman washing her hands, and she turned and yelled something vile at Jimmy. He didn't bother to explain himself. He took a quick glance at the open stall doors, in case Kira's plan had been to loop partway back and hide. They were open, the stalls empty. Still ignoring the glare from the woman at the sink, Jimmy pushed through the door to the other side.

He found himself staring down the polymer barrel of a very ominous looking pistol. His eyes met Kira's for just a second, and hers were hard and unblinking. Maybe, if he'd seen vulnerability in them, a hint of remorse, the fact that she was using his sister as a human shield might not have convinced him that Lance was right about Kira. Maybe—just maybe—Kira could have sent him a signal with her eyes that things were not what they appeared. But there was no such signal, and Jimmy knew he and his sister had been had. Well, he more than her. But that wasn't important now. What was important was getting Nicole out of this alive.

"Stay back or I'll shoot," Kira said, turning the gun from Jimmy to Nicole's side.

"No!" Jimmy yelled, putting up his hands. "No, don't hurt her." He looked frantically for Lance to do something, but the big man was standing firm.

"You follow, I shoot," Kira said, and started backing Nicole up again, past the green door to the dining room, and down the hallway to the back yard.

*   *   *

"Kira, please," Nicole said as she half walked, half was dragged backward.

"Keep calm," Kira said, then backed out the doors, still pulling Nicole with her.

Kira removed the gun from Nicole's ribs, spinning around to cover the back yard with her eyes. Nicole had heard that time slowed down for "operators"—the Navy SEALs and special forces guys. It was speeding up for her, and the back yard was a blur of people. Some recoiled at the sight of Kira and her gun, some were oblivious. Either way, she didn't give them long to react.

Releasing her grip on Nicole, she took hold of her arm. "Come on," she said, pulling as she started running down the alley to the north. Her grip was firm, and Nicole had no choice but to keep up, especially since she was convinced Kira would do whatever was necessary to keep her hostage.

When they reached the end of the alley, Kira slowed and so did Nicole. Kira grabbed her arm a little tighter and pulled her closer as they stepped onto the sidewalk. Nicole fell a step behind Kira, who looked right then left. Nicole followed her eyes, and thus was just grasping what she was seeing to the west when Kira pulled her tight again. Two deafening cracks sounded as Kira fired the gun at two men in black who had come around the front corner of Wall Drug. One bullet plugged into the wood post supporting the awning, and the other sailed to who knew where.

The men recoiled back around the corner, and Kira again started dragging and prodding Nicole, this time east, down the sidewalk. They passed a minivan and came to a black crossover vehicle. With another peek backward, Kira stopped at the front of the crossover, a Honda CR-V.

"Drive," Kira said.

"What?"

"Get in and drive."

Nicole started around the front of the vehicle. Kira's gun followed her, then panned back down the sidewalk. She fired again, just once this time, and it still caused Nicole to shudder. Without turning the gun, Kira said, "Get in."

Nicole was about to ask how when Kira cracked the passenger window with the butt of the gun. The window spider-webbed, then shattered into crumbles when she hit it again. She reached in to unlock the doors, then aimed the gun down the sidewalk again. "Get in," she said to Nicole, who opened the now unlocked driver's side door.

Kira was in the passenger seat by the time Nicole got in. "How—" Nicole started, while Kira leaned down under the dash and pulled a pair of wires. She used both hands to hotwire the CR-V, leaving the gun on the seat beside her. Nicole thought about trying something—reaching across Kira for the gun, opening the door and crawling out, reaching into the purse on her lap for the bear spray, attacking Kira's exposed head or neck. But, a basic self-defense class her freshman year of college aside, Nicole knew nothing about hand-to-hand combat, and it was clear from what she'd witnessed the last few minutes—especially with the security guard—that Kira was an expert. And Nicole was still frozen in shock.

It only took Kira a few seconds to ignite the engine, and she sat back up. "Drive."

"Where?"

"Just drive," Kira said, picking up the gun again.

Nicole nodded, reaching for her seatbelt by default, trusting that Kira wouldn't shoot her for doing so. She did not, and Nicole moved her purse to the console between the seats, still in reach but not unless Kira was seriously distracted.

"Go, Nicole."

With no other option, Nicole edged away from the curb, now truly alone with a woman she had no doubt was a cold-blooded killer.

CHAPTER FORTY-TWO

Jimmy had to applaud Lance's courage. Or maybe it was desperation. Despite Kira having a gun and, judging by the way she maneuvered, tactical knowledge of how to use it, Lance followed her. Down the hall, then out into the back yard. He moved slowly, non-threateningly, making sure Kira wouldn't harm Nicole. But he also wasn't letting her get away.

To his own credit, Jimmy continued to follow Lance. It was not nearly so courageous, and was absolutely motivated by desperation. If something happened to Nicole because of him, his insistence that they pick up Kira to begin with, his trust in her . . .

Gunshots sounded. Two of them, just as Lance and Jimmy emerged into the back yard. They both panned their eyes across the compound, searching for Nicole and Kira. Jimmy could barely breathe, expecting to see his sister lying in a pool of blood by the stagecoach or big jackalope. Instead, he saw wide eyes on a few patrons, and a couple of them pointing down the alley to the north. It took Jimmy a second longer than Lance to notice and get moving, and he hurried to catch up.

Another shot exploded just before Lance reached the end of the alley, and he paused, allowing Jimmy to join him. "Stay back," Lance said, putting out his arm. He peeked around the corner to the east, and Jimmy couldn't help himself. He scooted around Lance's other side and stepped beside him onto the sidewalk.

He was just in time to see the rear of a black crossover pull into the street and accelerate. He knew his sister was inside, and that she and Kira were about to get away.

*   *   *

"Where are we going?" Nicole asked as Kira directed her to take the first right, along the backside of Wall Drug.

"For now, out of town."

"Are you going to kill me?"

Kira made eye contact. "Not if I don't have to."

That was semi-comforting.

"Do what I say, and you'll be fine," she said, then whirled her head around, ponytail flapping with it, to look out the rear window. When she whipped back around, she said, "Take the next left."

Nicole did so, trying to get used to driving a new vehicle with a seat that was too far back while attempting to control her breathing and quell her fear. She straightened out, now heading east on 6th Avenue, past an empty parking lot on the left and a Methodist church on the right. She swiped a loose strand of hair from in front of her face, which caused Kira to momentarily flinch, and Nicole immediately dropped her hand back to the wheel. In so doing, she noticed a trickle of blood on her arm, from when Kira had adjusted her grip and slashed her with the mug shard.

"Right at the stop sign," Kira said.

"I need to adjust my seat."

Kira looked back. "Make it fast."

Nicole braked, a little too abruptly, then felt around for the buttons to adjust her seat. She found the seat back control first, and it snapped her upright. Then she found the controls to ease her seat forward.

"Let's go," Kira said, and Nicole made a right turn, south. She was getting comfortable in the CR-V, which she noticed featured a Bob Ross bobble-head doll on the front dash. There was a Dunkin cup in the passenger cupholder, with lipstick on the rim. A glance in the rearview confirmed the backseat was empty—no car seats or stuffed animals—and also that no one was following them. But Nicole was waiting for flashing lights and sirens soon.

They drove past the EconoLodge where Kira had temporarily taken refuge a few days ago, back when Nicole and Jimmy thought she was in trouble. Seeing it brought Nicole just a small measure of comfort, because she now knew where she was. They passed a Phillips 66 on the right as up ahead the interstate overpass loomed.

"Which way we going?" Nicole asked.

Kira turned her head from looking out the window to the right. "Straight."

Nicole looked the same way, out the vacant window, and saw two motorcycles turn onto South Boulevard.

"Step on it!" Kira said.

Nicole accelerated through the intersection.

"Faster," Kira said, pushing the gun a fraction toward Nicole for emphasis.

CHAPTER FORTY-THREE

Lance turned and ran west, toward the front of Wall Drug. Jimmy wanted to chase after the black crossover, but knew it was futile. So he followed Lance. By the time he caught him at the corner, Lance had joined up with several other members of Black Hills GOLD. He took just a moment to assess who was there and who wasn't, then said, "Frank, where's your bike?"

A man who resembled Lance in build but with a blond goatee instead of a white beard pointed to a nearby Harley.

"Go east on this street, make sure they don't loop back north or east."

Frank took off.

"Braden."

Kira's ex-boyfriend—theoretically, who knew anymore—nodded.

"Try to follow. They turned south on the next street."

"Check."

Lance looked around briefly. He spotted Cade and another man Jimmy didn't recognize who had followed them into the alley and then down the sidewalk to the corner. "Get to your bikes, head east on 90. Get ahold of your brother and Johnny and tell them to go west."

Cade nodded.

"Marlin, you're taking Jimmy. Follow me."

"Where are you going?" Jimmy asked.

"Whoever spots them first will alert the rest of us."

Jimmy nodded, then followed Lance's point to Marlin. He was older, decked in grayish blue jeans and a black vest over a black long-sleeve shirt. His silver-tinged black hair was pulled into a stub of a ponytail. He nodded for Jimmy to follow him. Head and heart spinning, he did.

Marlin's bike was parked across the street, facing south, and looked to Jimmy like all the rest but for a roaring lion painted on the fuel tank cover. It was standing in front of a hill, with three crosses painted on the hill and backlit by the glow of a sunset.

"Here," Marlin said in a voice that made Lance's sound like falsetto.

Jimmy looked away from the painting just in time to catch a helmet.

"Let's go get your sister."

*   *   *

Marlin's helmet was equipped with a built-in headset so that Jimmy could hear what everyone was saying, even if he couldn't identify the voices. A couple bikes had departed Wall Drug ahead of Jimmy and Marlin, so presumably it was one of them who reported seeing a black crossover going south on Glenn Street.

Marlin drove to the end of Main Street, then waited, idling until Lance turned his bike in a wide arc to the east. Marlin followed, as Jimmy heard Frank (who identified himself) report seeing nothing. Braden, presumably, said he hadn't caught up to or even seen the crossover.

Lance turned right at the Exxon station, and Marlin followed. The headset crackled. "This is Casper, on the ramp to 90 West. No black vehicles behind or ahead."

"Copy," Lance's gruff voice answered. He had just reached the Glenn Street onramp to Interstate 90, and now accelerated under the overpass. Marlin followed.

"I've got them southbound on 240 East," a voice said.

"Cade, keep going east, try to come from the next southbound exit," Lance said. "Everybody else, on Mike and Vic."

Up ahead, his cycle belched as it sped forward. Jimmy felt his body lag behind as Marlin's lion-emblazoned Harley followed suit, past the eastbound 90 ramps and south toward the badlands.

*   *   *

"Who are you?" Nicole asked. They were doing sixty-five on Highway 240, ten miles over the limit.

"Does it matter?" Kira asked. Her posture had calmed, the gun resting in her lap but still aimed at Nicole. She kept her eyes between the highway and the side-view mirror, and Nicole took a look back as well. There were two motorcycles in the distance, maybe more—it was hard to tell.

"We did everything we could to help you," Nicole said.

"Save me the sob story."

"I'm not sobbing. I'm saying we deserve to know."

"The more you know," Kira said evenly, "the more you're a liability."

Nicole swallowed. "CIA?"

Kira actually laughed.

"You're not Chinese, unless they hired you."

Kira said nothing.

"Russian."

Kira looked over.

"That's it," Nicole said. "You're a Russian spy."

Kira raised the gun. "Shut. Up."

Nicole swallowed and drove in silence for a few minutes, her eyes on the rearview mirror as much as the highway. She tried to remember how far it was from the Badlands entrance station to Wall—or in this case, vice versa. She wondered, what were Kira's plans once they got to the curving road that hugged the ridge atop the gullies and ravines? The CR-V handled nicely, but Nicole doubted it cornered better than the Harleys. Did Kira know of a hidden turnoff? Did she plan for Nicole to go off-road? A *Thelma and Louise* ending?

Another look in the mirror showed the motorcycles were gaining, and there were at least four of them. Nicole turned to Kira, whose eyes were on the side mirror. "Do you have a plan?" Nicole asked quietly.

"Yeah."

Nicole waited, but Kira said nothing. So she began trying to think of a plan of her own, because she was going to need some way to get out of this.

CHAPTER FORTY-FOUR

Rumble strips on the highway sounded as if they dislodged something from the bottom of the CR-V. Soon after, a sign on the side of the road warned of reduced speed ahead.

"Keep going," Kira said, as if reading Nicole's mind.

She had eased off the gas pedal, and didn't re-accelerate, but didn't brake either. She was still doing sixty miles per hour.

They thundered across a cattle guard—or, based on the fuzzy brown specks on the horizon, a bison guard—and Nicole again let her foot off the gas as they came to a "Speed Limit 25" sign, followed by a pullout where several cars were parked in front of the "Entering Badlands National Park" sign.

"What are you doing?" Kira asked.

"I'm not going to kill somebody," Nicole said. She flicked her head toward two small structures a few hundred yards ahead, where the southbound lane split into two lanes. "We have to stop up there."

"No," Kira said. "Keep going."

"It's a ranger station."

"I don't care."

"Kira."

"Blow through!" Kira said, raising the gun and pointing it at Nicole.

If Nicole remembered from the day before, there wasn't a gate, and she saw only two cars, one in each of the southbound lanes. She slowed to forty miles per hour, not having an opening.

"Nicole!"

"Where do you want me to go?"

The car on the right started to accelerate.

"There," Kira said, "and don't let up."

Nicole smashed the horn as she veered into the right lane. The driver ahead didn't notice. Less than fifty yards from the dual entrance buildings, Nicole laid on the horn again. The car suddenly swerved left as Nicole blasted past the entrance station at thirty-five miles per hour, missing the car's rear bumper by inches.

"Nicely done," Kira said.

"You're crazy."

Kira, who had lowered the gun, grinned. The smile vanished when she glanced in the side mirror. Nicole flicked her eyes quickly to the rearview and saw what Kira saw—four motorcycles following their path.

"Step on it," Kira said, and Nicole punched the gas pedal again.

*   *   *

"That chick's *loco*," one of the riders in front of Lance, Marlin, and Jimmy announced in his radio.

Lance's response as he flew past the entrance checkpoint at forty miles per hour was to ask his fellow Black Hills GOLD riders for a sitrep. Cade checked in, saying they had passed the missile silo on a side road running south several miles east of Highway 240. Casper had reversed on the next exit west of Wall and was a few miles behind on 240. Four more riders checked in behind Lance and Marlin, who were less than a hundred yards behind the two bikes that were less than a few hundred yards behind Nicole and Kira in the crossover.

"We're going to have lots of tourists in the park," Lance announced. "Don't be surprised if she tries to use them. We lose the drive before innocents get hurt, are we all clear?"

Several replies of "Copy" sounded in the headset.

The first voice, the one who had initially spotted the crossover headed south and who had declared "the chick" was crazy, interrupted them. "She's turning."

So far, Jimmy had tried to be a bobsledder, keeping his head in line with Marlin's, lest he throw them off balance. But he tipped his head marginally left, then right and saw the crossover taking a right turn. The lead cycles were hot on its tail, charging west into the dust created by the crossover on a gravel road. Absent a helmet, Jimmy thought Marlin might not follow. But he slowed just enough to safely make the turn on Lance's heels.

With endless prairie on the right, the road wound like a ribbon at the edge of the gorges and gulches of the badlands on the left. In addition to Nicole's safety, Jimmy now found himself worrying about the effectiveness of motorcycles on gravel with huge drop-offs just off the shoulder of the road.

*　　　*　　　*

The CR-V's tires kicked up a biblical cloud behind the women as Nicole pushed the accelerator to fifty miles per hour on the gravel straightaway. "Where does this go?"

Kira didn't answer right away, and Nicole concluded it went where it was hard for motorcycles to follow, through rolling prairie on the right and alternating short, grass-covered mounds and sudden drop-offs on the left. Nicole hadn't studied any maps of the area carefully enough to know if there was an outlet to the west or if Kira's next command would be to go off-road.

Kira looked behind them again, then turned her head. "Keep going."

Nicole assumed she meant fast, and checked the rearview as they crested a small rise. As she did, she saw chrome emerge from the dust cloud. Instinctively, she accelerated, which caused Kira to turn around again.

"Go!"

"I'm going."

"Faster."

"And skid into the canyon?" Nicole said as they approached a curve to the right. A slight rise on the left temporarily obscured the ridgeline, but she knew it was there, and also knew making a hard right at fifty-plus wasn't a good idea.

Kira flexed her fingers on the gun's grip, but said nothing. Nicole took the corner as fast as she dared and, as she straightened out, checked her mirror. Four Harleys were on her tail, one of them edging toward her blind spot on the left. The mounds on the left were gone, and the edge of the gravel drive was just yards from the side of the cliff.

"Go faster," Kira said.

"I can't."

"Nicole!"

"I'm barely in control now. You want to go over the edge?"

Kira whipped around to look back again. The revving of a motorcycle drew Nicole to her left, where she saw a Harley edging beside her, almost even. She had no idea how the riders were outpacing her on two wheels, and she coaxed a little more out of the CR-V without giving way to skids.

"Bump him," Kira said.

"What?"

"Bump him."

"He'll go over the side."

"I don't care. Do it."

Nicole kept the wheel steady.

"Nicole," Kira said evenly as she raised the gun, "do it or die."

CHAPTER FORTY-FIVE

A quick glance at Kira's pale blue eyes convinced Nicole she would in fact pull the trigger, whatever that meant for her as the passenger of a vehicle driven by a dead person. Nicole swallowed hard, feeling her heart pounding against her chest wall even more than it had been for the last half hour.

"Now, Nicole."

She swiped imaginary hair from her head with her left hand, then dropped it down beside her. "Just wait until he's not by the cliff."

"Now!" Kira screamed, jabbing the gun forward.

She was clearly over the edge, about to get them both killed. So Nicole resorted to desperation.

"Okay," she said, flicking her eyes to her mirrors. With her left hand, she felt the seat back control button.

"Nic—"

Nicole pressed the button to recline the seat and threw her upper body weight back into the seat, at the same time stabbing her right foot at the CR-V's brake pedal. She fell back, looking at wispy clouds through the sunroof. She felt her seatbelt digging into her stomach as her body slid forward and her foot slipped off the brake, causing the vehicle to fishtail.

It all happened in only seconds, which was also the length of time it took Kira to fire her gun.

*   *   *

From less than a hundred feet behind the crossover, Jimmy watched over Marlin's shoulder as one of the two bikes right on its tail veered left and began to pass the crossover. Jimmy had no idea what the rider was doing. A motorcycle couldn't possibly force a crossover off the road, or even force it to stop, could it? It was more likely to get run off the road itself, and not just that but run over the edge of the ridge.

Suddenly the crossover's brake lights lit up. Jimmy's chin inside the helmet bumped into Marlin's shoulder as he too braked as much as possible without losing control. He almost clipped the wheel of the bike in front of him, which also had braked and almost run into the crossover. Marlin, in the midst of gearing down, edged right, while Lance, on their left, edged farther left, leaving three bikes side-by-side-by-side just off the bumper of the crossover as it now accelerated moderately.

All sorts of thoughts ran through Jimmy's head. Nicole had wrested control of the vehicle away from Kira. Nicole had talked her into stopping. Kira was trying evasive maneuvers, trying to make the bikes behind her crash. A tracking chip inserted in Kira's brain by the SVR had exploded like in that *Mission: Impossible* movie. Or maybe Nicole was driving, and several of those scenarios were reversed.

Over the growl of four Harleys, a gunshot exploded.

Jimmy yelled his sister's name into his helmet, even as Marlin swerved around the crossover's bumper and accelerated beside it. The crossover coasted, then abruptly stopped. So did Marlin, skidding broadside beside the crossover's rear door. Jimmy was off the bike quickly, but was still third in line behind Marlin and another rider in approaching the vehicle with his sister and Kira inside, one of whom had just fired a gun.

*   *   *

Nicole's window exploded in fragments of glass and she heard herself scream. It was accompanied by a thud, and she saw a mass of brownish-blond hair in her periphery. She realized the CR-V was still moving, and found the brake pedal again with her foot, and pushed it to the floor. The vehicle jerked to a stop.

Kira had never buckled her seatbelt, and the sudden braking had caused her, turned sideways in her seat, to fly forward. Her head had cracked against the windshield and her body against the dash. She had reacted quickly, firing her gun at the space where Nicole's head had been an instant before she reclined. She had then dropped the gun, which now lay on the console next to Nicole's purse.

Kira groaned, reaching a hand for her head. She appeared woozy.

Nicole started to sit up, at the same time reaching for the gun or the gearshift, she didn't know which. The movement seemed to rouse Kira, who tilted her eyes toward Nicole. They widened, then darted around, looking for the gun. Both women grabbed for it at the same time. Kira's hand grazed the gearshift, while her other hand shoved Nicole's shoulder and knocked her just far enough off balance that her fingers touched the gun barrel but were unable to latch onto it. Kira shifted her body, giving her right hand a clear angle at the gun's grip.

The CR-V was still in gear, and Nicole was about to punch the gas pedal when two sinewy, tattooed arms reached through the vacant passenger window. The left hand clamped on Kira's wrist before it reached the gun, while the right arm wrapped around her neck. She screamed and flailed a kick that just missed Nicole's head as the arm yanked her back through the opening.

Her hand faltering, Nicole found the gearshift and pushed it to park. Then she collapsed back into her reclined seat.

CHAPTER FORTY-SIX

The next few minutes were absolutely bonkers.

Jimmy watched as Marlin went full King Kong and jerked Kira out of the crossover and onto the gravel road. Immediately, he had her flipped on her stomach, his knee in her back, and Jimmy seriously wondered if he was an undercover cop or a former Navy SEAL.

Meanwhile, the other biker on their side—Willie, as Jimmy later learned—beat Jimmy to the passenger window. Jimmy heard him ask "Are you all right?" and joined him a second later, squeezing in to see Nicole reclined in the driver's seat. At first, he feared she'd been shot, but he saw no blood, and then saw her nod when Lance, arriving at the driver's side window, asked the same question as Willie.

"Nic!" Jimmy said, and she turned his way. Her eyes were wide and her hands shaking, but she looked him in the eye. He was about to crawl through the window when Willie reached in to unlock the door and open it.

"Watch out for the glass," he said as Jimmy practically dove in. He stopped when he saw the gun.

"Why don't you both get out," Lance said, at the same time opening Nicole's door. She fumbled for her seatbelt, then took Lance's arm to keep from collapsing.

Jimmy backed out of his door, stepped around Willie, and nearly tripped over Kira's legs as she still lay sprawled under Marlin's knee. He rushed around the front of the crossover and enveloped Nicole in a hug. He alternated telling her "It's okay" and "You're okay" as he stroked the back of her head, then pulled back and made eye contact to ask, "Are you okay?" She nodded through tears, and he hugged her tight again.

Sirens sounded in the distance. Lance verified that Charlie—the rider who had come alongside the crossover's left side—was all right, then used his cell phone to call the rest of the gang and update them. Willie retrieved the gun from the console, removed the magazine, and cleared the chamber.

Jimmy and Nicole verified and re-verified that each other was okay, and babbled jumbled bits of their day that neither remembered later. When Lance came beside them and asked if they were both all right, Jimmy introduced his sister, forgetting that they had met under the South Dakota flag at Mount Rushmore.

The sirens grew closer.

Two more motorcycles arrived.

Marlin stood up with Kira's arm grasped firmly in his left hand. His right held up a small flash drive. "Secured," he announced.

Beside him, Kira's hair was a disheveled mess, a sullen stare on her face.

"You confirmed the serial?" Lance asked.

"I did," Marlin growled.

Lance opened his palm, and Marlin tossed the drive to him. He caught it and pocketed it. Then he looked around. "We've got LEOs arriving," he said in a loud voice. "Put all your weapons on the ground, give full cooperation."

Jimmy held his arm around his sister as almost every member of Black Hills GOLD removed from concealed holsters a gun, and in many cases a knife or second gun.

Nicole turned her head to Jimmy's ear and whispered, "Are we safe?"

"I think it's like C.S. Lewis said," Jimmy answered. "No, but they're good."

"Are you sure?"

"Ninety percent."

The first vehicle to arrive was a National Park Service SUV, light bar flashing. A South Dakota State Patrol cruiser was next, then a Pennington County Sheriff's Office vehicle.

"Are you going to faint?" Jimmy asked amid the sirens and pulsating lights and swirl of dust.

"No," Nicole said. "I'll be all right."

"Good. You can catch me."

She looked straight at him, and he grinned. Slowly, Nicole did too, falling back against the side of the crossover. It was a beautiful sight, his sister smiling after such a traumatic event was finally over. But Jimmy only reveled in it for a moment. Then a law enforcement officer of some branch, brandishing a weapon, told everyone to get on their knees and interlock their hands behind their heads, and Jimmy began to envision a night in the slammer with a motorcycle gang.

CHAPTER FORTY-SEVEN

"Now aren't you glad I talked you into this?"

Nicole looked at her brother as he spooned ivory-colored vanilla ice cream from a dish into his mouth. He was backlit by the setting sun, but his cowboy hat cast his face in shadow. It did not hide his mischievous grin. He swallowed the ice cream and turned from leaning on the granite railing. "I mean, is this perfect or what?"

She followed his gaze across the tops of sun-speckled pines to the faces of four presidents immortalized in granite. They were dark gray with the sun at their backs, still a brilliant yellow-orange orb just above the horizon. Nicole focused on Thomas Jefferson's slightly upraised face as she slowly licked a bite of ice cream—his recipe—off her spoon. She breathed in the pine scent, the clear air, the late summer sun, and looked at her brother. "Yes."

It had taken the better part of the afternoon for the various authorities to sort out everything—Nicole and Jimmy's accounts of the day, Lance and the other bikers' statements, and Kira's claims. While they were all on their knees in the gravel road, Lance looked right at Nicole and Jimmy and told them to speak freely and tell the truth. That would have been much easier had Nicole known the truth, but she was still putting together the pieces of what had happened and who Lance and his gang were.

Eventually, after questioning on the gravel road, back in Wall at a building kitty-corner from Wall Drug, and at the store itself, the truth came out. What she didn't pick up from the questions she was asked and the questions and answers she overheard, Jimmy filled in. She learned the basics of who Black Hills GOLD was and what they stood for—albeit not the intimate details Jimmy told her afterward. The sheriff also knew who they were, and held them in high regard. Together with Nicole and Jimmy's stories and Kira's inability to explain her actions, that was enough to convince him that Kira was ultimately the one responsible for the damage at Wall Drug, the attack on the security guard, the grand theft auto, and the high-speed chase into the badlands.

After providing their contact info, Nicole and Jimmy were released. Kira was not. She was being taken to the Pennington County Jail where she would be held on the day's charges until possibly handed over to the FBI or NSA or CIA as a spy. Lance and the sheriff arranged a handshake deal, which would need to be authenticated at higher levels, that would keep Black Hills GOLD out of trouble for their kidnapping of Kira in exchange for their testimony. The all-important flash drive that had started everything never left Lance's pocket, and the details it contained were never brought up.

In the gravel parking lot behind the building, Nicole and Jimmy swapped handshakes with the thirteen members of Black Hills GOLD present. All bad blood was gone, and they each thanked each other for their help throughout the day.

Lance also answered a few questions—such as how they'd found Kira in Denver (legwork by the American GOLD network and hunches), where they'd taken her (a member's cousin's hunting cabin), and who Travis and his unknown female associate were. Based on Nicole's description of him, Lance assumed it was Curt Travis, a low-ranking FBI agent who had been "buzzing around" BHG, trying to dig up something on the group. Lance guessed that Travis had deduced who Kira was and, when she'd made her breakaway, pursued her for the same reason BHG had chased her—to get the intel on that flash drive. His female partner/associate was an enigma, if she even existed at all. So was his appear then disappear behavior, but Lance guessed the BHG gang hadn't heard the last of him.

Before Nicole and Jimmy left, Lance also insisted on comping their vacation as a thank you, and since BHG had added to their expenses. Twelve other leather-clad, tattooed bikers also insisted, and Nicole and Jimmy capitulated.

A little after four o'clock, Nicole collapsed into the passenger seat of the rented Mirage. As Jimmy pointed it back to Rapid City, she had nothing more in mind than a nice, long nap upon their return. But Jimmy talked her into sleeping on the ride, freshening up, and grabbing a celebratory dinner at the Dakotah Steakhouse across the interstate from Cambria Suites. Thinking how hungry she was and how delicious a steak sounded—and because Jimmy offered to buy—she agreed.

It took a little more selling, after rehashing the day over a couple rib-eyes, to get her to agree to drive forty-five minutes farther to Mount Rushmore. But Jimmy was persuasive—they had yet to actually visit the landmark as tourists, they could get Thomas Jefferson's ice cream for dessert, and they needed to pick up the Jeep.

Full and exhausted, Nicole was now dreading the drive back to town. But Jimmy was indeed right, this was a perfect way to end a day.

"Do you have any regrets about what we did?" Jimmy asked.

Nicole frowned at her brother. "Today, you mean?"

"I mean from the moment we picked up Kira."

She thought over a spoonful of ice cream. "About a dozen of them."

"Really? I don't have one."

"Not one?"

"We never did get a proper goodbye. You know, she's bedraggled and handcuffed but stops and looks me in the eye, and I ask if any of it was real, and—" He stopped and winked at her. "No, not one."

"For real?"

He shook his head and dug his spoon into his dish.

"Not falling for the cute Russian spy?"

"Falling is a little strong, but it is a perfect plot for a late-night movie. And if we hadn't picked up Kira, who knows who would have." He shrugged. "Maybe she would have gotten away with that flash drive and BHG's secret would be out."

"And you're convinced that's a bad thing?"

"Ninety percent," he said, as he had all day when she'd asked him such questions.

"I'm still not sold on their methods," Nicole said. "But I guess desperate times . . ."

Jimmy nodded.

Nicole looked back at the presidents.

"Can I ask you something?" Jimmy said.

"Yeah."

"When you decided in that instant to slam on the brakes while reclining your seat in the hopes that Kira would shoot over you before crashing into the windshield—"

"Which worked perfectly, by the way."

"It did. But when you decided to do that . . ." He turned and looked at her. "What were you thinking?"

"W-W-J-D," she said. "What Would Jimmy Do?" She grinned. "I decided to fly by the seat of my pants for once."

"It's fun, isn't it?"

"It was terrifying. I almost start hyperventilating when I think about it now."

"You know what I keep thinking?"

"What's that?"

"How much like a *Dukes of Hazzard* episode that was," he said, draping his arm over her shoulders. "'Beats all you ever s—'"

Nicole elbowed him, interrupting his gravelly baritone singing. "Just eat your ice cream, Bocephus."

"That's Hank Williams, Jr," he said. "Waylon Jennings sang the opening—"

"I don't care."

"Noted."

They finished their ice cream as the sun sank behind the pines beside the mountain. Jimmy dropped his arm and turned around, leaning back against the half-wall again. "Ready to head out?"

Nicole swallowed the last spoonful of ice cream. "Yeah. I am dead on my feet."

"Two more questions then."

"Okay."

"Which vehicle you want to drive?"

"Your Jeep. Better odds if I run into an elk."

"That's fair."

"Number two?"

"Which of our seven hotels you want to stay at tonight?"

AUTHOR'S NOTE

The books in the Last Resort series have become odes as much as novels, and *Backs Against the Wall* follows that pattern. I've been to the Black Hills three times, twice on the way through and the third time as a destination. If you've never journeyed there, put it on your list. The rolling prairie is beautiful in its vastness, the badlands provide an otherworldly attraction, and Mount Rushmore is as awe-inspiring as it is reverential. (The ice cream is pretty good too!) And don't forget to stop in Wall on the way for five-cent coffee, good food, endless souvenirs, and a one-of-a-kind experience. The billboards along I-90 don't lie.

As always, I tried as much as possible (and as much as the story would allow) to be faithful to real-world geography and buildings. Where my memories and research failed or artistic license dictated and I strayed into imagination, I hope those who know better will forgive me.

I'm grateful for the support and help of my wife and parents as I wrote, edited, and proofed the manuscript. A special thanks to my nephew Caleb, my youngest reader, who kept me on track by asking when "your PG book" would be finished.

And thanks to those of you who are reading this, who made time to take this journey with me. I'll see you out on the open road . . .

ALSO BY NATHAN BIRR

The Douglas Files
Overnight Delivery
Three's a Crowd
All an Illusion
Shot List
Chasing the Wind
Blood and Treasure
One Life to Lose
Golden Key
Mine to Avenge
Nine Lives

Douglas Files Shorts
Black Male
WinterKill
Short Sail
As Good As Dead

The Last Resort Series
Fire & Ice
Broken Trust
The Fountain

Standalone Stories
God, Girls, Golf & the Gridiron
(Not Always in That Order) . . .
A Love Story

The Book of Levi

All is Calm?

Augusta Whispers

Final Rest

Non-Fiction
Rights or Wrong? Examining the
Declaration of Independence in the
Light of Scripture

www.nathanbirr.com

www.ingramcontent.com/pod-product-compliance
Lightning Source LLC
Chambersburg PA
CBHW032037240626
47154CB00003B/959